Aloha in Love

Jennifer Watts

Andy,

To the coolest Investment Advisor that I know. Thank you for all of your kindness and support.

May 30/19

Copyright © 2019 Jennifer Watts
All rights reserved.

No part of this book may be used or reproduced in any form or by any means (electronic or mechanical, including photocopying, recording, or by any information storage and retrieval system) without prior written permission of the author, except where permitted by law.

Editing by Creative Straight

Cover design by JCV ArtStudio

This book is a work of fiction. Names, characters, places, and incidents are either products of the author's imagination or used fictitiously. Any resemblance to actual events or persons living or dead is entirely coincidental.

To my uncle, Mike, who always had Hawaii in his heart. You are truly missed.

Playlist

1. Breakdown - Jack Johnson
2. Time Will Tell - Bob Marley & The Wailers
3. Santeria - Sublime
4. Pressure Drop - Toots & The Maytals
5. Here Comes the Sun - Peter Tosh
6. Sea of Love - Israel Kamakawiwo'ole
7. Somewhere over the Rainbow - Israel Kamakawiwo'ole
8. Sunshine - Matisyahu
9. A-Punk - Vampire Weekend
10. Say Hey (I Love You) - Michael Franti & Spearhead
11. Amber - 311
12. Stone Love - Pepper
13. High Tide, Low Tide - Ben Harper & Jack Johnson
14. Hawaiian Wedding Song - The Outriggers
15. Ku-u-i-po - Elvis Presley

Chapter 1

The over-produced sound of Boney M's "Feliz Navidad" plays over the satellite radio as I stare out the 30th floor window of my office. The bay skyline is foggy, and the view is obscured by gray clouds hovering in perfect harmony with my mood. Behind me, my office door clicks and my assistant, Terry, gives me a perfunctory nod.

"I despise this song," I announce, muttering just loud enough for Terry to hear. I try to tally up how many times I've heard the familiar refrain in the last twenty-four hours: at the grocery store last night, at Starbucks this morning, and during the elevator ride to my office.

Terry perches on the edge of my desk. "Whatever, Scrooge."

"Why does hating this god-awful song make me Scrooge? For the record, I don't hate Christmas, but this nauseatingly upbeat tune, with all its saccharine seventies keyboard rifts, really makes me want to hurl."

He gives me a knowing look. "Like I said…Scrooge."

"Does that make you Tiny Tim then?" I smirk, cocking one eyebrow.

"First of all…" He waves his finger at me like a stubby wand. "Terrance Jones has *never* been referred to as tiny—just ask my *Grindr* date from last night."

I ignore him, freeing my long red hair from its elastic band for the first time in eight hours. I've spent the entire day pouring over city permit applications for our newest condominium development. Glancing at the clock now, I realize that it's too late to chat with Terry—no matter how much I live for his wild dating stories.

"Terry, did you have something you needed from me?"

"What, you think I came in here to talk about Christmas carols?" He says, standing up from my desk.

"I should hope not." I yawn into my fist, pushing aside my paperwork as Terry replaces it with a spiral bound volume.

"The plans came in for the Rory Building."

"But the Rory Building isn't my project?"

"It is now. The big guy wasn't happy with Dylan's first draft, so he *ahem* 'asked' that you take over." Dylan is a junior broker, who seems to value cocaine and women much more than his position at the firm.

I roll my eyes. "We both know that Mr. Silver doesn't *ask* for anything."

The owner and CEO of Silverdale Developments, Mr. Silver or Dale Sr. as I know him, also happens to be my father-in-law. I was working for the firm when I married Dale, his son, who I'd been dating since college. Our union didn't curry much favor, but I gained a lot of respect for Mr. Silver over the years. He was your typical CEO—blunt and intimidating—but his fair and hardworking nature made dealing with him easy. Sometimes I wondered (although I'm ashamed to admit it) if that work ethic skipped a generation with my husband.

Sighing, I turn the proposal over in my hands, wishing Dale Sr. could entrust his son with the Rory Building instead. I know I shouldn't be so unfair; after all, Dale spent the last three days traveling for work. He travels a lot for Silverdale, but Lord knows that the time apart has taken a toll on our four-year marriage. I flip through the massive booklet as Terry adds (oh-so-helpfully) that it looks almost finished.

Just then, I flip to one of the renderings and gasp. "What the fu—"

"*Fuck,* Ashley. The words you're looking for are *What. The. Fuck.* Don't worry, I'm a big boy and won't rat you out to HR."

I ignore him—a true cornerstone of our relationship—scanning through the remaining drawings before landing on the final page. "I thought this land was slated for affordable housing? How did Dylan manage to pull a complete one eighty on this project?"

"Affordable housing?" Terry snorts. "That's an oxymoron if I ever heard one—we live in San Francisco." He walks around my desk and peers over my shoulder. "So what's the damage?"

An all too familiar feeling of anxiety creeps into the pit of my stomach. I've been feeling this way a lot over the past few months, raising serious questions about what I'm doing with my life. I'd love to bitch to Terry, but this isn't the appropriate moment to do so. I clear my throat and read aloud. "Luxury condominiums…marketed to off-shore investors…purchase prices starting at $1.9 million?"

"Well, a *fuck* is definitely in order then." Terry bends forward to pat my hand. "Maybe even a *fuckity-fuck*."

"I know you're just the messenger, Terry, but I thought Silverdale was doing something good for the community." Terry watches me with fascination. I think my erratic moods are the most interesting part of his day. "Sorry," I say, rubbing my forehead in frustration. "I should probably keep those things to myself."

"Nah, my lips are sealed." He mimes the action of zipping his lips closed. "Need any help?"

"I think I just need some time to sort through all of this."

"Say no more, boss." Terry turns and heads for the door. "But Ashley?"

"Yes?"

"I'm right out here if you need anything."

I flash what I hope passes for a smile, trying to ignore the dull pounding in my head. He disappears down the hallway and leaves me alone with my thoughts. For as long as I've been at Silverdale, Terry has been my assistant, and I know how lucky I am to have someone like him in my corner.

• • •

It's after 6pm and I'm ready to call it a day, exhausted after my 6am start this morning. I stuff the project plans into my credenza and lock the drawer more aggressively than usual. With some time to kill before spin class, I catch up on my favorite food blogs, hunting for a new recipe. The food pictures make my stomach growl, and I wonder how someone landed that kind of job—writing about food. I click one last recipe: a gruyère, mushroom, and caramelized onion French tart. My eyes drift closed, imagining a patio sunset meal complete with that flaky tart, some micro greens, and a crisp glass of Chardonnay.

I love cooking *almost* as much as I love food. I have a particular affinity for savory dishes, French cuisine, and anything fusion, but I don't cook much at home anymore. With Dale uninterested in trying my concoctions, cooking seems silly. My husband is always on some food program or cleanse. For now, it's no carbs and lots of eggs—some kind of "keto" thing. I literally watched him wrap three pieces of cooked bacon around a hunk of cheese last week, while he gave me hell for eating one *half* of a whole-wheat bagel. The last time Dale told me to *start watching my macros,* I saluted him with my middle finger, downing half a pint of salted caramel ice cream before his very eyes. Afterwards, he had the gall to send me a recipe for keto-tacos, with shells made from full-fat deep fried cheese—I'm no expert, but that sounds like a one-way ticket to a triple bypass.

At least he's temporarily off *intermittent fasting,* because we almost never have the chance to eat a meal together. I do believe in the health benefits of fasting, but Dale's a different breed—there are preachers' sons and there are CEOs' sons, and Dale was definitely the son of a CEO.

When he gets his mind set on something, that one track plays over and over until he's had his fill. I get it for high performance athletes, but my twenty-seven-year-old, one hundred and fifty pound, tennis-playing husband could probably go out for brunch once in a while and be just fine.

Thinking of Dale reminds me that I should call to confirm what time he'll be arriving home. I grab my cell and pull up his contact profile. It takes him five full rings to pick up, and when he finally does, he sounds distracted and out of breath.

"Hey babe," I say, just to piss him off.

"Ashley." He answers with a stern voice. "You know how I feel about such juvenile terms of endearment."

Oh do I ever, I think, but instead I try again. "Hello, Dale, my beloved husband."

"Better," he says, but I can hear the smile in his voice.

"How was the trip?" I ask.

"Fine." It sounds like he's still catching his breath. "I'm just leaving the hotel gym right now."

"What time do you think you'll be home?"

I hear muffled sounds in the background and assume he's walking outside. "Heading straight to the airport now. I should be back in town around 11pm." The flight from Vancouver was short and Dale always packed light, but the airport traffic was a killer.

"I'll wait up for you then."

"You don't need to."

"I'll probably be up and energized anyways," I say, fiddling with the rainbow colored post-it notes on my desk, "since I'm taking an 8pm spin class."

"Well, whatever suits you, Ashley."

"I love you," I say.

"You too. I should get off the phone if I'm going to make my plane."

"Right. See you tonight."

"See you." We both hang up, and I exhale in one big gust before tossing the phone onto my desk. Glancing out the window at the drizzly skyline, I decide to call it a day. I'm not due to meet my spin partner, Maggie from accounting, for another half hour, but I desperately need a change of scenery outside these four walls.

• • •

A few hours later, red-faced and drenched in sweat, I towel off in one of the spin studio change rooms. Tonight's workout was only forty-five minutes, but it still managed to kick my ass. Maggie bolted once the last cool down song finished, which (to my luck) happened to be a techno remix of Boney M's "Feliz Navidad." I hung back for a while to kill time, and that's how I ended up with the changing room to myself. As I open my locker, my phone rings and a number I don't recognize flashes onscreen.

"Hello?" I assume that it's Dale calling from the airport.

"Ashley?" The voice sounds familiar, but not enough to place it.

"Yes, and this is?"

"It's Erin. Erin Perry."

"Erin," I repeat back, hunting through the recesses of my mind, until it clicks: Erin Perry is a fitness instructor. "Did I miss a session or something?"

I'm joking of course, because the last time I met with Erin Perry was six months ago. Dale bought me an introductory personal training session for my birthday. It was my first, and last, foray into lifting weights.

"So you remember me then?" She sounds a bit strange, but of course I remember Erin Perry. It's hard to forget a woman with an eight pack, who loves burpees more than I love the Food Network Channel. She was pretty, blonde, petite, and constantly sporting a glow tan.

"Of course. What can I help you with?"

"Actually, I think I can help you. It's Dale."

"Dale?"

"Yes. He's not in Vancouver."

I feel the irritation seeping into my voice. "You know this how, exactly...?"

"Well, I was riding him—*hard*—this afternoon, and I for one am definitely not in Vancouver."

"Excuse me?" My mind works to process what she just said. When I don't speak right away, she sighs and continues.

"You don't have to believe me, but how else would I know that your husband has a thin dick and doesn't make any sound when he comes. It's actually really disturbing."

It actually was disturbing, but I still haven't managed to wrap my head around this new piece of information.

"I was at your house this afternoon, you know, while you were at work. You wash your sheets with Gain detergent, which Dale hates because it's a proletariat product, and you always have sweet and salty popcorn in your cupboards, which I only know because I ate a lot of it."

A long silence ticks by and I'm too shocked to react appropriately. Instead I mutter, *you don't touch another woman's popcorn,* almost to myself, as if I'm hexing her. From what I understand, if your husband is having an affair, there are often some common signs, but I honestly hadn't had any suspicions. However, the very next second, my phone pings with a text from Erin. It's a picture of my husband's thin dick, resting in her cherry-red manicured hand. Believe me, I'd recognize that dick anywhere.

"Anyways," she starts, as if she didn't just send me a dick pic. "I thought you should know 'cuz I'm done with his ass, but I have a sneaking suspicion that I'm the woman to another woman, if you know what I mean..." She trails off, maybe waiting for a response. "What am I talking about? Of course you know what I mean."

"*Why?*" I manage to croak out. "How long have you been sleeping with my husband?"

"Same amount of time that I've been training him."

My heart squeezes as I do the math in my head: it's been almost a year since they started sleeping together. She's silent for a beat, as if the air might crumble, and carefully chooses her next words. "As for why…to be honest, I'm not even sure. I don't love him. I'm not even sure I like him, but the idea of it all was exciting at first." She clears her throat. "I know it doesn't mean much now, but I am sorry. It was a shitty thing to do, and I'll have to own it for the rest of my life."

I let out a small cackle. "Yeah, Karma is a bitch, and so are you."

"I guess I deserve that…I hope it works out for you, Ashley, I really do, but if you want my opinion—"

"I don't." I try to cut her off, but she plows ahead anyways.

"If you want my opinion, he's not worth it. In fact, he's the most worthless piece of shit that I've ever made the mistake of fucking."

She hangs up abruptly, and I'm left gaping at the phone, thankful there's no one around to overhear. It's just me and that lone plastic Christmas tree in the corner, mocking me with its twinkling lights and colorful decorations. I get a text from Dale that says *just landed, home shortly*. It's like his ears are burning. I don't have the faintest idea of how to respond or what to do with myself, so I power down the phone, grab my gym bag, and embark upon the streets of San Francisco.

Chapter 2

Who knows how long I'm out wandering through my SoMa neighborhood, past the museums and art spaces and auto-repair shops. I loop around the block aimlessly, seeing the same shops again and again but only half-noticing where I'm headed. I walk until the soles of my feet burn, but this does nothing to distract me from the lump in my throat, nor the horrible sting of my unshed tears. It was already dark when I left the spin studio, but the moon has since dimmed. I feel my way to the front door of our walk-up townhouse with no idea of what time it is, but the glowing lights tell me that Dale is already home.

    I quietly let myself inside, dropping my gym bag before heading down the hall to our beautiful open concept kitchen. I love my townhouse, with its wide windows and sleek gray and white kitchen, almost as much as I love Dale, though at the present moment, love is precisely the opposite of what I feel. I find him seated at the breakfast bar, drinking red wine from one, among many, of the pretentious crystal glasses I so despise. They're some stupid name brand that Dale swears by and literally the only thing he'll use.

    He gives me a look that I can't place. "You're home late. Were the showers not working at the studio?"

    His eyes sweep over my workout clothes, clearly disappointed with my attire. Dale has this thing about sweat and showering immediately after exercise—come to think of it, Dale has a thing about everything. He doesn't say anything else, waiting like a faux gentleman in his overpriced three-piece suit. I laugh without humor, shaking my head. He's so committed to this façade that he actually took time to dress up.

"Is something wrong, Ashley?" His tone is off and the words come out like an accusation, though his face is blank.

I study his cornflower-blue eyes, soft chin, and the light blond hair slicked back from his baby cheeks. I've dedicated four years of marriage to that face, plus two rounds of unsuccessful in-vitro fertilization and one big fat piece of my heart. Dale sets down his wine just in time for me to approach and snatch up the glass, throwing it across the room. I watch it smash against the tile, exploding into a thousand tiny pieces, and damn if it doesn't feel good to destroy one of his precious pieces of crystal. I quickly pick up the second glass, which I assume he poured for me, launching it directly in his face. It bounces off his nose and sends red liquid gushing down his dress shirt before finally smashing on the counter.

"Christ, Ashley!" The sound of his voice adds fuel to my fire. I pick up the rest of the bottle and swing it around in a circle, finally slamming it against the refrigerator. By some miracle, it doesn't break, so I throw it on the floor as hard as humanly possible, entirely uninterested in miracles today.

"Ashley—the hardwood!" Dale screams, and I laugh out loud. Of course that's what he's thinking about, even in the midst of war.

Surprisingly, the bottle remains intact. I pick it up and raise it over my head. "Break, you motherfucker!" I shriek, heaving it at the polished floor with every ounce of my strength. This time, it does shatter. I let my shoulders sag in defeat, as if to mirror the broken glass. Dale is fixated on the floor, but his reaction tells me everything. His neck is flushed and the tips of his ears are red. He won't speak nor meet my eyes, almost like he's afraid of me.

"Really, Dale, an affair with your personal trainer? Could you be more cliché?"

He opens and closes his mouth like a fish flopping out of water, but no sound escapes.

"She called me, Dale. I know everything." I slump against the counter. "I'm not naïve enough to think that this doesn't happen in relationships, now and then, but we've only been married a few years. We promised ourselves to each other."

"Ashley, it was just sex—"

"Oh, don't start, Dale. Almost a year isn't just sex. It's pathological, a betrayal of the highest order."

"But it's over now," he adds, albeit feebly.

I snort. "Yeah, Erin filled me in on that too. I hear you found your next victim?"

His neck flushes full red this time, as his gaze trails out the window. "I'm a man Ashley. I have certain needs, and this past year was hard."

Oh no he didn't, I think, straightening up. "Please, Dale, tell me exactly how hard the last year was for you."

Dale runs one hand through his supremely gelled hair before shirking off his jacket and resuming his seat at the center island. I circle the kitchen to stand across from him, grateful for the physical separation, as the desire to claw out his eyes is building within me.

"It's just..." he stammers, "with the treatments—all those hormones and appointments and needles—it just became so clinical."

"Probably because it was."

"But it wasn't sexy anymore." He shrugs. "Besides, you changed. I mean, you gained some weight, but that didn't really matter. A few pounds are okay and I told you that, but you changed mentally, too. You were sad and crying all the time. The treatments became more important than anything, even more important than me."

The words leaving his mouth are surreal to me—even *unreal*. I can't actually believe I'm hearing this bullshit. Dale is acting like a wounded child.

"So, it's *my* fault that you cheated on me, because I was struggling with fertility treatments to which you subjected me, in order to have the family that you so desperately wanted?"

Dale slams his fist on the counter, raising one finger to scold me. "Don't you twist my words around, Ashley."

"What part of your words did I twist, exactly?" I cross my arms and shoot him a nasty glare.

"I still appreciated what you were doing, especially with all that you were going through."

"*Do* you though, Dale?"

"It was hard for me, too!" He argues, and I shut my mouth for a moment. It's true that I never gave much thought to how Dale was handling things, but it's not like he'd given much thought to my needs recently. He steals a glance at me, as if seeking approval. "You know I wanted a child—I mean, I thought I wanted a child. You've seen how my father is anyways, but I didn't expect that it would be so hard, and now I'm not so sure."

I shake my head, pacing back-and-forth behind the counter. "That's no longer of any consequence to me, because I'm not spending another second of my life waiting for you to grow up. This marriage is irreparable, Dale."

I take the two carat ring from my finger and toss it against his wine-stained shirt. For one last time, I scan the expanse of my beautiful kitchen and finally fix my eyes on Dale.

"You, Dale Silver, can go straight to hell. Take all this precious stuff with you, too, because I'm so done."

Chapter 3

I leave the house with nothing but the clothes on my back—sweaty Lululemon tights and a tank-top—ordering an Uber in a haze. All the way to my best friend Jamie's house, I alternate between hysterical laughter and crying, leaving behind one very confused driver. He appears to be barely out of high school, and it doesn't help my fragile state of mind that Boney M's "Feliz Navidad" was blasting from the radio the moment I stepped into the vehicle.

I called Jamie right away, spouting sentence fragments at her through the phone—about Dale's thin dick and how it feels to have another woman sample your salted popcorn. She demanded that I come over immediately; Jamie has always been my safe place, and I know that I can count on her always. She swings open the door to her cute Cathedral Hill condo, and I notice that she's totally decked out in party clothes. I peek over her shoulder and look for signs of whatever soirée I've interrupted.

"No one's here." Her almond-shaped eyes narrow, following the line of my gaze. "However, I'm technically supposed to be at an event downtown right now."

"Shit, I'm sorry. I didn't realize."

She waves her hand, as if to say *don't be silly*. "I invited *you* over, remember? Besides, you're coming with me."

"What?"

"You're coming with me."

"Oh, no way." I hold up my hands, taking a step back into the hall.

"Yes, you are. I simply won't take no for an answer. Besides, it's trance night at the Odyssey and this one is work-related, so I can't miss it." Jamie Chen, one of the most sought after club promoters in town, knows everything about the San Fran party scene. Her presence always guarantees a crowd. She fully opens the door and steps aside. "Now get in here so I can love on you."

I walk slowly into her living room, collapsing onto the worn but familiar sofa. I'd spent more than a few nights sleeping there during college years, but as much as I love the soft suede fabric pressing against my face, I have no idea why she keeps it. The thing totally clashes with the rest of her décor. Jamie's place is what I'd call *boudoir-chic*, with glittery pillows, hot pink lamps, leopard-print drapes, and one gigantic Marilyn Monroe poster framed in chrome on the wall.

I can't help but sigh, rubbing my forehead. "I understand if you have a work thing, but I'll just stay here until you get back."

Her full, red lips twist into an ugly grimace. Apparently I'm in trouble. "Did you not hear me? It's trance night. I won't be back until the sun comes up. I would skip for you in a heartbeat, but after what that piece of shit did, I think you need this." Jamie never hid her dislike for Dale from me, and vice versa, but they'd tried to tolerate each other for my sake. Dale thought Jamie was beneath me and had always treated her that way. Meanwhile, Jamie thought Dale was no less arrogant, condescending, or self-centered as he'd been in college.

Jamie and I had been friends since the first grade, when she moved to San Francisco from Hong Kong. I remember how she walked into my classroom with thick glasses and a bowl-cut, speaking barely any English. Some of the kids picked on Jamie, but I loved her right away. She's always had this quiet confidence, as if she couldn't care less what you thought of her, and she owns every room she walks into; our first grade classroom that day was no exception.

Eventually, Jamie's glasses gave way to contact lenses. Her bowl-cut morphed into a shiny bob; her skinny arms and legs transformed into a petite package complete with pouty lips, big brown eyes, and flawless skin. Once her looks caught up with her confidence, Jamie became a double threat. She has half a million Instagram followers and regularly gets marriage proposals from men and women alike.

"How is getting trashed at trance night supposed to help me get back at Dale?"

She leads me by the hand into her bedroom. "Because getting out there is the best way to avoid being stuck here, totally overanalyzing the last four years of your life." She sits me down on the bed, hovering like my very own guardian angel.

"God, even with a sweaty red face and bloodshot eyes, you're still stunning," she mutters, giving me the onceover. "Maybe you should give women a try?" She wiggles her eyebrows. Jamie swings both ways and has no reason to hide it, but after twenty years of friendship, I'm pretty sure that I'm not her type. I do, however, appreciate the compliment.

"I'm feeling more than a little raw here, Jamie."

"Sorry, too soon." She raises her hands in surrender. "I've never been a particularly nurturing individual, you know that."

I roll my eyes. "Understatement."

"See? You know me too well. That's why I don't own so much as a houseplant—it's far too much of a time commitment.

"You know, it literally takes only five seconds to water a houseplant. Some go *weeks* without water."

"Not the point. As much as I love you—and I do love you, so fucking much—I'm not going to let you lament some ungrateful shithead who you never should have married in the first place.

"Wow…" I say, getting to my feet.

"Wait—shit. That came out wrong. Look, I know you're hurting and I'm here for you. You can stay with me as long as you want. You can have my bed, the shirt off my back, I'll give you whatever you need. Not for one minute will you doubt that I'm on your side." She pauses, looking straight into my eyes. "I just meant to say that he never, not even for one second, deserved your love. I'm going to spend every day reminding you of that. In the meantime, I say fuck it—let's get wasted. Drinks on me."

With an epic groan, I flop back down on the bed. "Please, please, *please* just go without me,"

"*Lei yao mow low gah!*" She shouts, grabbing my hand and pulling me into a sitting position. It always spells trouble when Jamie starts yelling in Cantonese.

• • •

I don't have energy to argue with Jamie, so I find myself standing in front of the Odyssey an hour later. It's one of San Francisco's biggest nightclubs. Jamie has stuffed me into a black leather mini skirt and a hot pink tank top that totally clashes with my titan red hair. Both items are a tad too snug for my round hips and sizeable chest, but they were the loosest clothes that Jamie's tiny little ass had on hand. The ankle boots she lent me are also a size too small and already pinching my feet. Jamie flashes her killer smile, along with her VIP badge, and thankfully we're escorted past the huge line up. The club is overflowing with a mixture of LGBTQ folk and underage college students.

I lean forward and whisper in Jamie's ear. "Uh, I think we're about ten years too late to the party."

She dismisses my comment with a wave of her hand and leads me towards the alcohol-soaked bar. We double down on shots to the sound of hardcore techno and teeth-rattling bass. It's too loud to talk without yelling, so I throw back one more shot before Jamie guides me towards the VIP area, as if to say, *come with me if you want to live.* With the heavy electronic riffs, I can't tell where one song ends and another begins. In fact, I can barely hear Jamie shouting over the music. A distorted voice shouts *Wake the Fuck Up*—apparently a popular lyric—and the crowd goes positively wild, jumping up and down in unison. The display makes it clear that this is one hundred percent not my scene, but I can't deny that it's entertaining to watch.

After Jamie gets me all settled into one of the plush couches—and only once she's reasonably convinced that I'm not going to bolt and Uber back to her place—she hands me a cocktail and gives me a wave, disappearing into the pulsating crowd. I give her a half-hearted wave back before sinking into the oversized cushions, trying not to think about what germs might be lurking in the fabric. If I only had one of those fluorescent CSI lights, I probably could have the whole VIP section condemned. A waitress comes by and I start ordering another gin and tonic, only to be interrupted by a hard body sliding in beside me.

"Drink?" The cute face attached to the hard body flashes me a dimpled smile.

I raise my glass up. "Yes, it is."

He laughs as if I've said the most hilarious thing in the world. "No, I mean, can I buy you another one?"

I give him the onceover, only then realizing that he's young—very young—like barely twenty-one. He's pretty cute though, with his messy blond curls and sweet chestnut eyes. I can't deny that his eagerness is infectious, like a golden retriever with a tennis ball.

"Sure," I relent, throwing back the rest of my gin and tonic. "Thank you…" Right then and there, I decide to change things up. "I'll take a tequila and soda with lime please."

"Hardcore," he says, and I raise an eyebrow. "I don't drink tequila. Sometimes my mom does though."

Oh, this is going well. "On second thought…" I start to get up, but he beats me to it.

"Sorry, sorry! Let me grab you that drink."

He returns a short while later, bearing my tequila and soda, plus a bottle of beer for himself. I eye the drink warily before shrugging and taking a big swig. With the day I've had, I don't have enough energy to care about whether he laced it. Besides, buddy-the-golden-retriever is way too expressive to be a master of deception. I can't remember if he told me his name or not, so I decide to just call him Buddy.

We try to make small talk, but it's virtually impossible over the thumping bass. Instead we head onto the dance floor for a few songs (if you can really call jumping up and down in a circle *dancing*). The alcohol takes over and I let myself relax. Buddy has his arms bolted around my waist and the taste of tequila lingers on my lips. I let my head fall back and close my eyes, deciding to just go with it. The warmth flowing through me feels so right, and Dale is a distant thought in my mind.

• • •

My eyes blink open and my first thought is *oh hell no*. I release a muffled groan while the events of last night replay in my mind. Buddy and I left together and hailed a taxi back to his place. There was some heavy making out and a lot of awkward thrashing, but I'm pretty sure things didn't progress beyond that point. I seem to remember tearing at his clothes like an animal, but the booze caught up with Buddy before things could get too serious. One too many drinks for the baby-faced lightweight, I guess. Peeking under the covers, I'm relieved to see that both my bra and skirt remain in place. In fact, I'm still wearing my uncomfortable ankle boots, which protrude from the foot of the bed like I'm the Wicked Witch of the East.

My head is absolutely pounding. I grimace at Buddy, who's snoring peacefully beside me, before taking stock of the room—sweet Jesus, it's not even the basement suite that I came to terms with last night. The morning sun through the slot windows tells me that we're somewhere underground, but the space looks more like a rec room than a bedroom, complete with a mattress on the floor and a mini bar fridge. There's even an ironing board with freshly starched dress shirts strewn across it, but they're way too big to be Buddy's.

I squint at the cuckoo-clock across the room, hunting for my contacts and cursing my nearsightedness in the process. Luckily, I find them right away—on the bedside table, floating in a glass of water. I don't know whether to be proud or mortified for storing my contacts in such an impeccable fashion. I feel around inside the glass for the slimy little things, scooping them up and shoving them back into my eyes. They burn from the lack of lubrication, but when my eyes finally clear, I zero-in on the movie poster tacked to the opposite wall, a vintage Technicolor print for *Blue Hawaii,* complete with palm trees, bikinis, Elvis Presley, and plenty of butterscotch-sand. In that instant, it all clicks together for me. I need a new start, but not just any new start; I need a new start in Hawaii.

Honestly, Hawaii has been on my bucket list forever. I wanted to honeymoon on one of the islands, but Dale thought Hawaii was too pedestrian of a travel destination—his words, not mine. He insisted on Turks and Caicos instead. Nonetheless, studying the image of Elvis Presley playing a ukulele in short-shorts and a pink lei, I realize that I could really use some paradise in my life right now. While attempting to get up from the floor mattress, I hear a voice calling from upstairs. "Are you up yet, Chase? Breakfast is ready…I made pancakes."

Holy hell—it's got to be his mother. I mean, my first guess should be his wife, but her tone of voice is so maternal. Between the ironing board in the corner and the Xbox plugged into the TV, who else could it be? I find my tank top on the floor and quickly pull it over my head, frantically seeking an escape route but finding just one set of stairs leading to the main house. I definitely can't go up there—actually, it sounds like mommy dearest is coming downstairs. God knows what she'll do to me (or Buddy) if she finds me here. I bolt towards the half open window, my only other option, and begin to heave myself outside, flashing my ass cheeks in the process. My leather skirt bunches around my waist and I'm already halfway out the window when I hear Buddy speak behind me.

"Where are you going?" He croaks.

I glance over my shoulder and give him an apologetic smile. "Sorry, Buddy. Last night was fun, but it's not going to work out."

"Who's Buddy? My name is Chase," he asserts, half sitting up to rub his eyes. At the same time, Buddy's—or Chase's—cellphone starts playing the tune of Boney M's "Feliz Navidad."

"Oh, you have got to be kidding me!" I shout, but Chase is clueless. I hear the stairs creak at the same time that his mom comes *yoo-hooing* around the corner. I barely make it out in time, panting like a beast and 100% mortified about our *oh-so-sloppy* make-out session. Still, I'm grateful for the experience, thanks to the vision of Hawaii that Buddy's bedroom has burned into my retinas.

I hobble my way through the backyard and onto the main road, ambling along until I find a bus stop. There I sit down on the curb and rifle through my purse for my phone. Navigating to my recent calls, I dial Dale's number, altogether unsurprised that I have only one missed call and no messages. He answers right away, but I don't give him a chance to speak. Instead, the words come flooding out.

"I want a divorce." The next second, I hang up and burst into tears.

Chapter 4

A new year, a new start—once a familiar adage and now a painful reminder for my life. I've decided that January will be a month of rebirth, and the moment that we touch down at Maui International Airport, I feel that statement pulsing through my bones.

    1. *Resignation letter: check*

    2. *One signed separation agreement: check*

    3. *One BMW lease surrendered: check*

    4. *One townhouse in escrow: check*

    5. *One-way ticket to Maui: check*

    6. *One suitcase: check*

And a partridge in a pear tree. I'm so pleased that the holiday season is over, with all its in-your-face-joy and cheating-no-good-husbands. Now things can get back to normal, whatever that means. For a moment, I close my eyes in the center of the terminal, letting its energy hit me—the warm breeze blowing through the open air design with fresh leis everywhere and the heady scent of plumeria flowers lingering in the air.

Liquidating your whole life is actually much easier than it sounds. Once the townhouse sale has officially closed, I'll use my share to pay off my remaining student loans, then stash some savings away while I figure out my next move. One thing is for sure: I'm very glad to be free of the stupid Restoration Hardware furniture. When we first moved in together, my vote was for IKEA, but Dale being Dale wouldn't have it. I'd managed to sell a whole bunch of it on some community bidding site though, which padded my purse with pocket money and left Dale with nothing but a mattress on the floor (perhaps there was a thing or to I'd learned from Buddy after all).

I retrieve my single suitcase from the conveyor belt and head outside to track down a taxi, finding one right away. The driver leaning against the hood is what I'd describe as skinny-fat, with toothpick legs and a little round belly sticking out from beneath his open button-down shirt. I stare at his dirty flip-flops and work my way up to his face, watching him grin at me with tobacco-stained teeth.

"*Mahalo, nani wahine.*" His face is warm and friendly, with a soothing effect that matches the breeze itself. "The name's Paul, but my friends call me Pancho." He extends a hand and I shake it, unsure whether that means I should call him Paul, or Pancho.

"Hi Paul," I say, assuming that he and I aren't friends yet. "I'm heading somewhere called Paia Town. Do you know where that is?"

"It just so happens that I live in Paia. In fact, I'm heading home right now. Just finishing up my shift."

"Perfect," I exhale, finally able to relax. He pops open the trunk and reaches for one of my bags, but I packed light and manage to lope it inside on my own.

When I head for the back door, he shakes his head. "Sit up front and keep me company."

I shrug, joining him in the cab. He turns up the radio and Sublime's "Santeria" sounds from the speakers. I rest my head against the seat as he crawls away from the curb. Already I feel lighter, like I'm becoming one with the tropical atmosphere. The airport grounds alone are beautiful, but by the time we're cruising down the interstate, I've straightened out my neck to gape out the window. The road hugs the coastline and through the swaying palms, I see huge whitewalls crashing into the shore. It's worth way more than a postcard.

Paul (or Pancho) interrupts my reverie. "So what's in Paia? You got friends there?"

"What?" I say, running my hands through my hair, as if trying to tame a wild animal. I can already feel it frizzing in the humidity.

"No friends. I found a place to rent online. It looked very peaceful." I'd found the place on Airbnb, after searching for listings on the North Island. Google said that the island was more secluded in the north, and since I'm not into dealing with people right now, that was perfect. Besides, the rental was about a third the price of similar vacation rentals in many of the more tourist-popular areas, so it really was a win-win.

"It's peaceful for sure." Pancho nods. "It actually means peace."

"What does?"

"*Paia*. The word means peace in Hawaiian." He rolls down his window and hangs out his arm into the wind.

"That's pretty perfect then. It's my first time in Hawaii," I admit, and he whistles.

"Alright, an island virgin…" He draws out the last word, and I can feel the blush creeping across my cheeks. "How long are you here for pretty lady?"

I clear my throat. "In Paia? Not sure yet. A while."

"Well, you picked the right spot, and it's pronounced *Pah-ee-ya,* just to give you a heads up—locals can be fussy." He shoots me a wink. "It's the last stop on the road to Hana and a place where lots of tourists fill up on gas, but we get some of the most wicked swell here—surfers, windsurfers, you name it."

I've seen movies set in Hawaii, but experiencing it with my own two eyes is still surreal. I might only be seeing it through the cracked windshield of Pancho's cab, but it's already one of the most beautiful places I've ever been. Calling it paradise might seem cliché, but paradise is the only word that fits its impression upon me. Even the air smells different, fresher somehow—clean fragrance and fruity scents—and as we cross into more jungle-like territory, I see an actual, no joke rainbow curved across the sky.

"It's an awesome community, once you get to know the locals," Pancho adds.

His statement makes me wonder what the community is like if you don't know the locals, but I don't say anything. Instead, my eyes travel to the cubed picture frame dangling from his rearview mirror. It holds a photo of a little girl, probably no more than a few years old, with chubby cheeks and shiny black curls.

"Is that your daughter?"

He flicks the cube with his finger. It spins around in a circle and a huge grin spreads across his face.

"That's my Melia. She's eight now, but I can't bring myself to take it down—even though I know she hates it." He chuckles.

"She's beautiful."

His voice rings out with adoration. "You should see her now."

"Trouble ahead for you?" I tease, and he laughs at my comment.

"Nothing I can't handle." The way he speaks about his daughter tugs at something deep in my chest. It's a look that parents often wear on their faces, a feeling that cannot be replicated, characteristic of a secret club that no amount of money or favor can penetrate. I'm both in awe of and sick with jealousy at the same time. While starting a family was initially Dale's idea, it became my passion, until suddenly I had to manifest enough passion for both of us.

"*Ohana*," Pancho mutters. "It means family, and family is everything here in Hawaii. You'll see." He raises his eyebrows at me in the mirror. I stare out the windshield, watching as the road narrows and winds into lush vegetation. "Welcome to the North Shore." Pancho gives me a welcoming nod.

As we pull onto the main drag, he explains that it's literally a one stoplight town. I'm immediately drawn in by the Western-style buildings, painted in a patchwork of pastel colors. We pass a surf shop, café, gelato shop, and this place selling expensive-looking beachwear. The vibe is old country charm mixed with bohemian beachside funk.

"It's perfect," I say, my voice coming out all breathy.

He laughs. "It ain't perfect, but it's ours."

"About how many people live here?"

He shrugs. "A few thousand, I think, but it's busier with the tourists."

We cruise down the narrow main street, flanked by power lines and skinny palms. I read some of the storefront business names aloud: Paia Inn, Mama's, and Charley's, as Pancho gestures to the right.

"There's a great beach down there called Paia Bay," he explains, and I catch a glimpse of sparkling white sand and navy blue ocean between one of the buildings. The town center doesn't appear to be more than half-a-mile long.

As we head upcountry, the vegetation thickens for about five minutes until we pull off the road. The taxi bumps down an unpaved route, kicking up dust as it lurches to a stop before a beautiful house with a thatched roof, floor to ceiling windows, and a wrap-around verandah. Set back from the ocean by sixty feet, the house appears almost circular, allowing it to blend and camouflage with its surroundings. One glance at the place tells me that it doesn't match the pictures of the apartment that I booked.

"Welcome to Kane's place. He's probably not home, but I'm guessing you booked the Ohana suite."

He leans back against his seat and points at a smaller one story cottage situated even closer to the ocean. It looks cozy and inviting, with its pitched roof and plantation shutters. I hop out of the passenger-seat and head for the trunk, with Pancho following suit.

"Need any help?"

"I think I've got it. The owner left pretty detailed instructions." I haul my suitcase onto the pavement, struggling with the bulky handle.

"I'm not surprised. Kane likes his peace and quiet—the less talking, the better." He chuckles with a smile that touches his eyes.

"Thanks for all your help, Paul." I hand over a wad of cash and before I can say goodbye, he envelops me in a bear hug.

"Please, call me Pancho."

"Okay, Pancho. Umm…just curious though, why are you hugging me?" Even though it's weird and surprising, it feels kind of nice.

"You look like you need a hug."

His embrace matches the rest of him, from his cartoon-wide smile to that grounding deep-throated chuckle. I feel my eyes start to water; I cannot remember the last time anyone treated me so tenderly. Dale was definitely not a hugger, and neither was Jamie—not to mention that I grew up in a pretty formal household. My proper English parents never placed that much value on physical affection. I sigh when he releases me from his clutches, giving me a little wave before jumping back into his car.

"*A hui hou.* Hope to see you around, Red!" He shouts from the window, as the taxi pulls away in a cloud of dust.

The front door of the cottage is actually around the back, closer to the road. I pull up my email for the keypad combination, freeing the door from its hinges. Inside, I find a spotless white kitchen, scuffed wooden floors, and handmade rattan furniture. It's what I'd classify as "shabby chic" and far more space than I'd expected for the price. I fall in love with the round dining table set, the worn loveseat against the wall, and the back bedroom partitioned off with a wicker divider. The air conditioning is cool bliss, as I drop my bag on the floor and release a pent-up breath.

"I'm finally here," I say, to no one but myself, closing my eyes and meditating on everything that I gave up to arrive at this here and now—this little piece of my own freedom. I notice a set of glass doors just past the kitchen and slide them open with a well warranted gasp, for the view is something beyond beauty. My foot creaks onto the small lanai, a kind of Hawaiian patio that I've only seen in pictures, revealing an expanse of emerald green Bermuda grass. Beyond it lies the never-ending sparkle of turquoise ocean.

The view is the most impressive aspect of the property by far, and I don't have much to complain about. Still, I can't help but notice a big rectangle in the shape of a pool at the front of the house, long ago filled with lumpy, gray cement. It doesn't match the meticulously maintained property—in a word, it's ugly. I know the upkeep for pools is expensive, but surely there's a better option than plugging it with rocks. Despite the eyesore, I'm lucky to have found this little piece of paradise. I've pre-paid for a month's stay, but I'm thinking of asking the owner to extend the reservation. The wind chimes clanging together behind me are the only item that needs to go. They're cute and made of intricately woven shells, but I hate the clanging sound as much as Boney M's "Feliz Navidad."

Heading back inside, I spot an outdoor shower made entirely of bamboo beams. Showering outside wasn't generally acceptable in our upscale San Fran neighborhood, but I'm a long way from home now and fully intend to embrace my surroundings. I glance once more at the tidy little kitchen, and a handful of new recipes spring to mind, but first I need a shower and a moment to unpack. More importantly, I need to call Jamie. I dial her on my cellphone—the one possession that I couldn't part with—and she answers on the first ring.

"So, you're alive?" She says, dryly, before I can even say hello.

"I'm just calling to let you know that I made it here safely—as instructed."

She snorts into the phone. "I don't know whether to congratulate you, or hire some local to personally smack you upside the head."

"Congratulations will do for now, I think," I say, wondering where she'd find anyone so inclined in a town like Paia.

She sighs. "I miss you already. I hate Dale even more for driving you out of San Fran."

"He didn't drive me out, Jamie. I made this decision by myself. We both know it was time to go."

"Have you heard from him?" She asks, bitterly.

"Not since the day before yesterday. He's still pretending that I'm on vacation, and he definitely hasn't acknowledged that I resigned, despite that my signature's drying with HR as we speak. If I'm lucky, I'll only have to speak with him a few more times, about the house sale, as the final draft of our separation agreement is already in place."

She changes the subject then, probably sensing my fatigue. "So what's it like over there?"

"Well, I've only seen the coastline and the airport so far, but those were both stunning. The vacation rental I have is pretty perfect. It's right on the beach with a private outdoor shower! I basically have my own house."

"That sounds pretty incredible," she concedes. "Meet any hot guys yet?"

I roll my eyes, though I know she can't tell through the phone. "I've been here, like, an hour, Jamie. The only man I've met is Pancho, the cab driver."

"*Poncho?* Like the rain jacket?"

I shake my head and giggle. "His name is technically Paul, but friends call him Pancho." Jamie always has a way of making me laugh.

"Well, is he hot at least?"

I laugh out loud this time. "You're impossible."

The line goes silent for a moment, and then Jamie's voice echoes across the Pacific Ocean. "Ashley, just come home, okay?"

"I can't," I whisper.

"Then I'm coming to you."

"Anytime—the sooner, the better."

"Let me find some space in my work schedule, and I'll be there. You can be my unofficial host, provided you show me everything that Maui has to offer."

"Done. I love you, Jamie."

"I love you too, Ash. Call if you need anything."

Something gnaws at my gut the second that I hang up the phone. Did I just make the biggest mistake of my life? I tell myself that it's only day one. Until I've had time to clear my head and give Paia a try, I must not second guess myself. In the meantime, a short nap should restore my internal sense of carpe diem. I sleep for a while and awake to the blistering hot afternoon sun streaming in through the windows. I glance at my phone, realizing that it's already after four o'clock. The second that I rub the sleep from my eyes, my stomach grumbles in warning. I don't have any groceries yet, so I take a quick shower and throw on a knee-length turquoise sundress and matching sandals, setting out to find a restaurant A.S.A.P.

The walk into Paia Town doesn't take long, even at a turtle's pace, but I'm surprised by how undeveloped the area remains. It's got this great hippie-surf-town vibe that you simply couldn't fabricate—I know because Silverdale Developments had tried in planned housing communities on many occasions, but without much success. At the end of the day, you just can't manufacture laid-back. I stop and snap an iPhone picture of some colorful surfboards all bound together in a fence. Carrying on with my walk, I pass buildings trimmed with turquoise, street buskers playing acoustic guitar, and this one preacher trying to sell me salvation from a street corner.

I finally stumble upon an open air Tiki-style bar called Salty's, bringing to mind old memories of college trips and tequila shots, with its hanging bamboo sign and bright green façade. I wander inside through a narrow courtyard flanked by Tiki idols, which opens up into a magical little backyard haven. There are two deck levels shaded by wooden gazebos and one pergola teaming with lush jungle vines. Potted palms dot the space as colored Christmas lights zigzag across the ceiling. I notice a handful of tables with stools made out of tree trunks, plus an outdoor fireplace flanked by Adirondack chairs. There's even a large hammock at the back (currently occupied by a young guy with dreadlocks), but the bar seems quite empty for this time of day, with only half a dozen people scattered around. It's the kind a place a kid would design, with no limits placed upon the imagination, and it was easily my new favorite spot in town.

I make my way to the upper deck and take a seat at the most catching bar I've ever seen. The counter looks to be constructed entirely of driftwood, and there's a pitched tin roof over the whole area, which I bet sounds amazing in the rain. However, my attention doesn't linger that long on the countertop, my eyes locking with the bartender's deep set hazel eyes. He's big—really big—both wide and tall and honestly kind of intimidating with his arms like crossbones over his enormous chest—not that I was looking at his chest or anything. One might describe him as beefy, but right now he's glowering at me like I'm the last person on earth he wants to serve.

"What'll it be?" He barks, but I can't tear my eyes away from his face.

His dark brown hair extends to just below his ears, with sun-kissed highlights emphasizing the green of his hazel eyes. A full beard camouflages his notably square chin, and as I continue my perusal, I notice the makings of rough beauty: strong nose, full lips, and an inch-long scar bisecting his eyebrow.

"What do you want?" He repeats, louder this time.

I can't help but stutter. "What do you have to eat?"

"No food." He shakes his head, rattling the shell necklace looped around his neck. On anyone else, the necklace would look ridiculous—frat boy to the umpteenth degree—but on him it's just...*yum*.

"Nothing?" I ask, my stomach growling again.

"Popcorn." He shrugs. "Maybe some macadamia nuts in the back."

"Then I'll have both, along with the biggest margarita you can make."

He blinks and I can't help but notice his long eyelashes, or the adorable cluster of freckles under his left eye. Oh boy...for a woman who just swore off men, I'm paying way too much attention to his facial features.

He grabs a blender for my margarita, turning away just as someone snags the seat beside me. "Apparently this place used to have delectable food, at least until cranky old Keo here bought it."

So his name is Keo—that's one little detail out of the way. I glance over and see a shock of frizzy grayish hair attached to a very tiny woman. She's wearing a fringe suede jacket and bellbottom pants, plus a straw hat and oversized sunglasses, which she whips off and sets down on the bar top.

"I'm told they served fresh fish tacos and poke that would melt in your mouth," she adds, "but this big galoot gave it all up for booze and mixed nuts."

His shoulders stiffen, but I can tell that he's listening. "Ah well, at least he didn't let them tear it down and build a McDonald's instead. Right, Keo?" She waves at him, and I notice a collection of turquoise and silver rings all over her fingers.

"Pave paradise and put up a parking lot?" I say, and she cackles back.

"I'm going to like you. I can tell already. The name's Adele. What's your story, doll? Here on your honeymoon?"

I snort. "Not quite."

Keo sets my drink down, and immediately I throw half of it back. "Another please." His eyes narrow as I smack my lips together, but he nods nonetheless. I down the rest of my first drink and slam the glass on the counter. "It's nice to meet you, Adele. I just moved here—at least—I think I did."

"You think?" She answers, reaching over to grab some popcorn from the bowl Keo just placed before me. I glance at the popcorn myself and shake my head. I should be starving, but the ice from the margaritas is filling me up.

"I quit my job, sold all of my things, and now I'm starting over."

"Good for you!" She shouts, grasping my wrist with butter-coated fingers. "Fuck the man!"

"The man?"

"The establishment."

"It wasn't really like that, actually."

"What was it like, then?" She gives me an expectant look, and already I can tell that she and I will be friends. Keo sets another margarita down for me, and I proceed to order a tequila shot. He raises an eyebrow but doesn't comment. Three margaritas, one handful of popcorn, and ten macadamia nuts later, I'm giving Adele my life story. As I launch into another tale about my cheating soon-to-be-ex-husband, I notice that my tongue is numb from the frozen drinks.

"So it turns out that our two hundred dollar a pop trainer was working out more than my husband's quads." I snort, causing Keo to swivel around. "He even had a track suit custom-designed for him to wear jogging with her—some top of the line sweat-wicking material weaved with silver unicorn tears, or whatever nonsense like that. It cost two thousand bucks, too. I mean, it was for running—some sweatpants from Costco could've done the trick, right? Don't even get me started on his stupid espresso machine. It was this god awful looking thing with *revolutionary fine foam technology*. Apparently the thing won awards."

I lay my head down on the bar-top and make eye contact with Adele. "Want to know a secret?" I mock-whisper, and she nods serenely.

"I used to pretend to drink his expensive coffee before work, but then I'd simply pour it down the sink and make a Starbucks run."

"A true rebel." A much deeper voice cuts through our conversation, and I lift my head to see the hulking bartender. His voice is flat and unreadable, so I can't tell if he's teasing me or not.

"It speaks," I say, half-slurring.

"Figured someone else should get a chance."

"Hardy-har-har." I dismiss him with a flick of my hand, turning my attention back to Adele. "Not to mention all the nightgowns he bought me. He slept in silk boxers like some kind of Hugh Heffner wannabe, and I hate the feeling of silk, but he never got the hint. He'd buy me all these silky lace nightgowns, like it was the fifties or something, and I'd try— I'd try to sleep in the damn things, but every time I'd long for the ratty Bob Marley tee I'd worn since college. I mean, who on earth enjoys sleeping in itchy lace and gauzy chiffon? It's like being wrapped in expensive dryer sheets."

Adele sighs in ecstasy. "Ah, the sixties…I loved my husband so much that I spent fifty years wearing house dresses. Now I'm seventy-eight years old and the love of my life is gone, so I say fuck dresses. I've been reborn."

"Good for you." I push her stem-less glass of white wine towards her and raise mine up for a sloppy cheers.

"I think I want to be a lesbian," she states, matter-of-factly, making me spit out a mouthful of margarita.

"Sorry?"

"I'd like to give it a whirl, now that Hal's gone."

"I don't think it works that way," I counter. This conversation is careering off track faster than a runaway train, but Keo seems totally unfazed, continuing to towel off freshly cleaned glasses.

"I'm sorry about your husband," I half whisper, realizing that I've unleashed all of my problems onto this poor, unsuspecting woman without asking a word about her life.

"Pshaw." She squeezes my free hand, the one that's not wrapped around my margarita. "When I lost him a few years back, I decided that I needed a big change, and now I love my life in Paia. I'm truly blessed."

"To you then, Adele, and to your beautiful life." I throw back the rest of my margarita and shift my attention back to Keo.

"Another, please."

"No."

"No?"

"I'm not serving you anything else!" He barks.

"Why not?" I whine, but it takes all my effort to speak without slurring.

"I SAID NO!" He shouts so loud that I actually let out a whimper. I feel everyone turn to stare at us, and Keo looks even scarier than my first impression might suggest. I slide off the stool on shaky legs, and Adele does the same, linking one arm through mine. She leads me to the tree trunk stools and makes me sit down.

"Don't mind him," she says, reassuringly, slinging an arm around my back.

I inhale a shaky breath. "What's his problem?"

"I'm not really sure. I just know the rumors, but I've never put much stock in gossip."

"Rumors?"

She hesitates before answering. "They say he killed his whole family, but that's hardly possible if he's here running this bar in Paia."

"Killed his family?" I glance over my shoulder at Keo. His back is turned away, but his shoulders rise and fall in a broken succession of deep breaths.

"All I know is that Keo owns this place and holds the title of grouchiest-man-in-town, so most people tend to give him a wide berth. Consider yourself appropriately warned."

I look around the bar and see that she's not wrong; it's empty apart from the seats we just abandoned. The remaining patrons give Keo sidelong looks, and one woman even whispers something in her partner's ear. They share a worried glance, all fueled by his outburst, no doubt. I'm still feeling a little raw, but at least Keo's outburst helped me sober up. I tell Adele that I want to go home, and she insists on accompanying me, at least part of the way.

I spot a small pizza place along the main drag, and my mouth waters at the smell of fried dough and melted cheese. I'd forgotten how hungry I was—my last good meal was some granola before boarding my plane this morning. I devour two slices of veggie pizza and Adele keeps me company, eventually walking me home. She's pretty sprite for an old lady; in fact, I almost have to jog to keep up with her, but I do find her presence comforting.

"Do you have kids Adele?" She smiles in the moonlight, illuminating her forlorn features.

"Hal and I couldn't."

"I'm sorry. Dale and I couldn't either. We tried..." I trail off.

"Don't be sorry, my dear. We had a beautiful life together. Don't be discouraged either—you're young! It sounds like you're better off without this Dale anyways. Who knows what the future holds?"

"I hope you're right," I say, stifling a yawn with my fist.

"Don't hope so, honey—know so." She gives me a firm hug, and I find myself melting in her arms. I've received more hugs today than over the past four years combined.

"I like you Ashley," she says, pulling me tight. "I think I'll keep you. Now go and get some rest. I'll introduce you to Kayla tomorrow. She's a firecracker—you'll love her. I'll pick you up at ten."

I find myself nodding, despite having no idea to what I've just agreed. "Sounds good to me. Hey Adele, what's your last name?"

"It's Lucky. Adele Lucky." She shoos me down the path to my suite, and I find myself grinning from ear to ear.

"That sounds about right."

Adele's voice shouts after me in the darkness. "Dear, you've been drinking and traveling all day—go straight to bed!"

I give her an acknowledging wave, but I have no intention of following her instructions. The night is young and the amber moon sits high and bright in the sky. I stumble past my cottage and head directly for the stretch of ocean in the distance, climbing over a row of dense shrubs to reach a slice of rocky beach. The ocean looks almost silver in the moonlight, its white-capped waves crashing into the shoreline like musical chords. I jump from boulder to boulder, teetering in thin sandals as I move towards the tide line. I'm almost there when a huge hand plummets onto my right shoulder, jerking me backwards until I slam into a rock-hard body. I let out an ear-piercing shriek upon realizing that I'm staring over my shoulder into the dark eyes of our local bartender-slash-potential-murderer, Keo.

I heave air into my lungs, trying to find the right words, but nothing rational comes to mind. My eyes find fierceness in his gaze, and my heart hurts for the hard lines along his mouth, the dark secrets twitching in his jaw. He holds my back against his ferociously huge front, and I can't help but tremble.

"Just where do you think you're going, Ashley?"

Chapter 5

I manage to shirk out of his rough hold, whirling around until we're face-to-face.

"What are you doing here?" I sputter, but the rush of adrenaline leaves me breathless.

"What are YOU doing here?" He parrots, and I laugh because it's all so absurd.

I gesture to my right. "As a matter of fact, I'm staying here—in the guest cottage."

He looks down at the ground, then back up at me. "I live here."

"Did you not just hear what I said?"

"Yes, but I still live here."

"No, I'm renting from Kane. You're Keo."

"Kane Keo, the owner," he says, as if it's obvious. "And you're renting the suite, Miss Walsh, not the beach." The name surprises me at first, because nobody calls me Walsh anymore, but I do remember booking the accommodation in my maiden name.

"I didn't realize that the beach was off limits."

"It's dangerous out here—the ocean doesn't mess around."

"I was just having a look."

"Well don't—the last thing I need is a dead tourist on my hands. Use your head next time."

It's on the tip of my tongue to ask what he knows about dead tourists, but self-preservation wins out. I keep my mouth shut. The rumors are likely nothing more than rumors, but Kane has an aura of danger that I don't want to test. I step back a few paces and almost lose my footing on some loose rocks. He lunges forward as if he's going to grab me and then stops himself, so I take the opportunity to give him a onceover. He's barefoot and wearing low-slung board shorts, along with the same tattered t-shirt he had on in the bar.

I notice a large tattoo around his calf, a series of intricate looking black bands and shapes, extending from just below his knee to his ankle. It looks like some kind of tribal design, but it's hard to make out in the darkness. His hair blows wildly around his head, making him appear part-warrior and part-predator all at once. Honestly, I don't know men like Kane. My love life has been all fitted suits and shiny brown wingtips, whereas he is rawness personified, opposed to the cufflinks, manicures, and designer haircuts that otherwise characterized Dale. While I can tell that he's is getting more impatient with me by the minute, I can't stop staring. Instead, I give him a wink.

Immediately he growls at me. "Get off my beach"

"Done and done."

I stomp right past him, biting my tongue in the process. I'd love to tell him to shove the rental up his ass, but other than his major dick-vibe, Kane's place is perfect for me. I definitely won't find something comparable at this time of year, so I walk back to the suite with my head held high. I can feel his eyes trailing me all the way to the door, but I don't look back. I simply punch in the key code and slam the door as hard as possible, kicking off my sandals but leaving my sundress in place.

Sleeps seems near impossible, but my fiery mood leaves me the moment that my head hits the pillow. I feel my eyelids drooping like molasses. As I drift off, I can still feel Kane's rough calloused hands on my exposed shoulders. I wonder how they'd feel on other parts of my body, and my hand snakes under my sundress, dipping beneath my panties to find another outlet for my desire. I close my eyes while imagining those lustrous dark eyes—like magic eight-balls—full of questions and answers and mystery.

...

When I wake up, everything hurts: my pounding head, aching feet, and gurgling stomach. I touch my nose and feel the beginnings of my first Hawaiian sunburn. My shoulders are also on fire. Being fair-skinned, I'm usually more careful about the sun, but yesterday was a whirlwind. I groan remembering how I acted at the bar, my two slices of heavy pizza, and that run-in with Kane Keo. What a great start to my new life. I roll over and look at the time, realizing that it's a quarter to ten, and I'm fairly certain I agreed to some kind of activity with my new friend, Adele.

At least I made a new friend.

I chase two ibuprofens with an ice cold shower, throwing on a swimsuit and cover-up before heading outside. Kane's place is dark and the blinds are drawn. The house appears to be locked up like a fortress. Weird. I thought he'd be up early and working like a machine. A shiny silver Land Rover interrupts my spying, rumbling down the pathway and onto my driveway. Adele is at the wheel, her long silver hair whipping in the wind as she waves at me. Someone sits in the front passenger seat, so I happily hop in the back as Adele begins with the introductions.

"Ashley Walsh, meet Kayla Lee. Kayla meet Ashley."

Kayla whips around and gives me a smile, revealing a set of adorable dimples. "So you're the *malihini.* How ya goin'?"

"I'm not sure what that is, but I'm good, thanks."

"It means newcomer." It takes me a minute to place her accent: Australian. It seems at odds with her raven hair and deep caramel tan.

"Wow, you have the best tan I've ever seen."

She's gorgeous, like, catalogue model gorgeous. She laughs and blinks her wide-set blue eyes at me.

"I'm Greek Australian—the Greek part helps with the tan, the Australian part with surfing."

"Kayla here is an A.S.P. ranked semi-pro surfer," Adele explains.

"Wow, that's incredible," I chime, though I have no idea what A.S.P. means.

"American Surf Professionals." Kayla fills in the blanks, as if she can read my mind. I actually *have* heard of American Surf Professionals, which is incredibly cool. Apparently I'm riding with a big time athlete.

"She's sponsored as well," Adele adds with pride. "Yep, Kayla Lee for Australian Gold."

Kayla laughs off the comment, but the sound is like liquid gold. "It's far less impressive than it sounds," she says. "Being a sponsored surfer usually means a lot of time nursing injuries and sleeping on other people's sofas, but it helps with groceries and keeps me in the best gear." She gestures to her cute shorty wetsuit.

I take one last look at Kane's house before Adele peels onto the highway. Part of me wonders whether he's watching from the window, but another part of me isn't sure why I even care. After a short drive, we arrive at Baldwin Beach. I'm literally gaping at the ocean as I clamber out of the Land Rover. Mature palm trees blow gently in the breeze, framed by dense greenery, flowers, and driftwood, as sand dunes rise up to meet the clearest turquoise water I've ever seen. Kayla slings an arm around my neck to get me moving.

"See right across there? There you have one of the best views of the West Maui mountains." She gives me a quick squeeze before jogging off with her surfboard.

I knew she was beautiful in the car, but her body is actually insane—a serious athlete with tone, a compact chest, strong arms, and the loveliest long torso I've ever seen. Glancing down at my own curves, which Dale used to refer to as lush, I can't help but feel a little intimidated. Kayla would look incredible wearing just about anything. I find Adele down the beach, grateful to see that she's chosen a spot with shade. I set my towel down on the soft sand and self-consciously tug off my cover-up. Underneath I'm wearing a sea-green string-bikini which suddenly feels way too small for the expanse of white skin on display.

Adele unearths a little radio from her enormous straw bag, tuning into a station playing one of my favorite Bob Marley songs, "Time Will Tell." I recline back on the towel and let the late morning wind wash over me, planning to spend my time watching the sun climb higher in the sky. When I hear Adele rustling around, I crack open one eye, only to witness her pull out a legit flask and proceed to spike her travel mug.

"Baileys?" She asks, thrusting the silver canister towards me.

"Isn't it a bit early for Baileys?"

She snorts. "I'm seventy-eight years old, remember? For me, it's never too early for anything, Baileys included. I could die anytime!"

I give her a sidelong glance. Between her fit physique and weathered but healthy looking skin, I highly doubt she's in danger of keeling over, but I let it slide. "I'm good, thanks."

Listening to my own words, I realize that I am actually good. For the first time in years, I don't feel anxious, angry, or empty. With the hot sun on my legs, the gentle breeze blowing through my hair, and my hangover rapidly subsiding, it's the first time I've felt peaceful in months. I cast my eyes upwards to count the clouds, as a large shadow appears above my head, altogether blocking my view of the sun.

"You need to put on some sunscreen," grumbles the deep low voice of shadow-man. I groan internally, squinting my eyes to see Kane hovering over my towel. He's shirtless with a deep olive tan continuing all the way down his body before disappearing beneath his board shorts. There's a smattering of dark hair on his extremely wide chest, but I think it suits him. In the light of day, his calf tattoo actually looks even blacker, wrapping all the way around his leg. I take a moment to study the intricate geometric design of interlocking squares, circles, and diamond shapes.

"I put some sunscreen on already," I contest, wondering why I'm having this conversation in the first place.

"Put on some more." He barks the order before turning to go. "And get yourself a hat while you're at it. Might as well attempt to cover up at least one part of yourself."

I brace myself on my elbows, leaning backwards to stare at him with my jaw hanging open. "What the hell was that?" I ask Adele, who's watching him go with a smirk on her face.

"I have no idea, dear. That's the most I've heard him speak in a long time."

"It's really none of his business. Is he drunk or something?"

Adele shakes her head. "I doubt it. I've never seen him touch the stuff—he just doles it out."

"What's he even doing here?" I huff out. "Shouldn't he be at the bar?"

She shrugs. "It's Sunday."

"So?"

"So the bar is closed on Sunday."

"Oh."

Kayla catches our attention, shouting from the water's edge. I shield my eyes to get a better look, and what I initially thought was a surfboard now appears to be a boogie board. She's waving her arms like a madwoman and screaming for me to join her. I'm not the strongest of swimmers, but I'm here at the beach, so why not?

"When in Rome…" I hustle to my feet, walking towards Kayla and doing my best to ignore Kane, who seems to have planted himself in the sand just a few feet away.

"Sure you know what you're doing?" He cautions as I walk past him, his voice low and menacing.

"I think I can handle a boogie board," I drone, proceeding to join Kayla in the shallow waves. She shows me how to position the board before handing it over. I run full tilt into the waves, laughing hysterically as they crash and knead my body into dough. It feels so free and far more invigorating than spin class. Kayla and I take turns while Adele snaps photos from the beach.

A big one rolls in and Kayla tosses me the board. "I think you're ready, mate."

I release a battle-cry before charging straight for the wave. It rocks me hard as I crash into the breaking surf. The force lifts me backwards and rips the board from my fingers, but when I come up sputtering, I have a smile on my face. Kayla wades closer to the shoreline, shouting my name and gesturing like a wild woman. Confused, I look back towards the sand and notice that Adele is doubled over laughing. Only when I look down do I realize why—I've completely lost my bikini top! My chest is totally bare.

I scream and grapple to cover my sizeable chest. I'm at least a D-cup and my breasts are more than a handful. Instead, I mash my forearms against my nipples and hope for the best, trying to wave towards Kayla, but this is difficult with crossed arms and the baby waves breaking against my legs. Kayla is hunting around for my triangle top, but she cannot stop laughing long enough to really focus on the task. I look around myself, but the top is nowhere to be found.

I head for the shore with as much dignity as I can muster. To my shock, Kane meets me at the shoreline and wraps a button-down garment around my shoulders. The thing completely swallows me. I figure he's got to be a foot taller than me at five foot six, but I'm surprised by his gentleness nonetheless. The shirt is white, and damp enough to be see-through, but it's the thought that counts.

"Thank you," I meet his eyes, sliding my arms through the short sleeves.

His face is unreadable again, but I see the hint of a smile tugging at his lips—or maybe I'm just imagining it. "You ok?"

"Embarrassed, but I'll live."

Kayla runs to join us, hooting and hollering as if she just won the lottery. She whips my sea-green bikini top in circles above her head, and I understand.

"Oh, thank God," I let out a big breath. She slingshots the offending bikini my way, and I feel my face redden. It's extra embarrassing with Kane standing there, especially in that I barely know him, but anyways.

"I'll give you your shirt back," I mumble, bending down to retrieve my bikini from the sand. His eyes lock with mine as he runs a hand through his sun-streaked hair.

"Keep it." His eyes skim my face, seeming to linger a moment on my lips. "I'd prefer if you cover up anyway." With that, he shakes his head and jogs down the beach.

"What in the holy fuck does that mean?" Kayla says.

His words sting a bit. Is he worried about my sunburn, or is the sight of me in a bathing suit so offensive that he'd rather donate his clothes?

"That is one weird bloke," Kayla whispers, and together we watch him go.

"I can't figure him out—one minute he's snapping at me, and the next he's acting all gentlemanly."

"Forget about him. They're all fuckwits in my book." Kayla's lips curl into a sneer. I can only assume that she means men, and I figure that there must be a story there, but now is not the time to ask.

"It's getting too hot. I think we should head into town for some food, ok? I'll go tell Adele to pack up."

Back at the car, Kayla graciously holds a towel around me, allowing me to redress in my bikini top and cover-up. I fold Kane's shirt before inhaling deeply into fabric, but only after checking that no one is looking. It smells musky—tinged with salt, earth, and the tangiest bit of sweat; the scent of pure, raw man—causing a tingling sensation between my legs. I shake it off and quickly stuff the shirt into my bag. The last thing I want is for Adele and Kayla to catch me in the act, but the scent of him lingers all the way into town. We grab a late lunch and down a few beers at Mama's Fish House, where I'm treated to the most delicious shrimp ceviche I've ever tasted. I wonder aloud if living here always feels like a vacation, and Adele is the first to answer.

"I've been here for six months now, but it feels longer than that—in a good way, of course."

"It's been two years for me, and I wouldn't be anywhere else," Kayla adds.

"Do you miss Australia?" I ask.

"Sometimes," she says, wistfully.

"Your family?"

"Most definitely not." She shakes her head and I notice how her face transforms.

I add "family" to my list of off-limit topics for Kayla, stuffing the last beautiful bite of shrimp into my mouth. "Well, I know that I should be doing something with my life. Figuring out my next move, looking for a job…" I sigh, leaning back in my chair. "I'm still waiting for my share of our townhouse sale, but that cushion won't last long, not with rent and student loans. Still, it's hard to get motivated, especially with blue skies and company like yours."

Adele reaches across the table to touch my hand. "You're being too hard on yourself. It has literally only been two days! Relax, dear, you're on island time now."

After lunch, they show me around Paia, stopping at their favorite little boutiques and forcing me to buy a few cute sundresses that I can't actually afford right now. I also pick up some groceries for the cottage, and we all agree to meet in town tomorrow evening at Salty's. It's such a beautiful afternoon, so I take my time walking back to my suite, appreciating the lush vegetation bordering the road. After a hot shower, I change into a tank top and my pajama shorts, getting ready to prepare dinner. The kitchen might be small but it's fully stocked, and I'm totally in my element.

I decide to grill the white fish in a sesame oil, garlic, and ginger marinade, pairing my concoction with fresh diced mango salsa and a side of jasmine rice. In the living room, I connect my phone to the music dock and hum along with some *beachy* music as I work. I always feel happy cooking, but as the space fills with the rich aromas of garlic and sesame, it somehow feels more like home. Once it's ready, I take my time eating and savor every bite.

Afterwards, I pour myself a glass of white wine and enjoy the sunset on the lanai. I know better than to try and chase the waves again, coming face-to-face with the wrath of Kane, but luckily the view is stunning from here. I get cozy in one of the patio chairs and close my eyes, basking in the warm evening sun. After a few minutes though, I find myself craning my neck around at Kane's own lanai. Surprisingly, he's there leaning against the railing of his own deck. The sun has dipped low enough in the sky that it bathes him in an orange glow, and his t-shirt is molded to his body like a second skin.

He doesn't even look in my direction, not even once, but it's hard to deny how handsome he is, even from a distance. His posture holds great tragedy, his expression contemplating both sadness and beauty. He appears completely in his own world, where people like me do not exist at all. The thought tugs at my heart as the sun dips behind the horizon. I finish my glass of wine and head back inside, sun-toasted and belly full, drifting to sleep with a big ol' smile on my face.

Chapter 6

Life is literally a beach. I spend the next morning at Baldwin, this time without a boogie board. Despite Kane's highhandedness, I slather myself in sunscreen and even don a big hat. He's not wrong about my skin, though he was a jerk about it. I dig my toes into the fine grain sand, lulled by the waves and low hum of bass music playing just a few towels over. It's a perfect morning to clear my head, and I'm surprised by how the hours fly faster than the rising sun.

Back at the cottage, I take my time prepping for Salty's. Part of me still smarts from Kane's comment about covering up, so I intend to show him just how good I look dressed up. Even if he couldn't care less, I want to look nice tonight for myself. I select my white bandage-style mini skirt, along with a tight raspberry tank top that really makes my emerald eyes pop. The skirt does a nice job of showing off my round hips, and while it's a bit of a pain, I straighten my titan red hair into a silky curtain.

At last, I add some subtle makeup, trying to be delicate with my sweeps of eye shadow, bronzer, and mascara. My ensemble is complete with a touch of raspberry lip gloss—and damn if I don't look good. The slight burn on my nose has faded, while my peachy cream skin gives off a nice glow. Still, the sun has darkened the freckles scattered across my nose, with which I've always had a love-hate relationship. I select a pair of white flip-flops and set out for the village. On my way, I hear the sound of a horn and turn to find Pancho in his taxi.

"Hey, Red. *Howzit?*"

I smile and assume he's asking how I am. "Good, thanks."

"Hop in."

"But I don't have any cash," I protest.

"No need, Red, it's a lift between friends. Besides, I can't let you go all the way wearing only *slippahs*." He looks pointedly at my footwear. "Where you headed?"

"Salty's."

"What a coincidence, so am I."

I climb into the passenger seat and we make small talk on the way. He parks and comes around to offer his arm. I take him up on the sweet gesture, and we walk into the bar together arm-in-arm, where Pancho is greeted by a round of cheers.

"You're popular," I say, laughing out loud.

"You know it, Red."

Kane glances at me from behind the bar, and his eyes flash with something immediately—heat, or perhaps even anger; I can't seem to tell the difference anymore.

"Fire pit, or bar?" Pancho asks.

My lips curve into what I imagine is a calculating smirk. The girls haven't arrived yet, and I want to test the waters with Kane. The thought of antagonizing him excites me.

"Bar please."

He deposits me on a stool made of KOA wood. One stool over sits a handsome blond guy with surfer hair and a sloppy smile.

"Who's your friend, Pancho?" The surfer guy asks. His hair is shaggy and unkempt, but the rest of him looks well put together. He wears dark slim jeans and a fitted Billabong t-shirt.

"Lance, this is Red. Red, meet Lance…" He takes our hands and clasps them together, forcing us to shake.

"*Ok'den*, I'll leave you be." Pancho moves on to greet a table of fans.

"Are you new in town, Red?" Lance asks, inching his stool even closer.

Before I can answer, Kane appears. "Her name is Ashley, not Red." I was barely aware that he knew my name, but I guess that makes sense, since I'm renting his place. He has all of my information, social security number included.

"What do you want, Ashley?" Kane acts as if taking my order is an inconvenience.

"I'll have a glass of white wine." I level him with my own far less intimidating stare.

"Put it on my tab, Kane," Lance says.

Kane gives Lance a death stare. "No."

"Come on, Keo."

His eyes could drill holes in Lance's forehead. "You deaf? I said no. She's my tenant, and it's not happening."

I clear my throat to butt in. "If it's all the same to you, I believe I'm renting the room, not your babysitting services." He winces ever-so-slightly at the word *babysitting*.

"You're my tenant," he barks. "Drinks on the house."

"That wasn't true last night."

He cocks one eyebrow. "Do you remember paying last night?"

Shoot, I think. I literally dined-and-dashed. "Uh, I'm sorry. I totally forgot."

"Like I said, on the house."

"Good to know." It's my turn to cock an eyebrow this time, throwing back an entire glass of wine in the process, just to test the theory.

"Another please," I say, oh-so-sweetly.

Lance whistles *bad-ass* through his teeth while Kane pours me another glass. I do my best to make small talk with Lance about Paia. I laugh at his jokes, even the bad ones, grazing his arm at every opportunity. I might be laying it on thick, but it's been awhile since I've flirted and I'm a little out of practice. Besides, I'm only half-listening to Lance; the bulk of my attention watches Kane's reaction from the corner of my eye. He sets a new glass of wine down before me, slamming it a bit too hard against the counter. He's been prowling around like a caged animal back there, making me wonder why he even bothers bartending in the first place. I mean, he could probably hire someone to do it for him.

"Ashley?" Lance's voice interrupts my train of thought.

"Hmm?"

"I was asking if you've been to Hana yet—just up the road."

"Not yet, but I'm hoping to check it out soon."

"I'd be happy to show you," Lance offers, flashing me an easy grin. He's cute and comfortable to be around, so why not? I'm about to say yes when Kane reappears with another glass of wine, despite that I've barely made a dent in the last one.

"I'm taking her," he growls.

I gawk at him. "You are?"

His eyes travel down my neck, resting on my cleavage before flicking up to my face. I feel my skin getting hot under the intensity of his gaze. "I'm heading there tomorrow to pick something up anyway. It makes the most sense." He shrugs like it's no big deal.

Lance releases a throaty laugh. "Pity for me."

Kane's eyes cut into him like knives. Before I can read too much into the situation, I hear Adele's voice echoing from the front doorway. I hop off the stool and flash Lance the sultriest smile possible, satisfied to see his eyes widen.

"Bye, Lance," I say.

"Bye, Ashley. Hope to see you around." I graze his arm before walking away, hearing him mutter *the sooner the better* under his breath.

I rush over to Kayla and Adele, scolding them. "You're late."

"Her fault." Kayla points at Adele. "She changed her outfit three times."

"I had to get it right," Adele sniffs proudly.

"And get it right you did." I give her the onceover. She's wearing a floor-length, tie-dyed skirt with a sparkling peasant blouse and a thick macramé belt. It's dressy and a little over the top, but it looks good on Adele, whose silvery hair is tamed by a matching tie-dye headband.

"It's *chockers* in here. Let's grab some seats before they're all gone," Kayla says. She's not wrong—the place is filling up quickly. We snag an empty table in the gazebo at the back.

"Speaking of outfits," Adele begins, eyeing me, "you look like sex on a platter."

"Back at you," I say, but she just snorts.

"My tits don't quite fill out a halter top like yours anymore."

Kayla wears casual jeans and a flowing top. She looks effortlessly beautiful with zero makeup and dark locks falling across her face. Suddenly I feel overdressed—not Adele overdressed, but overdressed nonetheless.

"What did we miss?" Kayla asks, as Adele flits to the bar for drinks.

"I met a cute guy named Lance."

She scrunches up her nose. "Lance is okay for a yank, I guess. We surf together sometimes."

"You're not…" I start to say, worried that I've trespassed into forbidden territory, but she shuts me down in a heartbeat.

"Not a chance. He's not my type at all. You go right ahead."

"Honestly, I'm not sure I should think about that right now. I mean, five months remain until our divorce is finalized, so technically I'm still married, at least in the State of California."

"You're thinking of getting back together with him?" Kayla levels me with a look.

"Never."

"Then don't fucking worry about it. Consider your divorced finalized, by me and the fine State of Hawaii, but is Lance actually someone you're interested in?"

"Maybe," I say with a shrug, my eyes traveling to the man behind the bar.

"Kane is taking me to Hana tomorrow," I add, just as Adele returns to the table with a bottle of wine and three glasses.

"What?" She squawks, just as Kayla rolls her eyes.

"Apparently he's going there anyway."

"Kane Keo doesn't do field trips with tourists, my dear—unless…"

"Unless what?"

"Well that would be interesting," Adele mutters.

"What would be interesting?" I feel myself getting increasingly frustrated with the cryptic nature of her reaction.

"Nothing—forget I said anything," she says, but her grin tells me otherwise.

"Remind me again," Kayla interjects, "this is the same *dag* who lost his temper and insulted you multiple times?"

"No reminder needed." I hold up one hand, but she forges forwards anyways.

"It's a pretty remote stretch of highway to Hana. Aren't you worried that he might pull over, chop you into pieces, and bury you under one of the scenic waterfalls?"

"Hush now, Kayla. Kane is a good man," Adele says. "No matter what people think."

"Can we talk about something other than Kane, please?" I half-whisper/half-shout, feeling a tingle down my spine. "He's behind me, isn't me?"

Kayla nods with wide-eyes, and Kane responds in a flat voice. "It's good to know that I'm still the talk of the town. Uh, Ashley?"

"Mmmhmm…" I answer, afraid to turn around.

"Be ready for 8am tomorrow."

"Got it," I manage to squeak out.

I don't look behind me, but I hear his retreating steps—that is until he stops. "And Ashley?"

"Yes?" This time I swivel around in my seat.

"Stay away from Lance."

"Why?"

"I know him. He's my friend."

"Isn't that a good thing?" I counter.

"No, it isn't."

"Why then?"

He studies me for a moment, and I can tell from the grinding of his jaw that he's pissed. "Because I said so." He huffs out, proceeding to disappear behind the bar.

Because he said so? Seriously, *FML*.

Chapter 7

I set my alarm for 7am, giving me plenty of time to mentally prepare for the day, but Kane still manages to beat me outside. The sun is hot for this time of day, and I can tell that it's going to be a scorcher. Kane gives me a curt nod as I emerge from the suite, waiting for me in a cherry red Jeep. It's an older model—simple but spotless—and I run my hand along the passenger side door. "Nice color."

"Red is my favorite." He seems to catch himself, noticing my cheeks flush. "For a car, I mean."

I hoist myself into the seat. "Sure."

"I could have helped you into the car, you know?" He sounds pissed, but I have to wonder why everything makes him so mad.

"All good—as it turns out, I have a functional set of legs. Besides, I competed in high jump as a teenager."

He gives me a skeptical look. "You did high jump?"

"Yes," I snap. "What's so strange about that?"

"I don't know. You're just so *lili'i*."

"Li what?"

"It means small."

"Five foot six isn't small. You're just enormous." I cross my arms over my chest like a defiant child.

"If you say so."

The Jeep is even cleaner on the inside. Kane Keo is obviously a pretty meticulous guy. He switches the radio on but keeps it low, and we ride in amiable silence for a while. It's always rare to meet someone and immediately feel that silence is comfortable, so I bask in the moment and try to relax.

"So what are you picking up?" I ask after a while.

"What?"

"You said you had to pick something up?"

"Right. A car part in Hana."

It doesn't seem like he wants to chat, so I focus on the lush landscape, which seems to grow denser by the minute. The road thins into a maze of switchbacks, cute little roadside waterfalls, and glorious peek-a-boo views of the Pacific Ocean.

"You don't get car sick, do you?" He asks, finally breaking the silence. "It turns into a one-way winding road from here."

"Nope, I'm more than fine with a few bends in the road. In fact, I'm a freak for roller coasters."

"Huh. Never been on one of those."

"A roller coaster? Really? You've *never* been on a roller coaster?"

"Never felt the need. Besides, I've lived on the island my whole life. Gotta say though, I never would've pegged you for a thrill seeker."

"And why is that?"

He shrugs. "I don't know. You seem safe."

I laugh out loud—safe, because *that* is every girl's dream.

"If you must know," I begin, "I just quit my job of five years, sold everything I owned on a whim, and left my dirt-bag cheating husband in San Francisco." I pause to let it sink in. "So, do you still think I'm safe?"

"Point taken." He nods and the car falls silent. I see an adorable roadside stand selling fresh fruit, and I begin bouncing up and down in my seat.

"Did you want to stop?" He tries to sound irritated, but humor stifles his voice.

"Pretty, pretty please?" I bat my eyelashes and give him the biggest smile possible.

Ever so slightly, I notice his lips part. He veers off the road and I unclip my belt, rushing to the stand like Road Runner. From the collection of fruits and veggies, I pick out an avocado, pineapple, and some freshly baked coconut cake. I'm totally in my element, loading my arms with goodies. The proprietor, a sweet Hawaiian lady with grey-streaked raven hair and a kind, prune-like face, comes over with a box for my items. When I go to pay though, she shakes her head and points at Kane. I protest in every way possible, but she just smiles. Eventually, I frown and stomp over to where Kane is leaning against the Jeep.

"Did you already pay?" I snap, hoisting up the box to avoid bruising my precious avocados. He ignores my question though, extricating the heavy box from my hands with one arm, as if it weighs nothing.

"We'd better get a move on."

"I can pay for my own food, Kane!" I shout, but he's already inside the jeep. Totally miffed, I follow him into the car. It was a nice gesture, but somehow it pisses me off. Every move he makes seems highhanded and bossy.

"You gonna' pout the rest of the way there?" He stares straight out the windshield.

"I'm not pouting."

"Yes, you are."

"I'm asserting myself as an independent woman."

"Like I said, you're pouting."

"Kane!"

He chuckles. "Jeez woman, it's just a box of vegetables. Consider it a Hawaiian welcome."

"Fine," I snap, angling my body toward the window. Only a few minutes pass before I'm grinning though. "Okay, fine. Thank you."

"I'm glad that you came to your senses, because next we're stopping for coconut shrimp, and I don't want any shit when I go to pay."

"*Ohmyfreakinggod.*" I exhale in one big gust. "I watched a Food Network episode on those, last year. I swear, I could smell them through the TV."

"Yeah?"

"Hells yeah, I've been dying to try them. I'm the kind of woman who *capital-L* loves food, as you can probably tell." I gesture to my body, and his eyes linger on my bare legs.

"Actually, it looks pretty damn perfect from where I'm sitting." I'm so shocked by his words that it takes me a minute to respond.

Then I remember what he said at the beach. "Yeah, right. Why did you insist that I wear a shirt at the beach then?"

This time his eyebrows skyrocket. "You think that's why I told you to cover up?" He shakes his head. "You're nuts, woman."

I'm not sure how to respond, so I leave it be. The air crackles with a strange tension as we hunt down the shrimp shack. It's a cute open-air spot with a few plastic chairs and exclusively paper plates. The smell is pure heaven. I'm almost giddy when he hands me my first coconut-crusted fried shrimp, all golden brown and wrapped in newspaper. I take a bite and an actual moan escapes from my chest. Meanwhile, I notice Kane shifting in the seat beside me, his shrimp still untouched.

"You don't like it?" I ask, stuffing another bite in my mouth. "You'd better hurry up before I eat all of yours."

He picks one up and swallows it whole. "My problem isn't the shrimp."

I'm far too distracted by the sweet and salty deliciousness to bother with his comment. "OMG I swear these shrimp are even better than sex!"

He choke-coughs on the shrimp in that moment. After clearing his throat, he locks eyes with mine. "If you think that's true, you've never had great sex."

His eyes darken and I squeeze my thighs together in the heat of his gaze, very aware of the jolt of wetness between my legs. Thinking all at once about Kane, coconut shrimp, and sex is not something my body can handle, especially after such a long dry spell in the bedroom. Instead, I change the subject.

"Why don't you serve food at the bar?"

He smirks—I guess my subject change wasn't so subtle after all. "Don't see the point."

"You don't see the point of food?"

He shrugs. "People come to Salty's to drown their sorrows."

"But people need to eat, too, and food is love."

"I thought love was love," he corrects, but I don't miss the bitterness in his voice.

"Semantics," I say with a wave. "When you feed someone something made from scratch, it's like an extension of yourself. People taste the passion you put into cooking."

"But I don't cook."

"Well, you could hire someone."

"What, like you?" He teases, but I like his crooked smile.

"That's not what I meant—but it's not the craziest idea in the world. I need a job; you need a menu. It could be perfect."

"It sounds like a lot of work and a big headache."

"Just think about how it could bolster your sales, keeping both the locals and tourists happy in the process."

"I'll think about it," he says, but his words don't match his tone. He seems completely closed off to the idea.

We finish our shrimp and pile back into the Jeep, and Kane promises we'll stop at a black sand beach along the way. The road is narrow and the drive insanely curvy. On my right, the landscape is a forest of thick jungle, with spectacular ocean views on my left. I spy a new waterfall around almost every turn. When we arrive, we park in a hillside lot and I start to hop out, but not before Kane grabs the sunscreen and slathers it all over my shoulders. He rubs what's left into my forehead and nose, bringing us so close that I can see the pulse in his neck. We head down to the beach below, where the coarse sand is the color of wet coffee grinds. I've never seen anything like it before, but the spot still teems with tourists. Even so, Kane doesn't rush me as I shuck off my shoes, digging my feet into the sand and staring out at the violently crashing waves.

"Stunning, isn't it?" Kane's eyes are like lasers. His hair is pulled back into a low ponytail, but some of the loose strands whip around his angular face. He stands with his arms adrift by his side, his well-worn t-shirt waving in the wind, and I'm quietly envious of how comfortable he looks in his own skin. I start to wade into the shallow water, so distracted by Kane that I don't notice my foot scraping against a barnacled rock.

I let out a yelp and fall into the ocean, soaking my white shorts to the skin. Kane rushes forward and scoops me into his arms, carrying me back to the beach and conducting a thorough examination of my foot. There's a small round hole above my toes that's spouting red blood. "It's pretty deep, Ashley."

"It hurts." My voices shakes. I bend forward to ease the flow with my fingers. The blood pools beneath them and leaves me feeling dizzy.

"Damn, it's bleeding a lot." He looks around, but there's no lifeguard on duty. He tugs his shirt off instead, ripping it in half and wrapping the strands around my foot like a tourniquet.

"Ouch!" I hiss, as Kane tightens the tourniquet past the point of comfort.

"Just gotta' stop the bleeding."

My blood seeps through his shirt and stains the fabric, but his eyes are fixed on my legs. He runs a rough hand up my calf, stopping at the back of my knee as his calloused fingers trace circles on my skin. I watch him swallow and know that he wants to explore further. I want it too; in that moment, I want nothing more than to feel those big hands sliding beneath my shorts. I wouldn't object if he ripped them off and sunk into me right here on the black sand with everyone watching. That's how intoxicating his touch feels—but he doesn't do any of that—instead he pulls his hand away, as if my skin is on fire, and simply stands up.

I try to scramble to my feet, but before I get there, Kane has me back in his arms. I wrap mine around his thick bare neck like a koala bear. "What about my shoes?" I say, and he bends down to capture both flip-flops before carrying me up the hill.

Back at the Jeep, he swings open the door with one arm and places me gently in the passenger seat with the other. The movement puts him right between my legs, and I don't think I'm imagining his shallow breath, nor the heat rolling off his body. Seated high up like this, I'm closer to his lips than ever before, and the pain in my foot is next to forgotten. When I lean forward, his lips part slightly, and I want nothing more than for him to kiss me. I close my eyes and let my lips brush against his mouth, but he rears back as if I've burnt him.

"I can't with you. I'm sorry." Just six little words, but they're enough to make my face burn with rejection. He wipes a hand down his face. "I can't be with someone like you."

"Someone like me?" I say, bristling.

"I can't be with anyone."

"What does that even mean?" I ask, but I can't bring myself to look at him. I shouldn't be imagining his body's response, but I am. I know he must feel something, too, even if only physical. I'm okay with just the physical anyways; it's probably all that I have capacity for right now.

"This was a bad idea." He walks around the car and climbs back into the driver's seat. "I'll take you back."

"But what about Hana?" I say, disappointed by our change of plans.

"Maybe another time." I can tell by his tone of voice that another time means never.

"Maybe I'll ask Lance." I don't know why I goad him, but I can't seem to help myself. Believe me, I don't miss how his knuckles go white around the steering wheel, but he doesn't object this time. In fact, he doesn't say anything at all, and my heart dips in my chest. "Just so I'm clear then, you don't want me, and you don't think I'm good enough for your friend, either, is that about right?

He answers without taking his eyes off the road. "It's not that simple."

"It never is, is it?"

"This was a bad idea."

I let go of a little laugh. "You think?"

He makes a U-turn and speeds back in the direction we came. I ignore him for the rest of the ride, resolving to start focusing on my life here. My new start begins right now, and I'd rather have three orders of fried coconut shrimp then this frustrating man's hands anywhere near my body. So much for the Hawaiian welcome.

• • •

The jeep barely comes to a stop before I've unbuckled my seatbelt and leaped onto the dirt road. I huff it double time back to my cottage, half-expecting Kane to chase after me, but he doesn't—and why would he when he's made his interest, or lack thereof, perfectly clear. I chalk it up to a rare moment when he was helping me through a tough situation in close physical proximity. It may have jumpstarted both our libidos, but it was just a knee-jerk reaction—emphasis on the jerk.

I slam the suite door behind me, pacing the length of the small kitchen while cursing myself. I've only been in Hawaii for a few days, and already I'm acting like a lovesick teenager, pining over someone who's obviously emotionally unavailable. I'm a mature, responsible twenty-seven-year-old woman and I need to start acting like one. It's not like me to be so thrown off by a man, even Dale never made me feel this unbalanced. Dale and I were never butterflies though. As my nana used to tell me, butterflies are for fairy tales and romance novels, a beautiful idea but unrealistic and unsustainable. She always told me to find someone who loved me more than I loved them, because life was easier with the upper hand.

    Even with Dale, while he was charming, flattering, and persistent at first, our marriage mostly just made sense. We were both young professionals on the rise, both hardworking and driven. We liked the same movies, shared a similar sense of humor, and we wanted the same things, like the townhouse and the Prius. We were happy together for awhile. For the most part, I was perfectly content with our marriage—watching a movie on the sofa, sipping wine on friends' yachts, and at least one orgasm now and then. We were intimate enough, but Dale didn't like going down on me and he wasn't big on head, so my O's came every third or fourth time (if I was lucky). I knew from my conversations with friends that a thirty percent success ratio was better than nothing.

    Which begs the question, why am I now losing cool over the antithesis of sensible and responsible? Why am I fantasizing about a monosyllabic hulk of a man with hands the size of baseball gloves and a mysterious leg tattoo? I ponder the thought while standing by the glass sliding doors and gazing out at the ocean. I figure it must be the proximity, and there was only one solution to proximity: I have to find a job and get my own place A.S.A.P.

    Even though I paid for the suite through the month, I have no choice but to be proactive when it comes to my next move. I can't stay here forever, and the faster I'm gone, the better Kane will feel. I make my decision and march back to his place, knocking on his door to demand respect for the remainder of my stay. It's early afternoon, so perhaps he's back at the bar, but the Jeep is in the driveway and I figure it's worth a try. I rap on the door and there's no answer. After a minute or so, I knock again and wait.

He answers eventually. He's shirtless and soaking wet, and holy hell does he ever look pissed. "What?" He snaps.

The more I try to keep my eyes on his face, the more that they act on their own accord, traveling down his wide chest and onwards to his tanned stomach, his navel barely visible above his towel. I involuntarily lick my lips. When I look back up, his jaw is locked in a grimace and his neck muscles are strained.

"Forget something?" He says, curtly. I exhale a breath and avert my eyes. The respect I was about to demand goes out the window, and I search my mind for something to say.

"I'm sorry to interrupt your…shower?" I blurt out. "It's stupid, never mind." I turn to go, only to hear him sigh behind me.

"You came all the way over here for something, Ashley. What is it?"

As I turn back around, I realize that I have no idea what I'm doing here. I haven't thought for one minute about what to say. However, I'm nothing if not quick on my feet. "I need to look for a job, and I was wondering if you have a copy of that local paper I've seen around?" He begins to open his mouth, and I hold up my hand. "Before you even say it, yes, I know what Google is, but I find that sometimes, especially in smaller communities, the paper is your best bet."

He stares at me for a second before speaking. "You need a job so badly that you're almost breaking down my door?"

I roll my eyes. "I quit the job that I had back home, so the obvious answer is *yes*."

"I just thought…" He starts to say, but I cut him off.

"You thought that I was another mainlander playing Hawaiian holiday for a few weeks, at which point I'd chicken out and hightail it home?" I arch one eyebrow at him. "Well, sorry to disappoint you, but that's not me. I moved here. I live here now, so you better get used to seeing me around."

He shakes his head and floors me with an actual smile. It's not a full grin, but it's enough to show off his dimples and snowflake-white teeth. "I guess you better come inside then."

He steps to the side and gestures for me to enter. I look around, surprised, as an invite inside wasn't what I'd expected. In fact, I thought he'd throw the paper at me and slam the door. I walk in ahead of him, hearing him clear his throat behind me. "Head on upstairs, I'm just going to get changed." I watch as he disappears into one of the rooms on the main floor, before my feet carry me up a flight of beautifully polished wooden stairs.

The upper floor is shaped like a circle, with floor to ceiling windows on almost every wall, which look out over the wrap-around lanai. A large ceiling fan hangs from the peak of Kane's thatched roof, and the living space is open concept and sparsely decorated. It faces the unique raw edge wooden countertop in the kitchen. I spot the standard "guy" furniture, including a leather sectional, simple dinette set, and one surfboard mounted above the flat screen television, but otherwise the space is undecorated. The classy furniture doesn't exactly suggest that Kane lacks photos, paintings, or throw pillows, but still the surfboard is the only ornamental addition to the room.

Wandering over to the single shelf by the window, I notice one white candle burning down the wick, flanked by the tiniest pair of flip-flops. The sliding glass doors are open, so I walk onto the expansive lanai to appreciate the gorgeously unobstructed ocean view. There's one staircase leading from the deck into the lush but unkempt garden, which opens up to the rocky beach. The only eyesore is the hastily-filled cement pool, but otherwise it's a breathtaking place.

"Find the paper?" His voice surprises me, and I whirl around to face him. He has changed into comfortable looking sweat-shorts and a black tank top—barefoot of course, with his wet hair appearing even darker than usual. He looks delicious enough to eat.

"I didn't look for it."

He flashes me a grin. "I thought women liked to snoop."

"Wow, sexist much?"

"Well, do you?" He's so forward and direct—it's kind of unnerving—but after years of bullshit back-and-forth with Dale, I appreciate the change of pace.

"Maybe I do, but that's not the point." I respond with a smile on my face. It's the perfect ice-breaker moment to ask about the cement pool, the tiny flip-flops by the candle, or all those rumors about his family, but I can't seem to find the nerve. Instead, I pick the safest topic possible.

"You surf?" My eyes travel to the board above the TV.

"Used to."

"Were you any good?"

He laughs. "No one I've brought here has ever asked me that before."

No one he's brought here? It's obvious he's talking about other women, and the thought makes my stomach churn.

"Sorry, I shouldn't have asked," I mutter. He must notice the change in my mood, because he reaches forward and tips up my chin with his finger.

"Hey, it's a good question, says a lot about you. I'll bet you're the competitive type."

"Hells yah, I am!"

He drops his hand, and I fight the urge to rub where his finger touched.

"Yeah, I was good."

"Then why don't you surf anymore?"

"I just don't."

Aloha in Love 69

He cuts the conversation short and turns towards the kitchen. It's obvious that I've overstepped again. Apparently I'm still learning where the lines are drawn. He rummages around in the recycling bin and extracts the local paper. Adele was reading it on the beach, and if it's good enough for the locals, it's good enough for me. Kane passes the paper across the kitchen island.

"Thank you. I'll bring it back when I'm done."

"Don't bother." He shakes his head. "What kind of job are you looking for anyways?" He sounds genuinely curious. It might be the first question he's asked me that didn't come with insults and orders.

I turn the paper over in my hands. "Honestly? Just about anything at this point. I was a broker in San Francisco, but I'd have to relicense to do that here in Hawaii, and I did more corporate real estate development work anyway. With everything that's happened recently, I'm not sure it's something that I want to do anymore. Maybe I'll open a bar," I add, teasingly. "Nothing like a little friendly competition."

He chuckles. "I wouldn't recommend it. Margins are terrible, and it'll be the end of your social life."

"Food could help with that," I try. "With the margins I mean, not the social life."

The tone of his voice is full of warning. "Ashley..."

"Okay, okay, no food. Have it your way."

"I usually do."

"Why am I'm not surprised by that comment?" I roll my eyes, but there's a strange heat behind his words, like he's testing me. I catch his eyes in careful perusal of my body, and his penetrating gaze makes me feel naked.

"Thanks for the paper, Kane. I can see myself out." I head for the front door alone, but he follows me anyway, leaning his large body against the frame and crossing his arms.

I step into the sweltering heat, glancing back to see Kane eyeing me like a statue.

"See you around, I guess."

"You coming to Salty's tonight?"

I shrug. "Maybe."

"Okay, maybe I'll see you there."

"Bye, Kane," I say, and he grunts. Total caveman—and damn if I don't envy Tarzan's Jane right now.

Chapter 8

I find myself walking the road to Salty's again that very evening. Kayla is in Honolulu for some surfing event, and Adele confessed to spending the night with Tinder and a bottle of thirty-year-old scotch, in an effort to "suss out a suitable lesbian partner" (her words, not mine), so I'm flying solo. When I arrive, Lance and Pancho are by the bar with another man who I don't recognize, so I find myself a seat near the end.

"You look nice, Red. Paia looks good on you!" Pancho says, giving me a friendly whistle. He greets me with Hawaii's universal thumb-and-pinky-finger gesture, called *the shaka*.

"Thanks, Pancho." I give him a big smile. "How's your daughter?"

"She's amazing." I don't miss the look of love reflected in his eyes. "My wife and Melia are visiting family on the Big Island this week. I miss them both like crazy."

"He is *literally* going crazy," Lance teases. "He hasn't stopped talking about them all night."

"Well, I think that's pretty sweet." The man to Lance's right gives me a curious look, but he doesn't smile. He looks native Hawaiian with his dark hair and matching eyes. He's wearing a neat collared polo shirt and slacks, and he's handsome, though not in a way that makes my lady parts tingle. No, that honor seems to be reserved for—

"Kane!" Lance shouts from across the bar.

Kane shouts right back. "What do you want Lance?"

"Ashley's here. Free drinks for tenants, remember?" He says, shooting me a wink. Kane grumbles under his breath but then concedes, pouring me a glass of white wine and sliding it across the bar.

"What if I don't want wine?" I protest, and he snorts.

"Beggars can't be choosers."

"I'm not a beggar Kane—you offered. I can pay for my own damn drinks!" I say, through clenched teeth.

The unknown man in the polo shirt chooses this exact moment to introduce himself, leaning across Lance and extending his hand. "Hi Ashley. I've heard a lot about you. I'm Taylor Akana, Kane's oldest and dearest friend."

"Kane has friends?" I say, lifting an eyebrow, which earns me laughter from both Pancho and Lance.

"She knows you well already, Keo." Taylor shouts after his friend. "I'll let you in on a little secret, Ashley," he mock-whispers.

"I'm listening."

"Underneath that prickly exterior, Kane Keo is just a big softie. Hard on the outside and mush at the center—he's like a pineapple that way."

"Hmm…" I roll my eyes. "I don't know if I believe you."

"Dude, did you just compare me to a fruit?" Kane gives Taylor an incredulous look.

"Yeah, but you'd be a Maui Gold for sure," he teases.

Kane shakes his head and gives Taylor a look, throwing the bar towel over his shoulder and refilling everyone's drinks but mine. I barely have anything left in my glass, but I don't let it bother me. Instead I sit down beside Lance and fall into a conversation with Taylor; apparently, he operates his own tour-boat/diving franchise across the islands, and he's known Kane since they were kids. He's a nice guy and an excellent conversationalist; I wonder how he's lasted all these years in the company of Kane's ornery.

When Taylor excuses himself, I turn my attention back to Lance.

"How was Hana?" He asks, tossing the blond hair from his eyes.

"Oh, we didn't quite make it." I steal a glance at Kane. "But I did see a black sand beach!"

"Awe…that's a bummer. Why'd you stop?"

I feel Kane watching us from behind the bar, and I wonder if he'll say anything. When he doesn't jump into help, I have to think on my feet.

"I-I was feeling a little sick, so I asked Kane to turn back," I stammer.

"Understandable." Lance nods. "That road is hella windy. But if you're up for another try sometime, I'd love to show you Haleakala Park. It's the largest dormant volcano in the world. The summit is big enough to hold the whole island of Manhattan. It also has some pretty gnarly trails, winding their way around cinder cones and lava flows."

His description feels like poetry. "That sounds incredible."

"There's another trail we could try some time as well, through the bamboo forest. It's got all these cool freshwater pools and waterfalls." His enthusiasm is so infectious that I can't help but nod along.

"But the best is the Paliku backcountry campsite. It's an awesome hike on sliding sands with some switchbacks, but it's 100% worth the effort."

"Camping actually sounds pretty fun," I say, wondering how long it's been since I slept outside.

Lance leans back and slings an arm behind my stool. "Only got the one tent though," he says, winking.

I can see Kane's shoulders stiffen behind the bar. "That hike is dangerous," he snaps, his full attention on the conversation now.

"Why are you always eavesdropping?" I ask him.

"He's right, Red," Pancho pipes up. "It's pretty rough. If I were you, I'd take baby steps. Kipahulu is drive-in camping right on the water with views that'll blow your mind, and Keiko and I would be happy to lend you a tent." He gives

Lance a look, but Lance just shrugs and dazzles me with his smile.

"Maybe it would be good for you," Lance says. "To cleanse the bad and make room for the new. Seriously, it's like a religious experience."

I can't help but wonder if maybe he's right. I've travelled across the ocean for a fresh start, but have I really started living? I turn my attention to Pancho. "Can I borrow that tent of yours after all?"

"You betcha. I'll bring it by your place tomorrow. I have a backpack you can use, too, if you need one."

"Thanks, Pancho!"

I hear Lance chuckle from beside him. "Shame, I was hoping we could share." He shoots me a wink, and meanwhile Kane levels me with a nasty glare.

"Sure you know what you're doing though, Red? Haleakala is no joke," Pancho says, but Lance interjects before I have a chance to answer.

"I'll keep her safe. Ashley, how about I pick you up Sunday morning?"

"I was actually thinking about asking Kayla to join. Maybe we can meet you there?"

"Sure." Lance smiles, but he looks a little deflated. As much as I like him, I'm not ready for an overnight hike with a guy I barely know.

"But I'm really looking forward to seeing the crater from your perspective. I just hope I can keep up!"

"I have no doubt that you'll keep up with me." He brightens noticeably and gives me a friendly peck on the cheek. "I'll see you Sunday then."

Pancho whistles through his teeth. "Boys got some alas on him, that's for sure."

"Stupid." I hear Kane grumble under his breath, but I can't tell if he's talking about me or the hike. At this point, I don't even care. Of all the people I've met thus far, Kane Keo is the only one who thinks I'm incapable of doing things on my own. I'm looking forward to showing him just how wrong he is.

Chapter 9

"Sunscreen?" Kayla asks.

"Check."

"Proper footwear?"

I glance down at my sturdiest running shoes. "Check."

"Condoms?" She snickers, and I give her a look.

"Hardly, Lance is a friend."

"I wasn't talking about Lance." She points out the windshield as we pull into the car lot of Haleakala National Park.

I find the back of Lance's head first; he waits before a huge pile of bags, and only when he steps aside do I get a full view of the guy behind him.

"Oh no, not happening," I mutter, and Kane's head snaps up, as if he can hear me. He tracks the car's movement with a scowl.

I take a deep breath, evidently frustrated, and Kayla starts to laugh. "Camping with Keo…I never thought I'd see the day."

"Not just Kane," I say, pointing to Taylor, who just climbed out of the car beside ours.

"Bloody hell," Kayla hisses under her breath. "You're on your own, Ashley."

"No way, you're not leaving me! We're in this together." I shake my head vigorously. "What's your problem with Taylor anyway? He seems like a nice guy, at least a thousand times nicer than Kane."

"Listen to you!" She clicks her tongue and shakes out her auburn hair. "There is no such thing as a *nice guy*, and the sooner you realize it, the better."

I roll my eyes but don't respond. She hops out of the car like a bouncy ball, and I slide slowly out the passenger door, grabbing Pancho's backpack and tent in the process. Before I even have time to throw it over my shoulder, I've already tripped on my own two feet. An animal cry escapes from my chest as my ankle rolls to the side. I hit the dirt before managing to right myself, glancing up to see if anyone noticed, only to find a looming shadow altogether blocking out the sun.

"Nice shoes—ready for an eight-hour hike along the sand flats?" The shadow says, in the exact voice you'd expect from a shadow.

I whirl around to face him. "The shoes I choose to wear are none of your business, Kane." I reach for my bag, but Kane heaves it over his shoulder before I have a chance.

"What's in here?" He grunts. "More shoes and purses?"

"I didn't ask you to carry my bag." I speak through clenched teeth. "What are you even doing here anyways?"

He shrugs. "Camping."

"Yeah, do you like camping?"

"Not really," he says, a smirk tugging at his plump pink lips.

"God, you're so infuriating!" Clearly he's trying to get a rise out of me, but I won't give him the upper-hand.

I stomp over to Lance, who's fiddling with a set of headlamps. "What are those for?" I ask, squatting down on my haunches beside him.

"It'll get dark out there at night, so I brought them for us."

"Thank you, Lance." I give him a grateful smile. "So...you brought company?" To emphasize my point, I steal a look at Kane, who holds my bag and glares in our direction. I don't miss how Lance's eyes narrow either.

"Yeah, sorry. He insisted—along with Taylor. They said it was public service to ensure I didn't kill a tourist."

Public service? I shake my head. Kane's self-righteousness knows no bounds. "Well, I'll ignore them if you do."

He grins. "Sounds like a plan."

I walk over to Kane with folded arms, demanding that he return my bag. He hands it over but insists on holding the tent, even though his own load looks massive. We head to the Haleakala National Park Visitor Center for a ten-minute orientation video. I learn that we're responsible for our own water and garbage—both must be carried in and out of the park—and the video seems specifically designed to warn unprepared tourists. I see Kane watching me from the corner of my eye; even though I'm a little worried about the hike now, I won't give him the satisfaction of showing it. The video finishes and Lance appoints himself as "unofficial leader of our group," proceeding to circle us up and list off our supplies.

"First aid kit, extra flashlights, a cook stove, a water purifier, and biodegradable soap…just in case anyone wants to wash up this evening." He stares at me from the corner of his eye, and I feel my cheeks burning. "We'll tackle the Sliding Sands Trail and head for Paliku tonight. It's about ten miles in, so we'll hike out in the morning."

Ten Miles? It's like my eyes are bulging out of my head. I'm still trying to process the distance, but it's definitely longer than Bag Ridge Trail or Mount Diablo Summit, both hikes that Dale and I used to do on weekends. Since arriving in Maui though, my only cardio has been failing to run on the beach. It's before eight in the morning and the breeze carries a chill as we embark upon the trail. The first mile starts off okay, even though the air is thin and there's little time to acclimate. The Sliding Sands Trail, also called *Keoneheehee*, is composed of lava rock, sand, and some sub-alpine plants dotting the landscape. It looks part *Mad Max*, part *Star Wars*, and the experience is otherworldly, even beneath the radiating heat of the sun. Sweltering, I feel the sunscreen melting off my shoulders, but Kane is primed and ready behind me the very moment we stop to enjoy the view.

Having already bugged me about UV-protection twice, I'm not surprised when he snatches the bottle from my hands.

"Give me that." He flips open the cap and moves closer to smear some on my nose.

"I'm twenty-seven years old, Kane—I can handle my own sunscreen." I snatch the bottle back, waving him away while rubbing the white blob into my skin.

"You should put on a hat," he snarls.

"And you should mind your own business," I say, with mock-sweetness.

Lance mentions that the descent is over twenty-eight hundred feet into the valley, and that's before even beginning the steep climb back to Haleakala Crater rim. "*Wikiwiki* guys! We've got a lot of ground to cover before nightfall," he shouts over his shoulder.

I'd like nothing more than to punch him in his overly-energetic face. I try to match Lance's pace, but I end up sliding around on the loose sand. Every now and then, a pair of large hands shoots out from behind to steady me.

"Easy," Kane says gruffly. I shake him off without saying thank you, irritated by the warm tingle that his calloused fingers leave on my skin.

"Sure you're ok?"

"Just fine."

I take another couple steps and almost land on my ass again. This time, he grabs me around the waist and pulls me against his hard chest. We descend further into the crater, which is overwhelmed by switchbacks and plenty of loose black volcanic junk. The desert disappears and the terrain becomes rocky, as the sharp, jagged pieces poke through my rubber shoe soles. My feet are sore within half-an-hour. The sun dips behind the low-lying cloud formations, and all I see for miles is a rim of vibrant red cinder cones encircling the valley. How a place like this can go from blistering hot to ice cold in a matter of minutes amazes me, even understanding the significant elevation change. Entering the forested heart of the crater, the temperature drops low enough that I can see my own breath.

I slip on my windbreaker as an icy rain needles the fabric of my clothing. My layers seem useless against the cold now seeping into my bones. We feel our way through a patch of fog that leaves a lush cloud forest all around us. I have to rub my hands together to keep warm, but at least Kane isn't harassing me about sunscreen. Lance leads the group with a subtle smile on his face, and I stick my tongue out at the back of his head. I suppose I'm just jealous of his gear. He looks extremely warm, with a cozy hood that seems to keep him impeccably dry.

Behind me, Kane wears thin pants plus a light jacket with no hood, but he doesn't seem bothered by the temperature. Rain runs down his face in rivulets, wetting his dark lashes and slicking the long hair back against his head. He looks, quite literally, like a wet dream, and I hate myself for even noticing. Kayla stops to dig a yellow poncho from her bag, slipping it over her head in front of me. I silently kick myself for not thinking of that—then again, I never imagined we'd be hiking through a deluge.

Lance calls back to the group, letting us know that we're getting close to the Paliku Rainforest. Thank God—I'm chilled to my bones and my feet ache like small tragedies. I dressed in layers, but my cotton shirts are heavy with wetness and unlikely to dry anytime soon. We reach the east end of the valley and hike into the crater from the base of the rainforest cliff. There we're met with an eerie, dead silence. There are no birds chirping, not even any wind, just an ethereal sense of stillness, pulsing with energy throughout the crater.

The sun dips lower in the sky, and finally we reach the flat bottom of the crater: a grassy meadow against a backdrop of vibrant blue sky. There's a simple square cabin and a picnic table in the heart of the meadow, but according to Lance, Paliku is a popular spot and often reserved well in advance. I'm fully expecting to set up camp in the field; however, just then, the cabin door flies open and someone comes barreling toward us, screaming Lance's name.

"Buddy!" The shouting-blur-of-a-human-being halts before us, and Lance steps forward to give him one of those manly backslap hugs.

"Ethan, man. I'm surprised to see you here."

"We hiked in for Nic's stag weekend. Showed up yesterday—Joe's here, too." The stag weekend explains the slurred speech and his eyelids at half-mast. He walks with that kind of boneless quality to him, and I have to suppress laughter as he stumbles and almost falls.

I'm happy that we've arrived, but I'm also exhausted. I drop my bag and it hits the ground with a thud. Lance wanders over to check on me with a concerned look occupying his face. Ethan's eyes follow his movement, and he flashes me an easy grin.

"Is this your girl, man?" He asks.

"No," Kane answers, before Lance can even open his mouth. Drunken Ethan smiles even wider.

"Even better. So are you guys camping here for the night?"

"Yeah, we're going to set up in the field," Lance explains, gesturing to the meadow behind us.

"No need, man. There's like a dozen beds inside and we're only three people. You guys are welcome to join." After he extends the invitation, Ethan introduces himself to Taylor and Kayla.

"And you are especially welcome…" He says to Kayla, whistling low. I swear that I hear Taylor growl like an animal.

"We're fine out here," Kane says shortly, but apparently Lance disagrees.

"Are you insane, Keo? It's a cabin with a woodstove. These cabins are *never* available. The girls will definitely be more comfortable inside."

"Yeah man, it was crazy cold last night." Ethan steps forward to shake Kane's hand, but Kane just stares at it like he wants to chop his fingers off. Luckily, Ethan is too drunk to be intimidated. "Seriously though, I think my nuts crawled up inside of me."

Kayla snorts, pushing past Ethan on route to the cabin. "Charming."

Inside, we meet the soon-to-be-married Nic and his friend, Joe, who seem to be enjoying a similar state of inebriation. Still, they're friendly and easygoing. Apart from Kane, who's prowling around the cabin like a caged tiger, nobody seems to mind their company. The Paliku cabin is well-stocked, equipped with a stove, cookware, running water, a wood-burning furnace, and several bunk-beds with sleeping pads. We each pick a bed and I roll out my $20 Wal-Mart sleeping bag before sitting down to remove my shoes. My socks are damp from hiking through the rainforest—along with everything else I'm wearing—and I stifle my whimpering as I struggle to get them off. Lance must hear me, because he rushes to my side with the first aid kit, kneeling to inspect my foot.

"We'll have to get you some proper hiking boots next time," he says, gently lifting one foot up in the air. I give him a quick smile, but on the inside I'm screaming. *There will be no next time.* "You did great, Ashley, really great." He gives me a soft look, cradling my foot in his hands. It makes me a little uncomfortable, but I'm grateful for his warm palms on my skin. "Your feet are like ice," he says, running a finger along my archway. He adds another finger and begins massaging the sole, making me groan out loud.

"Let me see." Kane elbows his way between us, causing Lance to drop my foot.

"I think I've got it handled, Keo."

"She's bleeding," he snarls back, like an accusation.

"It's just a blister! I'll bandage it up once her feet are warm." Lance pushes Kane to the side and returns to my battered feet.

"You don't have to do this," I say, softly. He looks at me and smiles.

"I want to. It's the least I can do, since you were brave enough to hike through this with me."

The next thing I know, Kane has slammed his hulk-like body into the bunk above me, causing the whole contraption to shake.

Lance raises his eyebrows at my new bunkmate. "You got something to say, Keo?"

"Fuck off, Lance," Kane snarls.

Once my feet are bandaged, I join the group at the wooden table. It's getting dark and there's no electricity, so we light a few candles and Lance adds more logs to the furnace. One of the stag guys flicks on a battery-powered lantern, which seems to emit a decent amount of light. Kayla, who's been slaving away at the stove, hands out bowls of freshly warmed chili. Taylor shares a loaf of bread and some butter, and I throw in some of my homemade beef jerky. We demolish the food in a matter of minutes—even Kane decides to join us. Once our bellies are full and the dishes washed, I bring out my homemade donuts. They're the only thing I managed to vacuum-seal for this trip, but the bready treat should fill everyone up.

I offer some to the stag party and Ethan swallows his whole. "What are these balls of heaven?" I watch his eyes roll back into his head.

"Malasadas," I say. "It's basically a Hawaiian donut, but I'm sure you guys already know that. I filled them with coconut cream and rolled them in sugar."

"I've never heard of a Hawaiian donut, but these are so good!" Nic declares, and I'm grateful to have the groom's seal of approval.

"It's like a donut and also not like a donut," Lance mumbles, his mouth full of fried goodness.

"I used evaporated milk, which changes the taste a bit, I think."

"It's *onolishious* delicious," Ethan says. "What's it called again?"

I clear my throat, embarrassed to be the center of attention. "Malasadas. The word is Portuguese and means *poorly cooked*. Immigrants coming to work in the sugar and pineapple industries brought the recipe over in the 19th century."

"You really are a food nerd," Kayla says, snorting, but my trivia doesn't stop her from scarfing down another donut.

"I do love food," I say with a nod, watching Kane eye me. He takes a bite of his own donut and makes no effort to divert his gaze.

"So you're smokin' hot *and* you can cook?" Ethan laughs. "Dayum girl, if I was the marrying kind, I'd marry you."

"Hey bro, back off, okay?" Lance says under his breath.

I watch Kane give Ethan a look that could freeze over hell. It doesn't seem to faze Ethan though, who has graduated from half-drunk to full-drunk, and at least the guys are having fun. The wood furnace does a good job of warming the cozy space, and I strip off my layers until all I'm wearing is a semi-dry tank top. Apart from Kane, we all stay chatting and playing cards at the table. The stag guys fire up their portable music speaker, and Joe makes a very sloppy attempt at flirting with Kayla. She shuts him down so hard that everyone groans in unison.

"Do you want a drink?" Ethan hands me a silver flask, but I refuse.

"No, thank you." A warm mouthful of liquor sounds tempting, but I'm too much of a lightweight around hard alcohol.

Lance drapes one arm over my shoulders, reaching for the flask with the other. "I'll take some."

Ethan rolls his eyes. "I didn't offer you any, man."

"Come on, don't be like that." Lance reaches for it again, but Ethan simply holds the flask over his head.

"Tell you what, *Lancey-Boy*, learn to fill out a tank top like Ashley, and I'll give you all the whiskey you want."

The other guys burst into laughter, but it doesn't last long. Kane's heavy boots hit the floor and he sidles up next to Ethan at the table. "What did you say?"

The other guys look away, busying themselves with the deck of cards, but Ethan is drunk and totally unfazed by Kane's towering presence.

"Apologize to Ashley—now," he demands. His voice is dead quiet.

Lance shakes his head and mutters, "Yeah, not cool, Ethan," and Kayla joins in by calling him a pig.

"Whoa, relax everybody. She's sexy! It was just a joke. Take as much as you like, Lance."

"Apologize," Kane repeats, more forcefully this time.

"Leave it alone, Kane," I insist, thoroughly embarrassed at this point.

Ethan still slurs his words like a frat boy. "I'm sorry beautiful."

Kane slams his fists on the table top. "Ashley. Her name is Ashley."

"I'm sorry, *Ashley*. Well guys, I'm empty. Think it's time to refill."

I wish Ethan had kept his mouth shut, but I'm impressed at his ability to be unaffected by Kane's anger. I suppose he probably has the booze to thank for that. He walks into the kitchen, presumably to refill his flask, and meanwhile Kane heads back to bed. The candles have nearly burnt down when a wave of exhaustion hits me. I say thank you for the games and conversation before excusing myself for bed. I use some of Lance's boiled water and biodegradable soap to wash my face and brush my teeth, barely keeping my eyes open as I nestle beneath the sheets.

I wake up later to the sound of my teeth chattering. The temperature has plummeted, the wood furnace has gone out, and the cabin is pitch black. My cheap sleeping bag does nothing to protect me from the cold. I simply can't stop shivering, and falling back asleep feels like a miracle in these conditions. I can just make out Kayla's silhouette across from me, with Lance's ragged breathing sounding from above. The other three guys are still up, but they've turned the music off and now chat quietly in the corner, their conversation punctuated by muffled laughter and the clang of their flask against the table. I consider getting up, but my body is violently shaking. As I debate whether to redress in my wet layers, I hear a rustling sound from above me, just before a large body climbs into my bed.

"Kane?" I say, my teeth chattering.

"I can hear you shaking from up top."

"I'll be fine," I try, but I can barely get the words out.

"You're cold—and I don't trust them." He shifts around and I feel his bare skin pressing against me, realizing then that he's shirtless.

"But I should trust you?"

"Probably not, but I'm the best option you've got."

He's warmer than a furnace, even without a blanket, so I don't resist when he wraps his strong arms around me. My body temperature rises and I feel myself relax, the shaking finally leaving my body. It feels so good that I can't help but snuggle into him. He stiffens but doesn't complain, so I press my face into his bare chest and sigh myself to sleep.

"I won't let anything happen to you, Lani," Kane whispers, his breath tousling my hair.

I don't know who Lani is, but I'll have to save the thought for the morning, as my eyelids are suddenly thick and heavy with sleep.

Chapter 10

I sleep better than I have in months, despite my myriad aches and pains, but Kane is gone the moment I wake up. Still, I want to thank him for saving me last night. In the fuzzy blue light of early dawn, I can see that everyone else remains sleeping in their bunks, so I slip on my damp sweatshirt and head outside barefoot. The orange sun breaks across the horizon, as if setting the valley floor on fire. I spot Kane up ahead, staring into the distance with his back to me. I approach like a mouse in the light of the rising sun, burning red through the clouds. My eyes fill with watery tears as brilliant hues of pink and green streak across the sky, layered with shades of pineapple-yellow and orange, reminding me of Hawaiian shave ice.

"I'm not worthy of this life," Kane whispers, evidently aware of my presence. "I don't deserve this beauty."

His comment catches me off-guard, but its nature doesn't surprise me. "Everyone deserves beauty, Kane."

"You really believe that?"

"Yes. I think an appreciation of beauty is what makes us human."

"That Ethan guy was certainly appreciating yours," he grumbles.

"And that bothers you?"

"Haleakala means *house of the sun*," he says, ignoring my question. "It's a spiritually important place where the demigod, Maui, lassoed the sun to make the days longer." We stand together watching the sky light up like a painter's canvas, and he turns to face me. "Your hair reminds me of the sunrise. Like fire."

I'm drawn to him like a magnet at dawn. I keep my eyes locked with his and take a tiny step closer, noticing how his nostrils flare. I take another step anyways, craning my neck up to meet his eyes.

"Ashley, don't."

I feign innocence. "Don't what?"

"You know what." It feels like he's towering above me. His hands are clenched in fists by his sides and when I rise onto my toes, he steps back and looks away, breaking the connection.

"Ashley…" He whispers but doesn't say anything more.

A ball forms in my chest, and I try to clasp the pain with my hand. I've been rejected once again; in fact, I walked right into it.

"It's fine," I say, wrapping my arms around my body like a suit of armor.

Kane lets his hands fall to his sides. "Don't say it's fine."

"What do you want me to say? I get it, ok. You're not into me."

He fumbles for words. "It's not that. I can't…"

I've never seen him so uncertain, but I'm not in a particularly forgiving mood. "Just spit it out Kane! Whatever you need to say, just say it and put me out of my misery."

"It's not something I can easily explain," he hedges.

I laugh, perhaps a bit too harshly. "Then forget I even came out here. We should get back anyway." I take two steps away from him; a haunted look flashes in his eyes, but he doesn't argue.

Back at the cabin, Lance is awake and packing up. His eyebrows furrow when he sees Kane and I approaching, backs ablaze with the sun. "Everything ok?" He asks.

I swallow the lump in my throat. "Everything's fine. We were just checking out the sunrise."

"For sure," he says, relaxing at my explanation. "It's unreal isn't it?"

I nod and give him my best smile. After waking up Taylor and Kayla, I stuff my swollen and blistering feet back into my running shoes. The first few steps are painful enough that I don't think I'll make it, but Kane answers that question for me in a flash, sliding my backpack over his shoulder.

"You can hate me all you like, but I'm not going to watch you suffer."

"You can't carry two bags, Kane," I say, exasperated.

"I can and I will. Discussion over."

As much as I want to throw the gesture right back in his face, I probably do need his help. The stag guys are still snoring away when we depart. Lance leaves them a brief thank you note and proceeds to lead us out the way we came. A rainbow enrobes the sky as we ascend from the valley floor. Lance points out a cluster of Nene birds, which are basically Hawaiian geese. He tells me that Haleakala has more endangered species than any national park in the world.

We hike to the summit on a series of switchbacks, facing an elevation gain of about a thousand feet, our breath stifled the higher we climb. Only outside of the crater does the warm weather return and the familiar sliding sands finally come into view. The hike takes all day. When I finally catch a glimpse of the parking lot, I almost cry out in relief. Kayla and I say goodbye to Lance at the car, giving him a big hug with zero concern for his B.O. profile. He hugs me back and whispers in my ear.

"I know how hard this must have been for you, but you survived it—not a lot of people can say that. I'm proud of you."

He kisses my cheek, and I pull away before I start bawling. The words mean more than he knows. This experience isn't something I would have accomplished with Dale, and though it was grueling and out of my comfort zone, at least it's my own. Lance and I part ways, and Kane steps between us to hand me my bag. I mutter a thank you without meeting his eyes. Kayla is already in the passenger seat and she doesn't look happy—in fact, she looks pissed. I throw my bag into the back and ease myself into the driver's seat, nursing the rocks in my quads.

"Trouble in paradise?" I tease.

Kayla gives me an evil look. "I don't know what gives Taylor the right to think he can boss me around. We're nothing to each other—less than nothing."

I want to ask what happened, but she'll probably just bite my head off, so I go for solidarity instead. "Maybe they're all like that; Hawaiian men, I mean."

"Hey, don't blame Hawaii for their testosterone-fueled idiocy, but at least you got it half right: Men. You're learning, my little grasshopper."

I start the engine and pull out of the lot.

"So where we headed?" She asks.

"Well, I need a shower in a big way, but first...pancakes."

"Yasss..." Kayla hisses out, clapping with more enthusiasm than I've ever seen from her. "And bacon—lots of bacon. It makes sense. We should do something to celebrate your first backcountry hike."

"Correction, my dear friend. We are celebrating my first—and my last—backcountry hike."

"I'll eat to that," she says, and we speed off down the highway, in hot pursuit of an all-day breakfast joint.

Chapter 11

The following Tuesday evening, we're back at the bar sharing horror stories from our hike with Pancho and Adele. I can tell they're surprised that I managed to complete it without dying, especially as I describe my massive lingering blisters to Adele.

"Alright, okay," Lance begins, "maybe I got a little carried away with Haleakala. Am I forgiven?" He gives me a pair of puppy dog eyes.

"Of course you are!" I say, giggling.

"I can do baby steps, too, you know." He wiggles his cute eyebrows—and damn if he isn't totally into me.

He doesn't seem to think much of Kane's warning, so I match his smile with a grin of my own. "What kind of baby steps did you have in mind?"

Lance opens his mouth to answer, but we're interrupted by the sound of glass shattering. Kane has dropped a beer mug on the ground, earning him a collective groan from the other patrons. His back is turned away from us, and before I can offer my help, he stomps off into the back area.

"If you haven't seen Ho'okipa Beach yet, I could show you some of my surfing moves—or there's windsurfing, if you'd prefer that."

I shake my head, remembering my last mishap with water sports. "Probably neither, but watching you works for me. I'd love to see the beach."

"Then dinner in Makawao afterwards? There's an awesome Italian place in town that also features live bands."

Kane chooses this exact moment to return from the back, carrying a broom and dustpan. He looks even more pissed off than before, if that's possible. I watch as he sweeps up the shards of glass, but not even once does he look my way.

"Ashley?" Lance waves his hand before my face like I'm blind.

"Yes, Lance?"

"So what do you think? People watching at Ho'okipa, followed by dinner in Makawao?"

I'm about to spit out the word "no," but I can't think of any good reason not to accept his invitation. I'm here in this beautiful place, meeting new people and making new friends, and here's one right in front of me who's kind, uncomplicated, and willing to show me what makes Maui special.

"Sure, Lance. That sounds nice."

"How about tomorrow night?"

"I'm free."

"Then it's a date."

I cringe at the word date. He's cute, but my head is all over the place and I don't want to lead him on. Kane drops another glass and it shatters against the floor like a comet.

"Fuck!" He explodes. Everyone falls silent at his outburst. A tipsy young tourist stumbles to the bar and leans over the back of my chair, shouting at Kane.

"Dude, that's like seven years of bad luck!"

It's a stupid comment from some sunburned college kid, but as soon as the words leave her mouth, Kane's face blanches. I hear Pancho hissing through his teeth from a few seats down, as Kane tosses the bar towel on the floor and hightails it outside. Naturally, all I can think is *what-in-the-actual-hell* was that? Taylor appears behind the bar and exchanges a few quiet words with Pancho. His mouth is drawn and he looks worried.

On his way out, he stops by my stool. "Did you see which way he went, Ashley?"

"He went through the front, but I didn't see what direction. I'm sorry."

"Don't worry about it," he spits out. The accusing look on his face makes me feel that this is all my fault. I can't imagine how one little comment could set Kane off like that, but clearly he's no master of controlling his temper.

"Well, I think that's enough drama for one night, don't you?" Lance tips his glass at me, and I'm grateful at his attempt to lighten the mood.

"Agree. I think I'm going to head back home."

Lance slides off his stool. "Can I walk you?"

"I got her," Pancho says, appearing behind my seat.

"You don't have to, Pancho."

"Never mind, it's *a'ohe pilikia*...since you're staying right by me."

Lance shrugs and smiles, leaning in to kiss my cheek. I feel absolutely nothing when his lips graze my skin, not even the slightest tingle, but still the gesture is sweet.

"I'll pick you up tomorrow around two, if that works for you?"

"Sounds great," I answer, but my mind is elsewhere. I'm staring at the door through which Kane just disappeared, trying to ignore my disappointment about tomorrow's plans. If only it were Kane taking me to dinner; if only he wanted me more than Lance.

• • •

I thank Pancho for walking me home alone nonetheless. It's a beautiful night, the stars like a snowstorm in the sky, and I'm not ready to call it a night upon arriving at my suite. I kick off my shoes and roam around the grounds, taking care to avoid the beach. Kane never said anything about the yard, however, and I figure he can't yell at me for stepping on the grass. With my sandals dangling from one hand, I walk the perimeter of the lawn, stopping only to watch the impressive whitewalls cresting and crashing into the rocky shoreline.

The night feels alive with the hum of crickets in pitch black darkness, but it doesn't bother me. The air is a heady perfume of exotic flowers and the prickly lawn soothes my soles as I walk. There's something about this place that's hard to put into words, but it makes me feel safe in a way that I haven't known since I was a child. As I near Kane's house, I can make out one pinprick of light bouncing ahead in the darkness. It grows larger and brighter until I'm face to face—or rather face to chest—with Kane himself, his flashlight eyeing me like a lighthouse. I assume he's about to yell at me for invading his privacy, but instead he just hands me the flashlight.

"Thought you might need this." He illuminates his face with a second flashlight, and the lines of his skin are fierce, even in the muted glow.

"Thank you. It's really kind of peaceful without it though," I say, shrugging. "I like following the moonlight."

His gaze is unwavering. "I'd feel better if you had it."

"Then I'll keep it." I point the beam of light at him with a smile.

"What are you doing up?" I ask.

"I could ask you the same." He barks back, but the words are softened by the appearance of a half-smile.

"It's a beautiful night. I couldn't resist taking a walk around. Now your turn."

"I don't sleep much." He doesn't offer anything more, nor does he turn away. Instead we stare at each other in silence, bathed in the yellow glow of our flashlights.

"So you're really going to Ho'okipa tomorrow?"

"Why not? I've never seen it before, and Lance seems nice." I drop my eyes to the ground, shifting from foot-to-foot.

"Yeah, a lot of women seem to think so." He lets go of a short laugh.

If this is Kane's way of revealing that Lance is a player, fine, but he can save the passive-aggression for someone else.

"I'm sure I'll be in good hands."

I notice how his body tenses, and he speaks so softly that I almost can't hear him. "Don't go."

"Why Kane? Why shouldn't I go?"

The tension in the air is palpable; the only sounds are the crashing waves and Kane's uneven breath between us. I wait another full minute for an answer, and when I don't get one, I sigh aloud.

"Good night, Kane." I flick off the flashlight but keep it in my hand, choosing to walk in darkness back to my suite, guided by nothing more than my own sheer will and the dim light of the moon.

Chapter 12

Lance picks me up in an old mint green Volkswagen Westfalia. A couple of surfboards are mounted on the roof. I'm surprised that the car still runs, given the sputtering sound it makes. He parks and comes around to open my door, which I think is really sweet. Once we're both settled, he backs down the driveway and I peek at Kane's place through the windshield. Even though the blinds are drawn, I swear I see them move.

"So are vans like *mandatory* for surfers?" I ask.

He chuckles. "Easy on the old girl. She's all I could afford when I moved here five years ago. I love her too much now to part with her."

"Loyalty—I like that." I tap the glove box in front of me. "Sorry girl, I meant no disrespect."

When I glance over, Lance is watching me instead of the road. "With a smile like that, you're always forgiven." He gives me a wink and I feel myself blush.

"Where did you move from?" I realize that I hadn't had a chance to ask him, which was hardly surprising given all of Kane's interruptions.

"Big Sur." He smiles. "You're from San Fran, right?"

"Yep, we're both California babies."

"Through and through. I miss it sometimes, but Hawaii's just got this energy about it—this place is its own living, breathing thing."

"I think it's called *Mana*...Pancho was saying something about it."

"Sounds like Pancho," he says. "One thing is for sure, the beauty is undeniable."

"That's what I'm learning."

We chat like two old friends reunited at long last. The road winds and winds but time seems to fly by regardless. Lance points to a beach in the east, as we begin our descent down a steep hill. "There she is." He gives me a wild grin. "Ho'okipa."

We pull into the crowded parking lot and luck out with a free space. I clamber from the van and wander to the beach, while Lance hops up to deal with the boards. It's not as big as I imagined, but it's buzzing with energy. Skinny palms dot the short, dry grass, and everywhere there are surfers waxing boards, guys sitting on circles of coolers—drinking beer and laughing like Gods—while beautiful girls sprawl on tanning towels below. I approach the rock wall, noticing a lifeguard shelter on one side and a picnic shelter on the other, like a makeshift frame for the cresting ocean and thunderous waves.

Lance appears beside me, as my jaw drops open like a drawbridge. "You're going to surf *that*?"

"Nothing better." He bobs his head at two guys passing by with surfboards. "It's big today, so I'm going to get a tow out. You'll be ok here?"

He skims his free hand down my bare arm. It's not lost on me that the gesture doesn't even give me goose bumps. "I'm good here. Go do your thing."

He suits up and I learn what he means by tow out— there's a jet ski on the beach giving rides out to the expanse of ocean beyond the breaking waves. Already there are dozens of surfers on the horizon, alongside a congregation of windsurfers, their colorful sails making kaleidoscopes of the landscape. I walk down to the sand and dig a towel from my bag, figuring I might as well catch a tan. I shed my sundress and lounge out in my yellow bikini. It's one of my favorites, with straps that wrap all the way from my chest to my waist, but there's not much of it. I lather on the SPF60 sunscreen and settle in to watch Lance.

Set after set, I'm captivated by the physical and mental strength required by the sport. He looks so confident in the waves, even after getting pounded by the swell. It looks exhilarating until he's thrown from his board—and then it's terrifying—and certainly not something I'm brave enough to try. The wind is blowing like crazy, turning my hair into a rat's nest, so I pile it onto my head in what I hope passes for a bun. I'm sure it looks awful, but at least it lets me give Lance my full and uninterrupted attention. About an hour later, he paddles back to shore, grinning from ear-to-ear. I feel strangely proud—not that I did anything myself—but because I actually know someone who can do something like this.

Lance halts at the base of my towel, dripping all over my legs. His messy blond hair is now plastered to his head, and I release a squeal when he shakes it out on me. "That's freezing!"

He shrugs. "You'll get used to it." Lance plants his board in the sand and unzips his suit. His eyes don't leave me as he strips off his wetsuit, and I notice him swallow hard as they dip down to my chest. "You look like sunshine in that yellow bikini."

"Thanks?"

"Seriously. That fiery hair, jewel-like eyes, big red lips? You must know that you're a smoke-show?"

"Cut it out," I say, tossing my sunscreen bottle back at him.

He falls to the sand dramatically. "And she has good aim, too. I think I'm in love."

"I thought you were in love with Old Minty back there," I tease, hitching my thumb in the direction of the parking lot.

He wiggles his eyebrows. "I can make room for two."

"There's never room for two," I mutter, almost involuntarily. My mind flits to Kane, but Lance misreads my comment.

"Shit, Ashley, I'm sorry. That was insensitive, given what happened with your husband and all."

"So you know about my situation, too?"

He looks toward the waves. "Paia Town is pretty small."

"Right," I clip out.

"If it's any consolation, he's a fucking lunatic for messing things up with you."

I tilt my head. "Actually, it kind of is. Thanks for saying so." I get to my feet and brush off the sand.

"Are you getting hungry?" He asks. "I'm starving."

I shrug. "I could eat, but I'll bet you worked up an appetite."

His eyes go half-mast and he shoots me a lazy wink. "Some might say that my appetite is unmatched."

I release a nervous giggle. I know that he's flirting with me, but I'm not prepared to flirt back, as dumb as that sounds. I follow Lance back to Old Minty and we head for a place called Makawao in the upcountry valley area. As we pull into town, I feel like I've been transported to the Wild West, with its cowboy themed storefronts and pastoral vibe. It looks part spaghetti western, part tropical jungle, and it seems even sleepier than Paia.

The interior of the Italian restaurant is nicer than the exterior would suggest, with its open, airy ceiling and snow white tablecloths. We talk nonstop as I stuff myself with Linguine Pescatore and homemade focaccia bread. I'm feeling lightheaded from two martinis but soothed by the laughter shared between us. I manage to save just enough room to share a tiramisu with Lance. He pays the bill, despite my protests, slipping his warm hand into mine on our way back to the van. It doesn't feel wrong per se, but it doesn't feel right either. Nonetheless, it's been a great night so I simply leave my hand in his.

He's all yawns on the drive home, so I'm surprised when he suggests Salty's. I'd rather go home and fall into bed with a full tummy, but Lance has been sweet so I reluctantly agree. The bar is busy for a Wednesday night. At this rate, I figure I'll be deemed a regular in no time. All of the bar-top seats are taken, so we head for the outdoor sofa by the fire table. Lance sits close enough that our knees touch, slinging his arm over the couch until his fingers graze my shoulder.

"Why are there servers here?" I say, noticing two young women taking orders.

"Kane adds a few staff on busy weekdays and sometimes on Saturdays, to keep up with the tourists. There's often someone else here, unless they call in hung over."

I try to make eye contact with one of the servers, but they're obviously slammed. I stifle a groan when I see Kane heading our way, coming to a stop before us.

"Shouldn't you be at the bar?" I ask.

"It's busy, so I'm helping out. What do you want?"

Lance drops his hand from the seat back, closing his fingers around my shoulder.

"White wine for Ashley, the Maui Brew Lager for me."

It's weird that he's ordering for me, but white wine sounds fine and I'm not one to argue. However, I do tense when Lance's hand starts tracing little circles on my shoulder. Kane's eyes lock onto the movement for an instant before he turns back towards the bar.

"Might be awhile with this crowd," Kane calls back over his shoulder while stalking off. This man seems to do a lot of stalking around, like an angry six-foot-five tall bear.

I listen to Lance tell stories from home until our wine arrives, delivered by a younger server. Lance is funny and charming, and I laugh at all the right moments, but my head just isn't into it. I'm tired, full, and I want my bed—I tilt back my glass and down the rest before asking to leave. Lance doesn't hide his disappointment, but he plays the gentleman role and eventually agrees. He says almost nothing on the ride home to my cottage, and I notice his contemplative face in the moonlight as he delivers me to the front door. There he bends his head down and I realize a second too late that he's going to kiss me. His lips brush mine and the kiss is soft and feathery, but there's no fire in it. After a few seconds, he pulls away and sighs.

"You like him, don't you?"

My voice cracks. "Who?"

He gives me a look. "Kane."

"If you think that, why did you ask me out?"

"I guess I wanted to test the waters. Ashley, you're beautiful, smart, funny, and down-to-earth. That's a hard combination to find these days; a guy would be insane not to try."

"Well now *I* feel like a jerk," I say, letting my shoulders slump forward.

"Don't." He chuckles. "I knew what I was getting myself into, even if you didn't."

"And now that I know?"

"I guess I'll just have to find a dark place and slink off to lick my wounds."

"No!" I shout, grabbing his forearm.

"Relax, Ashley, I'm kidding," he says, laughing. "Friends?"

"Friends," I say, exhaling in relief.

He pulls me into a firm hug and whispers in my ear. "And if you ever change your mind…"

I pull back and swat him on the chest. "Masochist."

"You have no idea." His eyes glitter with mischief, making me laugh out loud.

"Goodnight then, friend." I kiss him on the cheek and he grasps his chest comically, but not before a flicker of pain flashes across his face. I've hurt him and feel terrible about it. "Drive safe," I mumble, before he gives me a wave and jogs back to Old Minty.

Once I'm inside the safety of my suite, I brush my teeth, wash my face, shed my clothing, and fall into bed naked. With tonight's revelations on my mind, I toss and turn for what feels like hours. It's too humid inside and the ceiling fan does next to nothing. I decide that I need some air. Remembering the outdoor shower, I grab a towel and head onto the lanai for a cold wash.

The moon is high and bright in the sky, but I plug in the outdoor string lights for extra illumination. I turn the shower to tepid warm and feel my muscles relax the moment I step under the spray. The fresh air smells sweet and tropical. I can hear crickets chirping and the sound of waves crashing and echoing off the shore. I realize halfway through my shower that I forgot to bring out soap, but I don't even care. I just close my eyes and tip my head backwards, letting the coldish water run down my face and breasts, dripping between my legs. A rustling sound startles me from behind, and I turn to see all six-foot-five inches of pissed off Kane Keo standing beside me in the bamboo stall.

Chapter 13

"Kane!" I scream, trying to cover my breasts with my arms and pressing my legs together in the process. He's breathing heavily, as if he ran a marathon to get here, with eyes dark and wild.

"He touched you." He growls and steps closer until he's under the spray. The water beats down our fronts and soaks through his t-shirt, sculpting the fabric against his muscled chest. "You let him touch you," he repeats, his tone even more accusing, and I can only assume that he means Lance.

"Hello? I'm naked here, Kane!" I shout. "Can't you see that?"

"Oh, I see you, Ashley. I always see you." He takes another step forward and backs me into the wall. The water wets his hair, dripping into his eyes and down his face, but he doesn't seem to mind. His jaw is firmly set and his gaze locked with mine. When he speaks, his voice is dangerously low.

"Did he kiss you?"

"We were on a date, Kane. What do you expect?"

"Do not say that word."

"What word? Date?" I don't know why I'm taunting someone who's clearly riled up, except that I don't appreciate him caging me in with those enormous arms. He leans his weight into the wall and I watch his triceps flex and pop.

"I'll ask again, Ashley, and I expect an answer this time. Did-he-kiss-you?" His breath is erratic and he pants out each word like punctuation, searching my face for answers. I can't lie to him, but I won't give him the necessary context either, not when he's mere inches from my naked body and my traitorous nipples are standing at attention.

"Yes." I let out a shaky breath and watch a look of pure determination cross his face.

"No. Fuck no!" He roars, right before pressing his lips into mine. The kiss isn't sweet or gentle—it's rough and needy and raw. He nips at my bottom lip, and when my mouth opens from the shock, his tongue plunges in to tangle with mine.

The sensation shoots right through my core and then even further down south. My legs are shaking and already a slickness builds between my thighs. My pebbled nipples rub against his wet shirt, and I let out a moan so loud that I nearly come right there. The sound of my moans seems to set him off; his breathing becomes frantic and he thrusts his hard self against my center, grabbing my ass with both hands and hauling me up against the wall.

"I've wanted to be between your legs since the moment I saw you." His panting lips move to devour my neck. "But I can't promise you anything more than that."

"Uh-huh," I mumble, rocking my hips against his wet shorts. At this point, I seriously don't care what he promises me, as long as he gives me relief—I want this—I want him so badly.

"Do you want me inside of you, Ashley?" His voice is low, and it takes all my strength not to melt into a boneless heap before him.

"More than anything. Please fuck me, Kane," I whisper, and he answers with a chest-rumbling groan.

"Bed. Now." He reaches behind me and turns off the shower, carrying me back inside with hands still cupping my ass. He pushes the sliding door closed with his bare feet, carrying me to bed as if I weigh nothing. I expect him to throw me down caveman style, but he surprises me by laying me gently against the pillows.

The bedside lamp is on, casting the room in a dim, orange glow, but it's enough to see him slowly shed his clothing. His wet t-shirt comes off first, revealing that wide and gorgeous chest of his, followed by his soaked cargo shorts. They drop to the floor with a slap. He isn't wearing any underwear and his hard thick length is on full display. He strokes it up and down with one of his large hands.

"Oh my," I say, because I don't know what else to say. He's *huge*—I try my best to control my reaction, but he sees my eyes widen and smirks.

"Change your mind yet?"

I bite my bottom lip between my teeth, my eyes traveling from his waist to his eyes. "Definitely not."

He approaches the bed at a leisurely pace, but I can read the desire burning in his eyes. His black hair is damp and mussed up, falling just past his chin. His trimmed beard glistens with cool beads of water from the outdoor shower. I watch one droplet fall from his chin onto the bed. All I can think about is how much I want to feel that rough beard between my legs. As if he can read my mind, he falls onto his knees and grasps at each of my ankles, pulling me to the edge of the bed. The air is so humid that I'm already slick with a combination of sweat and desire. The need between my legs pulses and throbs. He starts a trail along my inner thighs, the stiff coarse hair of his beard tickling almost to the point of pain. I feel his hot breath on my cool center, followed by a rush of cold hair as he blows between my legs.

"I've wondered if you were red down here as well."

"Keep wondering then," I breathe out, and he releases a husky laugh.

"Hey, I'm not complaining. I like bare too."

"Maybe I'll let you in on the secret one day—*ohmygod…*" I moan as his mouth dips below my waist. He doesn't do what most men seem to do down there—those gentle little circles that feel almost for show—no, he plunges right inside, swirling his tongue in the most delicious way possible and gripping the back of my thighs like I belong to him.

"I can't even describe how good you taste. You're like nectar," he says, pulling back for only a second, forever attentive to the building wetness between my thighs. The tip of his tongue finds my clit and he sucks hard, making my hips buck up off the bed.

"Kane!" I scream, not even caring how loud I'm being. Usually I'm embarrassed about making noises and do my best to hold back, but with his expert tongue that's simply not possible. Besides, who's going to hear me?

"Kane," I repeat, my voice shaking. "I can't." I know I must sound crazy, totally incoherent, but the sensation is simply too much for me. Never before have I found such release from oral.

"I'm not stopping until you come." From the tone of his voice, I have no doubt that he means what he says. At his nudging, I spread my legs a little wider and let him take charge.

The first wave of orgasm hits me so intensely that it's almost painful. I scream his name out as the second one crests over my body. I'm still riding the wave when it occurs to me that I've never had an orgasm like this in my entire life. Before I can catch my breath, he's climbing onto the bed and inching my head onto the soft pillows. He slides a hand between my legs before inserting one finger and then another inside me.

"You're so wet for me," he growls, gently circling his fingers around my flesh. Feeling sensitive, I instinctively try to squirm away, but he places his free arm around my waist and holds me in place.

"Stay still," he breathes. "I know there's another one in you."

It takes me a second to realize that he means another orgasm. Does he seriously think I'm going to have another orgasm? I barely orgasm on the regular, let alone have two back-to-back, so he's crazy if he thinks it's happening again.

"Kane, I'm not… I've never…" I try to find the words, but he silences me with a long, burning kiss.

"You've never been with me before, Lani." He watches me with his deep hazel eyes, taking his time as his fingers work their magic. He inserts a third finger inside me and my eyes roll back into my head. "You are so beautiful when you come." He dips his head down to nibble on my neck, favoring one spot where he'll surely leave a mark, but I just don't care.

"So beautiful. There's no guard up, it's just you." With his three fingers working in tandem, the sensitivity vanishes and I feel vibrations building low down in my belly. "Your body is mine now."

He growls again, increasing the pressure of his fingers, and I pant out a response.

"What about the rest of me?"

"I'm not good with the rest."

I run my hand along his hard chest, grazing the trail of coarse hair leading down to his hot, thick length. He's glistening with precum as I take him in my hand, but he hisses through his teeth, grabbing my wrist to remove my fingers.

"Not until you say it."

"Say what?" I moan, feeling the pressure build within me.

"Tell me. Tell me that this body is mine."

"Until when?" I gasp out, his thumb finding my clit and teasing me. It's more of a slow burn this time, but I'm close.

"Until I fucking say so."

He kisses me hard. I moan as my hands wrap around his hard large length all buried between my legs. I know I can't hold out any longer.

My voice rattles. "This body is yours."

"Good girl." He kisses my neck and rewards me by pressing his thumb down on my clit, hard.

This time I don't scream; this time no sound comes out. My eyes squeeze shut, and it's a long orgasm this time, not a wave, but a slow vibration that makes me want to cry. I go limp in his arms. He pushes my wet hair back and kisses my forehead, leaning back and bracing his knees on either side of my body. He strokes his massive length up and down.

"Are you ready for me?" He asks, giving me a lazy smile.

"Yes." I can tell he likes my answer from the way his pupils dilate.

"Then stay right there." He gets off the bed and retrieves his shorts from the floor, removing a condom from the pocket. He rolls it on before I can even ask what he's doing, and then he's back on top of me, bracing his weight on his arms.

"You drive me crazy, like no one ever before. The minute I saw your face at the bar, I knew I couldn't stay away." He shifts his weight into me, his calloused hands coming up to massage my breasts. "When you flashed these luscious tits of yours at the beach, you almost killed me, woman. They were meant for me—and only me—to see. And on the black sand beach? I could've taken you right there. I would have, too, if I didn't think it would land me in jail."

"But you pulled away. You wouldn't kiss me," I whisper.

He shakes his head. "I knew if I kissed you, even once, it wouldn't be enough. I wouldn't stop. Look at you—your skin, your creamy perfect skin. It drives me wild when you don't protect yourself and cover up. You're far too perfect to be ruined, especially by me."

"But you'll ruin me anyway?" I ask, half afraid of his response, because I don't want him to stop. He answers by positioning himself between my legs and easing into me slowly.

"I don't know if I'll survive you, Lani," he whispers through gritted teeth, before thrusting deep inside me. We both groan this time, our voices mingling together as one. The size of him stretches me to the limit. It takes me a second to adjust but then it feels too damn good to care.

"You ok?" He whispers against the shell of my ear, and I shake my head yes, unable to find the words.

"Good," he says, right before pulling back and slamming into me hard. He fucks me roughly, seeming both needy and intense. I start to feel the slow tingle of another orgasm building, but I doubt it's humanly possible to have three in a row. His lips find my nipple and he tugs gently before swirling his tongue around each peak with equal attention. He slams into me again and I cry out his name.

"Kane?!" I say it like a question, but he seems to know what I mean.

"Oh yeah, you're coming again, Ashley, but I hope it's soon because I don't know how much longer I can last. You feel incredible," he pants out.

He runs one of his big hands through my hair and gently pulls the ends while his teeth nip at my chin. "Come for me…one more time, beautiful angel." The sound of his deep, throaty voice is all that I need, and my legs come up involuntarily to wrap around his waist. I squeeze hard and the resulting friction has me screaming his name for the third time tonight.

"Fuck!" He curses loudly and his body spasms all over me. I can feel the heat of him shooting into the condom and his groan of pleasure draws out way longer than I'm used to hearing. When he's finished, he rolls to the side but doesn't let me go right away. One hand is around the condom while the other is tangled in my hair, and I literally have no words.

"Even better than what I imagined." He gives me a quick hot kiss, dipping his soft tongue between my lips once more. He gets off the bed and disappears into the bathroom before I have a chance to respond.

"Then you imagined?" I finally croak.

He reappears without the condom, still gloriously naked. "Yes, *Lani:* Imagined. Pretty much a dozen times a day since I met you."

"You've called me that before. Who is Lani?" I ask, immediately bristling.

He laughs. "It's not a person, beautiful. It's the Hawaiian word for heaven. *Mai Ka Lani Mai* roughly translates to *heaven sent.*"

"Why?" I whisper, even as the tightness in my chest starts to loosen.

He shrugs. "Because you are."

I don't know what to say, nor what to expect from him next. Is he going to leave? Insult me? Make himself a sandwich? Instead he just flops onto his stomach and yawns.

"You're not sleeping here?" It's unclear if I'm asking or accusing him, even to me.

"It's late. I'm tired."

It was pretty much the same monosyllabic-Kane-answer I'd come to expect, but still. "Are you sure this is normal?"

"Sleeping?" He opens one eye to glare at me. "Yeah, I think so."

It might be the first time I've heard him make a joke, but it doesn't sit right. "But isn't this, I don't know, more than just the body?"

He lifts his head and gives me a searing look. "You're overthinking it—and anyway, this is my *hale*, remember?"

"No, currently it's my house." I bristle, wrapping my arms around my chest. "At least for the next two weeks."

He frowns and yanks me down until I'm blushing against his body. "You can stay here as long as you want. Longer than two weeks."

I don't have the energy to argue, and there's no point in sharing that I've already emailed two apartment shares in Kihei regarding availability, so I just sigh and relax into his side. He slings one big, beefy arm across my middle and simultaneously nuzzles into the crook of my neck.

"Do you even fit on this bed?" I huff out, glancing down at his feet, which must surely hang off the edge.

"I fit just fine, now go to sleep." He lifts himself up to kiss the top of my head before flopping back down and closing his eyes. He's out within minutes, whereas I probably won't be able to fall asleep for a week, what with the number of orgasms I just had. Nonetheless, fatigue catches up with me before I know it and I drift off into my own blissful sleep.

• • •

Morning is a lot less blissful. I awake naked, frizzy-haired, and sweltering hot, still half-trapped under Kane's enormous body. He's pressed right up against me, his calf wrapped around both of my legs, and I'm coated in a fine sheen of sweat. I can only imagine what the tangle on my head must look like, having left it untamed after my shower. I start to freak out a little about my morning breath, exhaling into my hand to check the smell. It seems fine, but I also have to pee, so somehow I need to get Kane off me. I start to shove his cement-like arm, but he only squeezes me tighter.

"Goin' somewhere?" He asks, an adorable sleepiness in his voice.

"I need to get up."

He mumbles into the pillow. "No."

"You say that word a lot."

"Mmm…" He hums, followed by the sexiest sounding chuckle ever. My nipples immediately stand to attention. "Am I really that bad?"

I snort. "You are positively mercurial."

"Never heard that before. Guess I should be flattered."

"You shouldn't be. A normal person wouldn't be flattered." I flip over until I'm facing away from him, and soon he lets me go, but not before thrusting his hardness against my backside.

"You can go, but get your fine ass right back here. And don't think you're leaving this room without a round two."

I race to the bathroom to pee and brush my teeth, washing my face with cold water and attempting to tame my wild hair. When I look in the mirror, I barely recognize myself. My eyes are bright, my skin is glowing, and I look relaxed. Who knew that all I needed was a bossy but sexy landlord giving me three stellar orgasms.

"Ashley!" He calls from the other room. "Time's up."

I brace my hands on my hips and walk back to the bed, not even caring that I'm completely bare. "That's rude!"

"I missed you," he says, sheepishly, and I roll my eyes. I can't deny that he looks delicious though; his bottom half is covered by a thin blanket and his inked calf sticks out from below.

"What does your tattoo mean?" I ask, staring appreciatively at the detailed lines.

He sighs like I'm testing his patience. "Leg tattoos were traditionally worn by Polynesian warriors. They can mean lots of different things: stamina, longevity, leadership, ferocity, birth rank, or a reminder of battles won—but honestly, I was nineteen years old and thought it looked cool. Now get your ass back into bed."

"You're so bossy."

"And you like it. Get. In. Bed."

I climb in but face away from him in silent protest. I can hear the rustling of a package and feel the bed dip beneath me. The next thing I know, he's sliding into me from behind, his rough hands coming around to capture both of my breasts. He eases himself in and I let my head fall back against his chest, the wetness building like a tidal-wave.

"I could stay here inside of you all day. You're addictive."

I rock back against him, looping my arms around his neck, which lifts my sensitive breasts even further into his hands. He pinches my nipples in response, twisting them ever-so-slightly as I chase my release.

"How are you built this way?"

"What way?" I stammer.

"Perfectly." His hand skims along my side and dips into the curve of my waist. "So smooth," he whispers, nibbling my earlobe. "And this ass." He gives my ass cheeks a firm tap. Within no time, I'm smothering my cries of pleasure with the pillow, and he follows closely behind, cursing out loud before burying his nose in my hair.

"Coconut," he mutters, having correctly guessed my shampoo. I laugh because it's a strange thing to say right after sex. In fact, this whole situation is strange, mostly because I have no idea what happens next.

I lay there feeling boneless—it's his turn to get up first. He dresses in his shorts and t-shirt from last night, both of which still look damp.

"Do you want some coffee?" I ask.

He smirks. "You don't need to make me coffee, Ashley. I gotta' head to the bar anyways, but I'll be back here later." He heads to the kitchen and pours himself a glass of water, while I wrap a sheet around my body and follow him. He downs the water in four big gulps and places the cup in the sink before starting towards the patio doors. On his way out, something on the kitchen table stops him dead in his tracks. I glance down to see the newspaper I borrowed, open to a page encircled by red.

"What is this?" He picks up the paper, shaking it in my direction.

I sign and pull the bed sheet tighter. "What does it look like? It's the classifieds."

He brings the paper closer to his nose and begins reading aloud. "Waitress in Lahaina, Head of Service Staff in Kihei, receptionist in Kihei?"

"They're jobs, Kane, so what? I've also applied for some remote, home-based positions, but those are a lot harder to come by and there's nothing available within my field. I'm not even sure that I want to do real estate anymore, so I have to be open to whatever is out there. It's not like I'm qualified for most of these positions anyways—I mean, I served a little in college, but that was years ago."

"Lahaina is a forty-minute drive, on a good day. You want to do that every day?" I must look guilty, because his eyes narrow into slits. "Ashley, what aren't you telling me?"

I cringe when he flips to the rental section. The two places I've inquired about are highlighted there, with my notes scribbled in the columns. "You're not leaving," he asserts, his voice flat.

"I can't stay here forever, Kane. This is a vacation rental, and things between us were already complicated. Now they're just…"

"Just what?" He challenges.

"Just…I don't know, Kane! Why don't you tell me?"

His voice softens, but he's not giving up. "This one is for February 15th."

"That's weeks away!"

"It's too soon." He shakes his head. "You've barely gotten settled in Paia. Think about Adele and Kayla. Besides, Pancho loves you."

"And Lance?" I regret the words as soon as they leave my mouth.

"Don't test me, Ashley." His voice is dead calm. "Unless you want the spanking of the century."

His total jackass, caveman response sends my mind in all sorts of inappropriate places, so I change the subject. "If not February 15th or March 1st then when? When is the right time?"

"You can work at the bar!" He blurts out, dropping the paper to the table.

"What?"

"The bar. The food thing. I gave it some thought and it's actually a good idea. I think you should try it."

"Really?" I say, hope blooming in the pit of my stomach.

"I already have a valid restaurant license. I just don't use it." He shrugs and gives me a smile. "I'll cover the cost of supplies, and you do all the menu stuff—you know, the cooking and serving. You can keep sixty-percent of the gross sales."

"That's generous."

"If I'm being honest, I'm still skeptical that people want to eat at Salty's, but I'm willing to give it a try. Remember though, sink or swim, it's all on you. If the food goes to rot and no one's interested, we'll have to revisit the plan."

"I wouldn't expect anything less." Already I can hear the excitement creeping into my voice. "When can I get started?"

"Whenever you like. Believe it or not, I was going to come over tomorrow and let you know, but my timeline got a little accelerated." He smirks, and I feel a low heat in my belly, remembering how he surprised me in the shower yesterday.

"How quickly can you get supplies in?" I ask.

"We can start using local ingredients. If I need to order in bulk, we'll cross that bridge when we come to it—it usually takes a day or two for deliveries from the mainland."

"Let's start tomorrow then. I'll put together a menu and do the shopping today." I'm literally bouncing off the balls of my feet, basking in the smile tugging at the corner of his mouth.

"You're cute. And fucking sexy."

"Thank you, Kane! Thank you for this opportunity!" I jump up and throw my arms around his neck. He catches me midair, letting my kisses reign down his cheeks before placing me safely on the floor.

"Okay, enough. In case you forgot, you're naked under that bed sheet. Jump on me again and you'll be on your back faster than you can say *aloha*."

"Sorry!" I take a step back. As much as I want him again, the idea of planning out a menu has my creative senses firing in overdrive.

"Come by the bar later. You can show me your ideas."

"Yes! Absolutely, you won't regret this—I promise."

He heads for the lanai, pausing at the doorway. "And Ashley?"

"Yes?"

"Call back those apartment rentals. Tell them you're not interested. I won't have my only chef commuting to work every day. Got it?"

I give him a mock salute. "Message received." I swear I hear him laughing as he closes the door.

Chapter 14

I spend the morning surfing through my favorite food blogs, searching for inspiration. I want to give Salty's something more than simply bar food. My mind goes to locally-inspired and oh-so-elevated bar tapas. Anything organic and sustainable, and the Paia crowd will literally eat it up. I'm so in my element that I forget the time. It's already past 5pm when I check the clock. I'm still wrapped in the bed sheet, having had nothing to eat or drink all day, apart for half a cup of cold coffee, which still awaits me on the table.

I make myself a bowl of granola and fruit before jumping in the shower. After throwing on my go-to ripped jean cutoffs, plus a cute navy blue crop-top and flip-flops, I head out the door with wet hair and barely any makeup. I'm so excited to tell Kane about my ideas that I run halfway to the bar, my laptop clutched against my chest. It's beyond busy when I arrive. No seats are available at the bar, and Kane has his hands full pouring drinks. While it's almost physically painful, I manage to wait my turn.

He catches my eye soon enough and his body is pure sin: deep tan, close-cropped beard, and his hair pulled back into a low ponytail. He's wearing a short-sleeved t-shirt that's unbuttoned halfway down his chest, along with low-slung board shorts and eyes that flash hazel when he sees me. It's no wonder that half of the bar stools are occupied by women, of various ages and stages, but all with their eyes locked squarely on target. It pisses me off more than it should, but Kane has made it clear that this thing between us is purely physical, and I don't have much say in the matter.

When he finishes pouring drinks, he slips out from behind the bar, scanning me from head to toe while frowning and pursing his lips. "What the fuck are you wearing?"

I look down, confused. "It's a crop-top." Half the bar is in beach wear, so I don't understand his problem. Sure, it shows some midriff, but it covers up my girls and has super cute cap sleeves, not to mention the name of my sorority scrawled across the front. "What?" I say, jutting out my bottom lip.

He stares at me like he wants to devour me right then and there, his eyes falling to my waist with a sigh. "You're killing me right now, woman."

"We're in Hawaii, Kane, and it's ridiculously hot today. People are half-naked most of the time."

"People," he snaps back, lowering his voice. "People, but not you."

I stand my ground. "Yes me."

He rolls his eyes skyward. "Forget about it. Come to the back and show me what you've got." He leads the way and I follow. "Hell, maybe I can find you an apron, or some other shit to wear back here."

I choose to take the high road and ignore his comment. Once in the back, he closes the door and pushes me against it. His thumbs push my crop-top away, sliding beneath my lace bra. I moan and my head falls back and smacks the door. "Ouch."

He soothes me with a kiss, swirling his hot tongue around my mouth. He tastes like toothpaste and pure raw man. "I want you right now. Can I take you?"

He pushes my top up all the way, tugging at my bra until my nipples are exposed. His eyes and the cool air of the storeroom have me heavy with need, and I find myself embarrassingly wet for him.

"Kane," I moan, my knees shaking. He lifts me by the ass until I'm level with his hard length, before thrusting against me.

"Feel what you do to me, Ashley."

"There are customers out there," I pant out. "What about their orders?"

"I have staff working today. The customers can wait. Please, let me inside of you."

Never have I heard Kane say *please*, so I find myself nodding in consent. He carries me to a small sofa and lowers me down onto the cushions, so that I'm facing away from him on my knees.

"Take off those shorts," he commands.

I fumble with the zipper before pulling them down my thighs. There's the rustle of a condom wrapper and his shorts hitting the floor, while he braces himself behind me. One of his large hands finds my lower back and pushes me forward. I lean into the sofa, and he slides into me from behind, driving himself in with gusto and making my trussed up breasts bounce. When he reaches around to massage my clit, I feel my orgasm like an earthquake.

"I love that you can't be quiet with me," he says, covering my mouth with one of his big, calloused hands. "But we don't want people talking."

The sensation of fullness from our position—combined with my aching nipples and the cage he's made around my body—all send me over the edge, and I'm shaking as I come.

"Oh, Ashley," he whispers, picking up his pace and slamming into me so hard that I fall forward against the sofa, sending my ass straight into the air. He holds my hips and drives into me. "You have the most gorgeous ass," he growls, his fingers skating and stroking between its crevice.

"Kane!" I jerk away from his touch, but he just chuckles.

"Don't worry, beautiful. I won't take you there until you're ready." His voice is thick with need. It's not long before his own body jerks violently, forcing him to smother the sounds of his release between my shoulder blades. I've never had so many back-to-back orgasms in my life.

"Can you die from too many orgasms?" I wonder aloud, earning me a full-on laugh from Kane.

He eyes glitter greenish-brown. "There's only one way to find out."

I dress quickly and Kane does the same. This time, he actually does lead me into the kitchen. There's a double fridge, six burners, a stand-up freezer, and a portable island packed with pots and pans. He lifts me onto the island and settles himself between my legs, running one hand through his long hair.

He loosens his luscious locks from his ponytail. "*E kala mai*, I couldn't help myself. You're just so easy to pick up and move around."

I snort. "That's not something I've been accused of before." I look down at the island that I'm using as a chair. "But this probably isn't the most professional way to have an employee to boss conversation."

"*Mmmhmm...*" he hums, rubbing his scratchy beard against my chin. "I'm not your boss. Consider yourself an independent contractor."

"Still," I protest. He shakes his head but helps me down. Meanwhile, I reach up to caress his beard. "I've always wondered what you'd look like without this—" Just then, a sense of 21st century dread floods over me. "Shit, my laptop!" I dropped it on the floor of the back room. Kane steps away to collect my precious hardware and sets it gently on the island. I power it up, making my way through the list of menu items I've brainstormed so far. I've decided to do a snack-food menu (or *pupus*, if you ask the locals) with a Hawaiian-fusion theme. He bends down to read my draft menu, but instead I start reading aloud.

"I'm thinking of a few different options, like pulled Kalua pork nachos, Lomi salmon bruschetta, teriyaki and pineapple beef bites, fried spam and cheese balls..." I take a deep breath before forging forwards. "Also some more substantial items, like grilled Mahi Mahi sliders, coconut shrimp tacos, mini poke pizzas, and maybe a Loco Moco but with veggie burgers and mushroom gravy? I don't have anything vegetarian so far."

Aloha in Love 121

Kane simply rubs his chin. I'm freaking out because I can't read his face at all.

"It's impressive," he finally says. "The locals will love it, as will the tourists searching for a taste of Hawaii. Are you sure it's not too much for you?"

My voice brims with excitement. "I can handle eight menu items."

He steps closer and tips my chin back, swiping the rough skin of his thumb across my lips. He bends down for a long, slow kiss, making my toes curl into my flip-flops. I never would have guessed that the short-tempered, cantankerous Kane Keo could be so affectionate.

"Lose the Loco Moco—it's too messy. Though I wouldn't mind if you made it for breakfast tomorrow—that is, *after* I fuck you until the sun comes up."

A shiver passes through me then. "How old are you Kane?"

"Thirty-one. Why?"

"I thought that men were supposed to slow down after thirty, you know, sexually."

"You thought wrong." He kisses the corner of my mouth, but my mind wanders to Dale and his exhaustive list of reasons why our love life fizzled out.

"Someone told me that once."

"Well, he's an idiot." Kane's deep voice rumbles, hearing the subtext in my comment. "I could be eighty, and I'd still want to take you on that little couch. Now get out of here—before I decide to take you again." He pats my ass and points me towards the door.

I can only imagine how I must look upon emerging from the back room with my hair tousled, cheeks flushed, and crop-top askew. Lance is sitting at the bar. He raises his eyebrows at me, so I adjust my top and turn my attention back to the restaurant, spotting Adele on the last bar stool. She waves at me from her perch.

"There you are, dear. I've been looking for you!"

"How was your date with Tinder?" I ask, coming around the bar to claim the vacant seat beside my friend.

"Terrible, darling. The lesbian hunt is proving more difficult than I imagined." Lance overhears and literally chokes on his beer.

"I'll leave you ladies to it." He hurries away, as if his stool just caught fire.

"But that's not what I wanted to talk to you about. I'm thinking of having a dinner party at my house on Saturday—just a few close friends. Are you free?"

A dinner party seems like the perfect opportunity to use my friends as guinea pigs, so I tell Adele about my menu for Salty's.

"That's a delightful idea! I'd love for you to cater, but you must let me pay you, both for the supplies and your time."

"Yes to the supplies, if absolutely necessary, but definitely not for my time."

I agree to give her a list of ingredients, and we plan to meet on Saturday morning. Adele will fetch me at my suite and I'll spend my day prepping. I hop off the stool, already preparing to leave when she calls after me.

"And Darling?"

I turn around to face her. "Yes Adele?"

"I'm so glad that you let that lovely man inside of you." Her voice is far too loud. My jaw drops, leaving me at a total loss for words.

"Oh, don't look so surprised. I've been on this earth long enough to know what freshly fucked smells like, and you, my darling, absolutely reek of sex. Ta ta!" She sends me off with a wave.

I open and close my mouth as the words fail to come. She saves me by turning her attention to Kane, who has just appeared behind the bar. I'm surprised to see that he doesn't look mortified at all; in fact, he winks at me. I rush from the bar with my face on fire, trying to occupy my mind with shopping lists and dinner menus and the fastest route to the grocery store.

Chapter 15

The next day, I borrow Kane's jeep and head for the Costco in Kahului. It's much busier than Paia. The line-ups and parking lots stress me out, making me realize how much I've already adapted to the lifestyle. I can't imagine going back to how things were before, especially after this week. The next few days, I split my time between testing recipes in the small kitchen and spending evenings wrapped in Kane's arms. He stays over most nights, but we barely talk. I realize after a while that I don't know much about him. I begin sharing details of my life (my parents, my old job, and some details about my marriage that make him tense up). He listens intently, asks great questions, and never judges my past, but I find myself wishing he'd open up even more.

Saturday rolls around, and Adele arrives bright and early to collect me from the curb. One day soon, I'll need to get a car, but I'd rather spend my money on the restaurant right now, and the escrow on our place in San Fran is killing me. I'm dressed in an old Bob Marley tank top and cutoff Levi's, having made sure to send Kane home last night, because I don't want to give Adele any more material. It's only about a ten-minute drive. The birds are chirping and the morning sun is rising as we pull into her driveway. She punches a code into the speaker and the front gates open like a demigod spreading her legs. I actually gasp aloud as we roll down the driveway. I never would have expected it, but Adele lives a very comfortable life.

"Did I forget to mention that I'm fabulously rich?" She says with a *tsk*. "Close your mouth, darling—it's just a house."

Just a house is definitely an understatement; estate fits much better. Her property is complete with a sprawling green lawn and a manicured garden of hibiscus and heliconia. Adele tells me that the house lies on waterfront land with fifty yards of white sand beach. We pull up alongside her monster of a house with its plantation columns and triple car garage. I can do nothing to stop myself from gaping. We park and head up the front stairs, through the massive foyer, and onwards to the back of the house.

"How big is this place, Adele?"

"Oh, maybe six thousand square feet." She leads me into a restaurant-grade kitchen complete with an entire wall of ovens and a refrigerator so big that I could probably rent it. "Hal came from a wealthy family. They owned sugar cane plantations. He actually spent his early years on the island, and that's one of the reasons I decided to move here. In a way, it felt like I'd be keeping a piece of him with me."

"That's sweet."

I smile, and Adele smiles right back. "It is, isn't it?"

The back wall of the house features a series of French doors, all hanging wide open in the breeze. The turquoise water is visible from every angle of the room, and a long chef's table is set up on the lanai, with white-covered chairs and delicate silverware. Tall glass candlesticks and vases of Birds of Paradise dot the table, while a pristine looking plumeria flower rests on every setting.

"Oh Adele!" I walk outside to get a better look. "If I'd known it would be like this…" I trail off.

"Then what?" She raises an eyebrow.

"My food won't stand up to this. It's not fancy enough."

"*Psh*, fancy is overrated. Flavor is everything." She brushes off my comment with a wave of her hand. "Make yourself at home. If there's anything you need, just text me. I'm off to the salon for some primping. Oh, and I'm bringing a date tonight. I call her *Maui Maude*. She's sixty-four and recently divorced."

"A younger woman—nice, Adele!"

She looks quite proud at the thought. "I imagine Kayla will come find you, that is, after she wakes up."

"Kayla lives here?" I ask, feeling like an idiot for not knowing.

"In the Guest House." She gestures towards the white sand beach. "At least for the time being. *Ta ta*, my darling."

She breezes out of the kitchen and I get straight to work, setting the pork to low in one of the ovens while frying up the spam for cheese balls. About two hours into my prep, a sleepy-looking Kayla pads barefoot into the kitchen. She extracts a whole carton of orange juice from the fridge and hoists herself onto the counter.

"Morning," she says, releasing a huge yawn.

"Don't you mean afternoon?"

"I got up before 5am to catch a sick break. Then I went back to sleep." She shrugs, and I notice she's still in sleepwear, wearing boy-short black underwear and a white men's tank top. Her tanned legs are almost a mile long. They slap against the cupboards as she swings them to and fro.

"So you and Keo, hey? I know you're fucking him now, but this whole cooking-thing seems like too much effort for a man." She gestures at the dirty bowls and cookware that I've scattered everywhere. I give her a sharp look, but she just laughs. "Adele might have let the shagging-gossip slip, plus you got *pash rash* on your neck."

"I don't know what that is. Besides this isn't for him— it's for me," I argue, and it is for me. I'm so in my element cooking that it doesn't even feel like work.

"He's making money on this project and leading you around by the vagina in the meantime."

"Trust me, Kayla, my vagina has nothing to do with this." I stop stirring to stare at her. "Maybe that's your own baggage talking?"

She looks away, taking another swing from the carton. "Maybe." She wipes the back of her hand across her mouth.

"But please tell me that you won't serve all this delicious food to Kane Keo looking like a servant."

I run a hand through my messy ponytail, taking inventory of my tank and shorts. "I actually hadn't given it much thought. I did bring a sundress to change into, along with my flip-flops."

Kayla rolls her eyes, hopping down from the counter. "You will not wear a boring old sundress to your big debut—I won't allow it. Once you're done here, give me a half hour for makeup and hair."

"You can do makeup and hair?"

"I do a lot that you don't know about." She walks around the gigantic granite island, stealing a handful from my pile of sliced pineapple. "I have something in my closet that's perfect for you."

"Nothing too sexy," I shout at her from behind, but all I hear is a trail of laughter as she disappears around the corner.

• • •

"No way. It's too sexy," I whine, surveying myself in Kayla's bathroom mirror.

She nods her approval. "It's off the charts."

Kayla has managed to stuff me into a dove-gray body-con dress, complete with side cutouts and a deep v-neck showing far too much chest. We're such different shapes; I have no idea how it even fits me, but she swears on her life that it looks good.

I skim my hands over my hips. "It's tight."

"It's supposed to be, and the color is banging with your eyes. You look like a goddess." She blows my hair out into soft, loose curls, finishing my makeup with smoky-gray eye shadow and pale pink lips.

"You are amazing at this." I blink at myself in the mirror. She somehow managed to make my green eyes look huge.

"It's a bit of a hobby of mine." I don't miss the pride in her voice. She looks effortless, of course, wearing a tight black romper with her auburn hair pulled into a sleek topknot.

"It's too much though, right?" I ask.

"Look, you need to relax. You look smoking hot. Your scary but equally hot fukboi will be here soon, and the food smells delish. You did it girl—now it's time to enjoy."

When we get back to the kitchen, Adele is already home. She looks polished and put together, with her hair pulled into tight curls, a massive string of pearls, and dark red lips to match. She's lounging on the lanai, flanked by two male waiters in tuxedos.

"Adele," I say, exasperated. "I'm more than happy to serve the food."

"Not looking like that, you're not," she snorts. "Besides, I always have extra help at my parties. It would be unusual if I didn't."

One of the waiters lights a few candles, their hurricane vases protecting them from the balmy breeze. The other escorts Kayla to her chair, just as the doorbell chimes. Pancho and his wife, a petite Japanese woman named Keiko, arrive with Lance and his date—a stunning blond. Lance gives me a hug right away.

"And just like that, I'm replaced," I whisper. He laughs and gives me a wink.

An older woman with a brown pixie cut arrives next. I can only assume that this is Maui Maude. Adele greets her by kissing both cheeks, and the two fall into hushed conversation. Kane's friend, Taylor, arrives alone, carrying wine and flowers for the host. He immediately takes the seat across from Kayla, and I don't miss how his eyes linger on her face. I take the seat closest to the kitchen, so that I can run back and forth between courses. One of the waiters pops a bottle of champagne and fills each of our glasses for a toast.

Kane is the last to arrive and I notice right away his crisp white button-down with the sleeves rolled up to his elbows and black dress pants. He looks mouthwateringly good and I jump to my feet when I see him, his eyes drinking me in from head to toe. His initial smile is soon swallowed by a frown, like one wave break collapsing into another, but I'm too nervous to worry about what's eating him. I sit back down as he takes the empty chair beside me, slinging his arm over the backside of my own. Adele taps her champagne flute with her knife, whistling as if she's thirty years younger.

"Friends, and lovers…" She shoots a look at Maude, who flushes. "Thank you all for joining me on this beautiful evening to celebrate our new friend Ashley's business venture. We're here for pleasure, of course, but there's work involved, too. You've entered our test kitchen and Ashley is awaiting candid feedback on her debut dishes. Each of you has a card next to your plate—mark down what you like and don't like. Don't be shy or afraid of hurting her feelings. The greatest gift we can give each other is honesty, and real friendship means sharing the truth above all else. So cheers to you, my darlings, I am grateful for your friendship. Every one of you is like family to me. *Mahalo*."

"*Mahalo*," we say in unison, clinking glasses.

The waiters turn on the music and the conversation begins to flow to the tune of Israel Kamakawiwo'ole's "Somewhere Over the Rainbow." Once I see that everyone is settled, I steal away to ready the first dish of Kalua pork nachos. To elevate the presentation, I've deconstructed the dish on a white circular plate. I'm in the process of garnishing it with avocado crema when the waiter joins me in the kitchen. He's cute with curly brown hair and big dimples, but he also looks much younger than me.

"Are they ready to go, miss?" He grins as if we know each other from another lifetime. "I'm Noah."

"Ashley." I give him my hand, keeping my voice neutral, which he holds a tad longer than appropriate.

"You're very talented, Ashley."

"And you're very forward, Noah." A deep voice rumbles from behind me. I can feel Kane's hard chest press against my back, and Noah's eyes widen when they meet his.

"I'm sorry...I-I didn't realize..." He stutters. "I'm just here to serve the food and keep an eye on the guests."

Kane wraps one thick arm around my waist. "Do me a favor, Noah, and keep both of your eyes off this guest."

"Yes, sir," he says, pulling his hand away from mine.

"The plates are ready to go, Noah," I mutter. "Thank you." I try to meet his eyes, but he won't even look in my direction—poor Noah. He loads his arms with appetizer plates and scurries from the room. I whirl around and whack Kane in his big, stupid, immoveable chest. "What the hell was that?"

"What the hell is this dress?" He snaps back.

"It's Kayla's, as a matter of fact, and I think I look damn good." I'm positively scathing from his territorial caveman B.S., and I make no effort to hide it.

"Make no mistake, Ashley, you look good. Good enough to be on the menu yourself." His thumbs caress the bare skin of my waist, right where the cutouts are placed. He yanks me against him until I feel the hardness through his dress pants.

"Kane!" I squeal. "You can't go outside like that!"

"And whose fault is that?" He says, but there's no real menace in his tone. "Just tell me—is the dress to tease *me* alone, or is it for Noah and all the other eyes in the room?" He threads his fingers through my loose curls and gives them a little tug. I gasp from the sensation of pleasure mixed with pain.

"For you alone," I whisper.

"Good answer," he says, covering my mouth with a kiss so intense that the space between my thighs dampens.

"Kane," I murmur, pulling my mouth away.

Aloha in Love

"Yes, Lani?" He licks a path along my collarbone, finding the dip between my breasts.

"I just thought I should let you know that this dress is too tight for underwear," I whisper, and he releases a deep agonizing groan. I turn my attention to the remaining plates of Kalua pork nachos.

"You're going to pay for that comment later, Ashley Walsh." He growls, stalking out to the lanai like a lion. I watch him go, admiring the outline of his firm ass in those sleek black dress pants.

• • •

I hold my breath all throughout the first two courses, but I start to relax as my friends' portions disappear from their plates. It's a beautiful, clear night, with laughter, wine, and the ocean sparkling beneath the light of the moon. I take a deep breath and inhale the heady scent of plumeria.

"Pancho, you know this is a tasting menu, right?" Taylor jokes, observing Pancho eating the remains of his wife's mini poke pizza.

"I'm a growing boy." He licks his fingers. "And these grinds are super *ono*—delicious. For a mainlander, you really seem to know your way around Hawaiian food. Seriously, Red, you broke da mouth with this one."

"Thanks, Pancho. I'm flattered." At least I think so, though I can't understand Pancho's Pidgin half the time. "Is *broke da mouth* a good thing?" I whisper to Kane, who chuckles.

"It's a very good thing." He slings one arm around me and plants a soft kiss on my lips. Pancho stops chewing mid-bite, glancing between Kane and me, his dark eyes noticing the arm draped around my neck.

"So you and Red?" He asks, but his words are muffled by a mouthful of poke.

Kane gives me a quick look before answering. "Yes. We're...hanging out."

The pause between his words makes my stomach bottom out, but I slap on a shaky smile. "We're just having some fun." The words feel like lead on my tongue, but I think they're what Kane wants to hear—at least what he's ready to hear. I glance over at Taylor, who looks neither surprised nor pleased about the news.

"Congrats, guys." Lance raises his glass in a toast, but his smile is tinged with the slightest bit of sadness.

"It's about time," Adele chimes in.

Kayla just snorts. "Yeah, it's a real shock, with the way you've been mind-fucking each other since the day you met."

"Mind fucking?" Maui Maude asks, turning to Adele for clarification.

"Foreplay!" Adele shouts, and I can't suppress the groan that escapes from my mouth. "Whenever those two were in a room together, you could cut the tension between them with a spoon."

"Knife," Maui Maude corrects. "I think the expression is *cut the tension with a knife*."

Adele just waves her newly manicured hand. "Whatever the utensil, you get the picture."

"The Kalua pork is delicious, and I loved the poke pizza as well," Keiko says. I shoot her a grateful smile, appreciating the change of subject.

"I hope you guys aren't full yet, 'cuz I have another taster on the way—spam and taro eggrolls with pineapple-pepper dipping sauce." I signal for the waiter to bring out the next appetizer, noticing Lance feed his date the last appetizer by hand, which is both cute and a little disgusting. For about the millionth time tonight, Taylor is staring at Kayla. My heart goes out to him. He tried to engage her in conversation a few times, but she's a master of the one-word shutdown.

"This food is resort quality," Lance's date pipes up, and I give her a warm smile back. "If you keep cooking like this, maybe the resorts will head up here."

"Over my dead body," Pancho snorts. "Paia is Paia, and it's going to stay that way."

"But why *wouldn't* hotels want to set up here?" Maude asks, turning her attention to Pancho. "Lahaina is expensive and busy. I'm sure there's huge demand on the North Shore."

"Paia has zoning districts and prescriptive community plans to avoid negatively impacting the local community," Taylor explains. "The county made it almost impossible to establish mass developments in Paia, so our piece of Paradise can remain mostly untouched."

The conversation conjures up memories of my old life, and a sick feeling grows in the pit of my stomach. I do my best to change the subject. "Okay, who's ready for my fried coconut shrimp tacos?"

I get a few whistles, plus one groan from a very stuffed Keiko, who gives her stomach a pat. "I don't think anything else will fit inside this body."

"I don't know how that's possible, since Pancho ate most of your food," Kane says, dryly.

"Hey now." Pancho tosses his napkin down. "Tell you what, man, you can have my tacos then, since they're your favorite."

"Tacos are your favorite?" I look at Kane, who just shrugs.

"I thought Korean beef was your favorite?" Taylor asks.

"No," Lance cuts in, "that's his second favorite."

"Makes sense." Taylor nods. "We used to stuff our faces with tacos after a long day of surfing."

"Way back when Kane Keo was *the shit* on the competitive scene." Kayla tips her glass in his direction.

"You surfed competitively?" I ask, my head whipping back-and-forth, as I try to keep up with the conversation.

"Sort of," Kane says, looking uncomfortable.

"He was ranked," Kayla interjects.

"He truly could have been one of the greats," Taylor adds, his tone wistful.

"Then why did you stop?" The table goes deadly quiet. Kane looks down at his lap, and Taylor glances out towards the ocean. Obviously I've entered some kind of dangerous territory. "What else don't I know about you?" I say, my smile wavering.

Kane remains calm, but I can sense the shift in mood around the table. Just then, Pancho starts throwing out random facts about Kane, attempting to lighten the mood. He was born and raised in Hana by his grandfather. In high school, they called him *Ke alii* which means "king," and he almost joined the military. My friends go around the table sharing details about Kane, while I glom to their stories like a starving woman. I know absolutely nothing about him, no details from his past or plans for his future. I'm not even clear on what motivates his present. The only thing I'm familiar with is his big hard body and oh so talented tongue.

While I knew not to expect anything from our fling—or thought I did—the realization rocks me all the same. Kane doesn't value our connection enough to share even the smallest of details, and I'm kicking myself for allowing this to happen. I sink into my chair, deflating like a leaky balloon as the tide comes in on my emotions. Kane glances at me, and I notice how his brow furrows. He doesn't seem to appreciate not knowing what I'm thinking, but I literally never know where his head is at—ironic to say the least. I do my best to keep up the façade, but my shaky bottom lip betrays me and I take refuge in the kitchen before I burst into tears. Only two more courses to go; then Adele will bring out the coffee and fresh fruit platter for dessert, and by that time, I should be able to slip out unnoticed.

The last two courses go smoothly, and I collect up all the comment cards. The waiters have already scoured the kitchen and there's really nothing left to tidy, so I resolve to pick up my dishes and containers in the morning. Adele, deep into the red wine and fully immersed in conversation with Maui Maude, doesn't give me a hard time about leaving. I say goodbye and thank every guest one by one, whose kind compliments make my eyes water. I wait until Kane is distracted by Taylor before heading inside and grabbing my purse. On the condition that I drop it with her tomorrow morning at Baldwin Beach, Kayla lends me the keys to her car. I limp down the long driveway in her high heels, which are half a size too small and pinch like hell, as I head for the rust-speckled gray Toyota. After a few yanks, I manage to get the driver side door open, hearing it creak like a haunted house.

"Where do you think you're going?" His voice cuts through the night, sending a chill of pleasure down my spine, but I find my resolve before turning to face him.

"Home, Kane."

"I'm taking you home."

I sigh dramatically. "No, I'm taking myself home. Can you please just back off, for once?"

The driveway is unlit and the moon obscured by Adele's massive home, so I can barely make out Kane's large silhouette. "What happened back there? I thought everything went perfectly."

"You would," I mumble.

"What does that even mean?"

"It's not important."

"Clearly it is, if you're leaving."

"I just want to go home, Kane."

He takes a step closer. "Then go home with me."

"Why?"

"What do you mean *why*?" His silhouette takes another step in my direction.

"I don't even know you—that's why!" We're both silent as the words sink in. "If tonight showed me anything, it's that I know nothing about you, Kane Keo. So let's stop pretending this thing between us is anything besides what it is."

"And what is it?" He steps so close that the only thing separating us is the car door.

"It's *you*, Kane Keo, fucking some tourist, at least until you've had your fill."

He stumbles backwards as if I've hit him, his eyes widening like a predator, before letting out a full blown roar. I feel scared—not of him exactly, but of the situation. I want to hop into the car and drive away, but my feet are nailed to the ground.

"That's not what this is."

Kane pulls me into his arms and slams the car door.

"Then what is it?"

"I don't know yet, but definitely not that." He scrubs a hand down his face. "Shit, Ashley, I didn't mean to make you feel like that. I told you…I'm not good at the rest of it, but I want to be. I want to take you out. Please let me take you out."

"Don't do me any favors," I grumble.

"Don't be a smartass," he shoots back. "I'm taking you out because I want to. Tomorrow. I'll take care of everything, and I promise to tell you about myself then."

"Tomorrow?"

Kane smiles and nods. "But first I'm taking you home tonight."

Before I can protest, he lifts me over his shoulder and smacks my ass. "And you'd better tell Kayla not to expect this dress back, because I'm going to tear it off you with my teeth." My laugh gets swallowed up by the darkness, as Kane carries me back to the warm glowing light of the house.

Chapter 16

The bar is closed on Sundays, so Kane keeps his word and arrives on my doorstep at 9am the next morning. I almost fall over upon glimpsing him at the door. He has shaved his beard to reveal a pair of high cheekbones, square jaw, and one strong straight nose. He has also trimmed his sunlit hair, which rests now just above his ears. I don't know if the changes in his appearance are a literal attempt at being more open with me, but holy hell is it ever hot.

He gives me a strange look. "What?"

Moving closer, I run my hand down his freshly-shaven cheek. "I thought I liked the beard, but you're even more handsome like this, if that's even possible."

I continue to stare and he actually blushes, which is kind of adorable.

"You look pretty *ono* yourself."

His eyes scan my white strapless sundress, and I look down at my outfit.

"Nah, you definitely win. There's no competition standing next to you."

"C'mere," he says, pulling me against him and taking a deep breath. "Mmm…coconut and jasmine, my favorite." He buries his nose in my hair, which I've pulled to the side and styled into a loose braid.

"Should we get going?" I ask.

"We'd better, or else I'll have you naked on your back in less than sixty seconds."

I smack his shoulder. "Play your cards right and maybe you'll get some at the end of the date. But I want to see how hard you work for it," I tease. He laughs as I pull the front door closed behind me.

He walks me around the side of the jeep and helps me in. Once inside, I do up my seatbelt and give him a look. "Where to?"

"I have a few ideas." He speeds away into the overcast morning.

The sun works hard to break through the clouds, but the breeze is rejuvenating and I roll down my window to inhale the fresh air. Kane takes the highway. We drive for about half an hour before pulling up at the Maui Ocean Center, where he parks the car and turns off the engine.

"I know you're not a tourist anymore," he says, "but I feel like you might have missed out on that part."

"So we're tourists for the day?" I say, touched by the gesture, and he gives me a warm smile.

Kane pays our entry fee, and we spend the first hour exploring the outdoor area and tidal pools. It's a lovely tropical space with a stunning view, but the wind is impassioned and I'm thankful for having pulled my hair into a braid today. We walk through the shark's mouth and onwards through the aquariums, stopping to hear a guided talk about the center's conservation programs. Kane presses his hand against the glass just as a spotted tiger shark glides by, and his face appears faraway as he speaks.

"I took my son here a few times."

"Your son?" I should be surprised by the admission, but I guess I've been waiting for this moment. More than anything, I'm grateful that he's finally opening up.

"I had a son, but he died."

"When?" It's a strange opening question, but I have so many left to ask, and who knows when Kane will retreat into his shell again.

"It'll be seven years in March." He clears his throat. "He was three years old when he died."

"I don't even know what to say. I'm sorry, Kane. I cannot imagine that."

"You can't imagine it, no, not until it happens." He looks off into the shark tank. "I still remember how he smelled when I held him up to see the tank—like sunshine and salt and indescribable sweetness." He sighs and takes the deepest of breaths. "They say it's instinctual, smell. We're like animals that way. Before having a kid, I never would've thought that was true, but I'm telling you, I could've found my boy in a pitch black room with scent alone."

Still he stares off into the distance, the turquoise glow of the aquarium highlighting his face. "I remember holding him up to watch the Manta Rays. I remember feeling his soft, chubby arms wrapped around my neck, and the pressure of his small warm body against mine."

He's painting such a vivid picture that I can feel a tear slip out and escape down my cheek. I swipe it away before he notices, not wanting to make the moment about me. I want to ask how his son died, but I chicken out and go with the safer option. "What was his name?"

"Kaiden."

"And his mom?" I'm trying not to push, but curiosity has gotten the best of me.

"After Kaiden died, she couldn't deal. She committed suicide."

"Oh God..." I cover my mouth with one hand, trying to process how anyone could survive one tragedy after another like that.

"It was about a year afterwards. We tried our best to stay together, but we were both lost. One night, while I was at the bar, she swallowed a whole bottle of Xanax that the Doctor prescribed for sleep, chasing it down with a bottle of vodka. I found her later that night at home."

"Kane..." I sigh out his name at the same time that a group of children walk by in matching yellow bibs, probably on a field trip. Their excited chatter ruffles the air and drowns out my own voice. "To lose them both so close together..."

"The funny thing is—Kaiden's death didn't break us up. We were already broken. We dated in high school. She got pregnant at twenty-one, and we married right after Kaiden was born." He takes a deep breath, his eyes flitting around the fish tank. "She struggled with mental illness back then, but having a kid hit her hard. Her moods were all over the place already, long before Kaiden died. I used to worry about leaving them alone together, believing she'd make a careless mistake and that would be it, but it was me I needed to worry about."

I'm about to ask him more when he pushes himself off the aquarium glass and turns to walk away. "You wanted to know more about me? Well, there it is. That's why I don't do relationships. I haven't dated since my wife died, because how would that work, anyway? It's not like I've had anything to celebrate. Still, I'm a man with limits. I'll fuck when I have to, but nothing more—I don't deserve more."

"What makes you think that?" I whisper, standing on my tip toes and looping my arms around his neck. To my surprise, Kane gently lowers them to my sides.

"I don't deserve happiness. No man should ever bury his child."

I know better than to argue right now. Even though I don't agree with his logic, I understand that the statement is true for him. Besides, his outwardly caustic personality is now starting to make sense.

"Come on, let's check out the tropical fish," he says.

In his words, I hear everything that he can't say yet. For now, this is all he's willing to give, but I'll take it. Kane holds my hand and tugs me forward, his neutral mask falling right back into place. We leave the ocean center and head for a nearby food truck serving Thai fusion. Kane opts for the pad thai with chicken; I choose ginger shrimp stir-fry and we share an order of veggie spring rolls. He tells me about his grandfather and growing up in Hana. He tells me how he started the bar, his friendship with Taylor—in fact, he talks about everything except the giant pink elephant in the room. As much as I want to continue our conversation from the ocean center, I won't push him until he's ready.

After a late lunch, Kane suggests that we head to Kihei for some shave ice at his favorite place, which turns out to be the cutest outdoor stand, painted in vibrant greens and yellows. We sit side-by-side and share a Papa-Nui-sized order of red raspberry and pineapple. Midway through our feast, it starts to downpour with rain—big, warm, tropical drops that soak through my dress before I even have a chance to think. I laugh and hop off my stool. Kane joins me, unbuttoning his short-sleeved shirt to shake off the wetness. He wrings out the hem and leaves it hanging open, as my eyes find their way to his smooth, muscled stomach and dark trail of hair disappearing beneath his shorts. I take a step closer as the heavy rain comes down in a barrage, running my hand across the hot, damp skin of his chest. He shivers, a low noise rumbling from the back of his throat.

"You are so beautiful." With my eyes locked on his, I stand high on my toes and use his collar to yank his mouth down to mine. His lips are cold when I kiss him, still frozen from the shave ice, and he tastes tart from the raspberry flavor. His hot tongue slips inside my mouth, and the combined sensation almost makes me combust on the spot.

"We need to find a bed," he croaks, breaking the kiss momentarily. The rain has slowed and a few people watch us kiss from the street. One tourist holds up an expensive looking camera and snaps an actual picture, which sends me into a fit of laughter. I'm laughing so hard as I wipe my eyes that Kane breaks down and joins me. The sound of his laughter is hands down one of the most gorgeous sounds I've ever heard.

"Well that was a mood killer," I say, having finally calmed down enough to speak.

"I don't think that's possible with you, *Lani*."

"Do you think he'll frame it?" I wonder aloud, earning me a chuckle from Kane.

"If it's a picture of you, definitely." He looks over my shoulder. "Since we're here, I might as well take you to the *Barmuda Triangle*."

"The what?" I say, thoroughly confused.

"The Triangle. It's a bunch of different bars in Kalama Village with live music and plenty of dancing." At the mention of dancing, I literally clap my hands and jump up and down. The movement must make everything bounce because the look he gives me is a little dangerous. "But maybe you should wear my shirt, since that dress is looking a little see-through."

I glance down at my white dress; it's slightly more translucent than before but definitely not see-through. "I'm not going into a bar with a shirtless, Kane Keo," I say, crossing my arms. "I'll get trampled by all the women trying to maul you. Besides, it'll dry quickly, especially if we're working up a sweat on the dance floor."

He rolls his eyes but concedes, and we head to the first bar to do just that. The song playing is Matisyahu's "Sunshine," one of my favorites, so I grab his hand and tug him onto the nearly empty floor. Though I never would have expected it, Kane turns out to be an incredible dancer. He has a natural rhythm that hints at some sort of formal training from the way he dips and spins me around. As one song bleeds into another, he pulls me into his chest and dips his head down to kiss me breathless. We make out on the dance floor like teenagers until someone asks us if we wouldn't mind moving out of the way, and we stumble off in search of a table. The dive bar we're at isn't very big, but it's great for people-watching and I settle in as Kane goes to get me a drink. He returns with a Corona for me and a can of Coke for himself.

"So you really never drink?" I ask, as he takes a swig from the can.

"I haven't in years."

"Is it because…of your son?" I don't know why I'm bringing it up again, especially when he seems so relaxed, but there's so much left unsaid.

"I guess partly it is." He shrugs. "After Kaiden died, I drank—a lot. I'd go on benders to forget everything, then I'd hate myself in the morning for doing just that. My doctor gave me these pills to level things out, but all they did was make me feel like a zombie. After a while I stopped taking them; I'd rather be in agony and remember my son then feel nothing at all. I guess in the end, I figured that I didn't—that I don't—have the right to drink away my pain."

"And surfing?" I press on. "Did you stop that after Kaiden too?"

He ignores my question and answers with his own. "Why should I be allowed to live my life when my boy is buried in the ground?"

"So it's kind of like an eternal self-inflicted purgatory for you then?" I say, the first few sips of beer making me bold. "That hardly seems fair."

"Life isn't fair." He laughs without humor and just like that the moment between us is broken. We finish our drinks in near silence, but luckily the DJ cranks the music and it feels a bit less awkward.

"It's how I got the scar." He breaks the silence then, pointing to the raised white line bisecting his eyebrow where the hair hasn't grown back. "I was on a bender and got into a bar fight. *Sonofabitch* cracked a bottle in half and sliced me. I was lucky he missed my eye…his aim was bad."

"Wow." I don't really know what else to say. Feeling like I've ruined the mood for the night, I suggest that we go.

It starts to rain on the drive home, and I watch the raindrops race down the windowpane in pairs of two.

He finally breaks the silence with a relenting sigh. "I didn't tell you about myself to scare you off, Ashley. It's the opposite. For the first time in seven years, I actually have some hope. I feel like smiling again, and when I do smile, I feel less empty. You've made me laugh more in the last few weeks than I have in years, but I carry so much guilt around that I'm not sure how to deal with this feeling."

I turn to face him, blinking back tears that threaten to fall. "That's not what I want to be for you, Kane. I don't want to cause you any guilt or anguish."

"But there's good, too," he says quickly. "Seeing you light up on the dance floor, watching you smile. Discovering new things with you, or the old things again—it's something I haven't wanted for a very long time, but with you it somehow feels right."

I reach across the center console to grab his wrist. "Then hold onto that feeling now. We can see where things lead. No promises, no pledges, just us getting to know each other better."

He exhales, then nods. "I can do that."

"That's a start."

He seems to relax as he switches on the radio, but meanwhile I find myself tensing up. As happy as I am that he's opening up, part of me wonders to what I've agreed. I know he's told me a little about his past, but there's so much left unsaid. I can't help but wonder why he doesn't trust me with the rest.

• • •

We park at Kane's place, and the dashboard lights fade as he switches off the engine. "Do you want to come up?" His voice floats through the darkness. I'm surprised that he's asking me inside, since we never go to his place. The only time I've been there was that day I borrowed the paper.

I unclick my seatbelt and mumble a quick "sure" before following him to his front door. It's dark inside, and humid. "No air conditioning?" I ask, climbing the stairs after him to the living room, where he flicks on the overhead lights and fan.

"I don't use it much. I like sleeping with the windows open to hear the sound of the waves. Do you want something to drink? Wine?"

"Just some water, please." I can't help but wonder why he has wine at all. My stomach hurts as I imagine all the other women he likely brought here in the past.

Kane pours me a glass of water and opens the sliding doors to the lanai, letting in the salty, cool air. He seems nervous with me in his space, like a teenager with a girl over for the first time. I circle the living room and stop beside the shelf where the little shoes are resting. Suddenly they make more sense to me, and I stare at them a moment before speaking.

"What did you want to be when you grew up?" I ask him, looking over my shoulder.

He laughs and then stops short, apparently lost in thought. "A professional surfer, of course. You?"

I run my fingers over the tiny shoes. "A famous chef, like Martha Stewart, minus the jail time."

"You always loved cooking?"

"I did," I say, nodding.

"Then why not do it?"

"My parents didn't think it was a practical career choice, which is true in some ways. The hours are terrible, the pay isn't great, at least until you work your way to the top, and it's crowded at the top. My parents are older and very traditional—they said culinary school was like a trade and thus not meant for women. I honestly think they looked down on it."

Kane picks up the glass of water and walks over to pass it to me. I gratefully take a big sip before handing it straight back to him.

"You don't talk about your parents." He says it like a fact, rather than a question.

"We aren't close. We barely speak, especially since the move. They think I'm being ridiculous—that I'll eventually come to my senses and return home to work on my marriage. I guess a lot of people think that."

"And what do you think?" He puts down the glass and takes a step closer.

"I think life is too short to waste it on people or things that don't feed your soul."

"You've got that *mana* spirit inside of you, Ashley. It shines so bright."

He flashes his gorgeous white teeth, as if to embody his point, but I turn back to the shoes and change the subject. "These are so small. It's hard to believe they actually fit someone."

"Nah, Kaiden was actually a big boy for his age, like his daddy."

"When Dale and I were trying for a baby, it felt so hopeless that I couldn't bring myself to buy anything for the child. One time, after the second unsuccessful round of IVF, Dale brought home this tiny pair of blue Lacoste sneakers. I think he was trying to cheer me up—I don't think he meant it to be cruel—but I couldn't even look at them. I gave him my best smile and said thank you, shoving them into the bottom of the Christmas decoration box the moment he left for work. I cried my eyes out for hours. Everything set me off back then: friend's baby shower invites, Facebook feeds, diaper commercials, and everyone with their advice—try acupuncture, try gluten free, try supplements, don't try at all because it'll happen when you're not trying."

As I'm speaking, Kane takes another step closer to put his arms around my waist. "You're young, Ashley. Just because it didn't happen with him, doesn't mean it won't happen."

I look up at him and tilt my head back. "That's the funny part...they couldn't find anything wrong with me." I break from his inquisitive gaze. "A few cysts here and there, but they took care of those and still the problem persisted. Dale was tested, too, but he never shared the results, insisting he had a strong bloodline and it couldn't possibly be him. It makes me wonder now if he really even wanted a child, or if his attachment and frustration was all about our inability to conceive. The idea of struggle, of difficulty, of not being good at something—it didn't fit into his plans." I release a big ol' sigh. "But maybe I'm being unfair. I'm sure it wasn't easy for him either…"

I step back to inspect his face, but it reveals nothing. "Oh my God, listen to me spouting-off about Dale and my nothing problems when you…" I trail off, casting my eyes to the ground.

"You can say it, Ashley… *When I lost my son.* I buried my boy and no one should ever have to do that. There's no feeling in the world like having to pick out a tiny casket so that you can put your kid in the ground." His nostrils flare, a signal that he's trying keep it together.

"I wish I knew what to say to you, how to relate," I admit.

"At least you're honest. Most people say nothing. They avoid you like a leper from Molokai. People give you a wide berth, or they whisper and make up stories—I'm sure you've heard enough of them during your time here. They stare at you in the grocery store with that horrible mixture of pity and relief—relief that it wasn't them, wasn't *their* child. Some days…most days…I have to force myself to breathe."

"You are the strongest person I know," I whisper, running the back of my hand down his smooth cheek.

"I'm not."

"You are." I gently pull his head forward and our lips meet in the sweetest, softest kiss, our tongues intertwining in a slow, languorous dance. Without touching each other, we take our time exploring each other's mouths, until I tear my lips from his with a moan.

"Take me to bed, Kane."

Needing no further invitation, he scoops me into his arms and carries me through the kitchen and down the stairs to the main floor, where he kicks open the bedroom door with a chuckle. His bed is a massive canopied structure facing a lush back garden and the crashing ocean waves in the distance. The lanai doors are open to let in the thunderous sound of the sea. He sits down and sets me in his lap, and we continue kissing as we undress each other piece by piece. He pushes the straps of my sundress off my shoulders and out spill my bare breasts.

"No bra?" His voice is low and hoarse.

"A bra doesn't work with this dress," I pant out.

"I agree." He takes my breasts in his hands, both aching and heavy with need, and massages them gently. He shifts me off his lap to remove his pants and underwear, before scooting back against the pillows and taking me with him.

"Tell me what you want." He mutters against my lips, trailing fiery kisses across my neck and shoulders.

"I want to sit on you," I say, barely above a whisper, feeling the flames in my cheeks.

"That's so fucking hot. Tell me again."

"I want to ride you," I repeat, louder this time, and he growls.

He reaches for the side table for protection, but I put my hand on his arm to stop him. "I want to ride you with nothing between us."

He freezes. "Are you sure?"

"I'm clean—I mean, I got tested after Dale, after his escapades—and with my other reproductive challenges, let's just say I'm not worried."

"Me too. I always use protection—always—but are you absolutely sure, Ashley?"

"I want you like this," I admit, feeling my face go an even deeper shade of red. "More than anything."

He exhales with a curse and leans back against the pillow before speaking. "Then you can have me. C'mere."

He pulls me forward until I tumble into his lap, giggling and moaning as his hot, hard length presses up against my thigh.

I loop one leg over his hip until I'm straddling his body. I'm so ready for him as I lower myself down, but he's thick and stretches me at this angle. He hisses through his teeth as I proceed to lower myself down all the way, throwing my head back as I take in all of him. The sensation of fullness is so intense that a loud cry escapes from my lips.

"Fuck, Ashley. It's so good. I can't describe it."

I start moving, slowly at first and then faster and faster, making my breasts bounce as our slick skin slaps together. I come hard and without warning, and when the last cry escapes my lips, Kane flips me over and eases into me at a painfully slow pace. I lock my legs around his hips to urge him on, but he reaches back and lock my ankles in a vice grip.

"No, beautiful. I'm taking my time with you tonight."

He draws himself almost all of the way out before slamming right back into me. He repeats the movement, rocking into me slowly as he rotates his hips. I moan with a mixture of frustration and pure pleasure.

"Don't tease me, Kane," I say, my mouth open and my head back. I can feel the intense ache of the next orgasm building like a tsunami.

"I never tease." He continues to circle his hips, hitting just the right spot each time. I come again, this time screaming out his name. He gives me a wicked grin and winks as I come down from the high, but when I clench my muscles around his length in response, it wipes the grin right off his face. "Fuck, as much as I love watching you come undone," he groans, "I can't wait any longer."

Kane drives into me without restraint as sweat beads drop from his brow onto my chin. I skim my hands over his slick chest, right down to his firm tight ass. I squeeze his cheeks and pull him closer, feeling his entire body lock as his own release cascades into my body. I can actually feel his warmth emptying into me. He rests his full weight on top of me for a moment before rolling over.

When I look at him, he's breathing heavily with one arm slung over his face. Neither of us speaks. I'm not sure what to say or do next, since it's the first time I've been in his bedroom. It's his house, his sanctuary, and I find myself in unfamiliar territory. I mean, sure, he's opened up a lot this evening, but I doubt very much that he wants me to stay in his marital bed. I quietly move to the end of the enormous mattress and hop off to find my sundress.

"What are you doing?" He says, sitting up.

"Getting dressed?"

"I'd prefer that you sleep naked."

"You want me to stay?" I stare at the floor, the sundress, my hands—anywhere but him.

"I always want you to stay."

"That doesn't even make sense, Kane. This is the first time I've been in this room."

He sighs. "Like I said, I'm not good at the other stuff. I'm not even sure what I'm good for anymore, but if you're okay with that, I'd like nothing more than for you to climb up here and sleep next to me."

I can feel the smile spreading across my face as I let my dress fall to the floor. I crawl back into his bed and pull the covers up over me, nuzzling my back against his front. He wraps one arm around my chest, locking me into his body. I stretch out my legs but only reach the top of his knees.

"You're so tall."

"You make me feel tall." He laughs into my back. "But I love it. You're the perfect size for me—the perfect everything, from that tiny waist to your beautiful round hips and those creamy white thighs. Not to mention the lovely freckles on your nose."

"I HATE them," I start to say, but he silences me, tipping my head back and kissing a path across my cluster of freckles.

"No, they're perfect. The perfect blend of sweet and sexy, just like you."

I run one hand down the corded muscle in his forearm. "You make me feel safe."

"You are safe with me, Ashley," he whispers, his voice hoarse. "Now stop talking and go to sleep." His arm tightens as he kisses my ear, getting a mouthful of hair in the process.

"*Aloha po, Mana'o nahenahe*. Sweet dreams, *Lani*."

The dreams that finally come are sweeter than I can remember dreams being in a long time, thanks to the beautiful man wrapped around me.

Chapter 17

It is a struggle to slip out of bed the next morning, surrounded by the warmth of Kane's arms, but anything is possible when you need coffee. We were up late and Kane roused me before sunrise for a second round, so I'm already yawning on my way to the kitchen. Not wanting to wake up Kane, I tip toe from the room like it's just another one-night-stand. When I get upstairs, I glance at the clock above the stove and see that it's just after 8am.

I find the coffee grinds in a cupboard and tinker with his coffeemaker until I've got it figured out. With my caffeine fix on the way, I decide to make some toast, rummaging through Kane's refrigerator to see what's there. I'm pleasantly surprised to find it stocked with all kinds of fruit; however, breakfast is soon forgotten when I stumble upon some crab meat and a new recipe starts forming in my mind. I take out the eggs, mayonnaise, and red pepper, even scrounging up some breadcrumbs from the pantry. I'm so deep in preparation that I have no idea how much time passes before Kane's arms wrap around my waist and bring me gently back to reality.

"Did I wake you?" I say, glancing at the clock before realizing it's almost 9am.

"No, the smell of coffee woke me up—but this certainly isn't coffee…" He rests his forehead against the back of my head, eyeing my culinary creation. I can feel his breath on the nape of my neck and my whole body tingles in response. "What have you gotten yourself into here?"

I take a break from chopping the red pepper and turn to face him. "Crab cakes are what I've gotten into. I felt inspired."

"Crab cakes for breakfast?" He asks, looking contemplative. "We could do worse."

"I can make you real breakfast as well," I say, feeling shy about the bits of red pepper stuck to my hands.

His fingers brush against my chin, and he tilts my gaze to the ceiling. "I can think of better ways to channel that energy."

"You are insatiable." I stare at his full mouth, and he hisses with flashing hazel eyes.

"Keep looking at me like that, and I'll show you how hungry I really am."

He lifts me onto the wooden countertop and lowers his nose into mine, but before our lips meet, my phone vibrates with an incoming call.

"Ignore it," he commands, but I roll my eyes and snatch it off the counter.

"Ashley speaking." I speak breathlessly into the phone, but my greeting is met with silence on the other end.

"Hello?" I can hear the faint sounds of breathing and know that someone is there. "Dale, if this is you..." I start to say, feeling my face get warm, but a voice interrupts me.

"So my son *has* been calling you then?" It's the refined, slightly accented voice of Dale Silver Sr.—I recognize my ex-boss' voice right away.

I clear my throat. "No, he hasn't. Not recently anyway."

"Hmm..."

That's literally all he says.

"How...how are you, Mr. Silver?" I stutter.

He laughs, but not unkindly. "Please, Ashley, you've known me for close to a decade. I saw you walk across the stage at the University of San Francisco. I gave you your first desk in this industry. Even if my son has piss poor timing and non-existent self-control, we can probably still dispense with the pleasantries."

"Fair enough," I say, realizing that Dale Sr. hasn't said so many words to me since our wedding four years ago. Not that he's been cruel or unkind; in fact, I've always liked Dale Sr., harboring deep respect for his hard work and clear vision. He built his business up from nothing, and he deserves every accolade and ounce of success—Dale Jr., on the other hand…

"What can I help you with then, Dale?" I try to whisper the last word, but Kane's head still whips up. He grabs for the phone, but I give him a look, pulling back and covering the microphone. "It's his father!" I hiss. He looks no less pleased, but at least he backs off.

"I understand from my son that you're on an extended vacation; however, the agent selling your townhome seems to think otherwise."

Of course Dale Sr. is talking to our agent, screw all that pesky privacy stuff. "This is not a vacation, you know that." I speak as politely as possible. "We're getting a divorce. I quit Silverdale, and I'm taking my life in a new direction."

Dale Sr. is silent as falling snow. I inspect the panko breadcrumbs caked under my nails, hearing the faintest sigh through the phone.

"As much as I wish that my Dale had a little more decorum and gratitude, I do know that you're good for him, Ashley—very good indeed. Is there any way that you'd reconsider…"

"I'll stop you right there, Mr. Silver—there is absolutely no chance that your son and I will ever reconcile. What's done is done, and it was a blessing in disguise for us both. There is no going back—not now, not ever." I can feel fire singeing through my veins, arming me with invincibility as I speak the words aloud. Surprisingly, Dale Sr. doesn't put up much of a fight.

"I understand, dear, you probably don't believe me when I say that, but I do. While I did call you my daughter in-law for a brief time, you were—more importantly—one of my most promising employees. If you refuse to go back to Dale,

I can't force that life upon you, but I would like you to reconsider coming back to Silverdale."

"I'm not moving back to San Francisco," I spit out.

The energy through the phone is like hearing a patient flat-line.

"I meant for you to represent Silverdale in Hawaii."

"You don't have an office here," I counter.

"We may well soon." His voice is practically humming. "There is untapped opportunity on the islands, and we signed an engagement agreement with a local developer last year, with the aim to develop multi-family residences in the Maui area, along with the possibility of a luxury resort in the community."

I steal a glance at Kane, catching only his backside, but his posture is stiff and I can see that he's listening. "If you want my opinion, Mr. Silver, that last idea is impossible here, given the strong sense of community and their commitment to preserving the natural environment."

"That's just it, Ashley, I do want your opinion. This is precisely why I'm asking you to join us."

"I'm not in the business anymore."

"Never say never." He chuckles. "Don't answer me yet, not until you've seen the initial plans. I'll have them couriered to you overnight—and I am truly sorry, Ashley. I'm sorry for my son, but most of all, I'm sorry that he didn't appreciate what he had right in front of him. Goodbye, dear."

Before I can protest, Dale. Sr. has hung up the phone. I stare at the thing in my hand. Those might be the nicest words he's ever said, but if he thinks I can be swayed by project plans and development proposals, he's wasting his breath. That ship has long since sailed. I mean, look at me elbow-deep in my coconut milk and ginger crab cake batter. I toss the phone down and wash my hands before shaping the mixture into little patties.

"What do you think about a papaya salsa to accompany these? Or maybe a basil remoulade?" I ask, and Kane looks at me like I've lost it.

"That's it? That's all you have to say after being on the phone with *him*?"

"With my old boss," I snap back. "Who also happens to be my former father-in-law, and as you just heard, I'm not interested in having either of them back—not a chance in hell."

Kane's hands form fists at his sides. He stares through the sliding doors and onwards to the lanai and ocean beyond. "So why does this Dale Sr. guy think that you getting back together with your ex is an option?"

I sigh inwardly, already dreading the direction of this conversation. "It appears that Dale hasn't been totally upfront with everyone about how serious and final our situation actually is."

"Explain," he barks out. I have to bite my tongue to keep from snapping back at him.

"My friend, Jamie, mentioned something similar the last time I spoke to her. She mentioned that he told a few people I'm on an extended vacation, even claiming that we're on a break, but our temporary separation agreement is already in place and he hasn't tried to contact me yet, so I doubt he has interest in reconnecting. If anything, he's downplaying it to save face."

Kane smirks at me. "You really believe that?"

"I really do. The most important thing to Dale—and I do mean the most important—is his reputation. What people think of him is everything, but when the divorce is finalized and I haven't come crawling back, he'll find some other way to spin it—he always does."

Kane exhales a gusty breath. "Can we not talk about him anymore?"

"With pleasure." I snort. "Now get over here and help me cut up these papayas. We have a salsa to make."

· · ·

I'm not even surprised when a thick brown envelope shows up on my doorstep the next day. I don't know how Dale Sr. knew where I was staying, but I'm guessing Kane must have brought the mail over this morning. I roll my eyes but scoop it up and carry the thing inside, planning to ignore it for the next several days, but curiosity gets the best of me and soon I'm tearing it open and extracting the heavy folders. They contain the spiraled and bound project summaries, along with some draft blueprints.

I sit down at the breakfast table to skim through the information, but my heart sinks upon realizing that the luxury resort they're planning is a monstrosity. The very essence of the place is garish and overblown, a total slap in the face to Hawaii's natural beauty. It's meant to be a themed hotel, thereby making no effort to fit in with the landscape. In fact, it calls for the destruction of a good portion of the natural environment, and by some cruel twist of fate, the proposed location is not just in Maui, but specifically Paia town—my vibrant and unpolished little speck of paradise.

My stomach rolls like the swelling sea. I shove the folders into the closest kitchen drawer, having no interest in seeing them again. I wonder to myself if they're an omen of some kind, or perhaps I'm just bad luck. As hard as I try to escape, the past seems destined to follow me wherever I go. All the skeletons in my closet are intent on ruining any chance I have at happiness, at least it feels that way. Nonetheless, I shake off the thought and choose to be in the here and now. I chose this life for myself, and an envelope of paper and pipe dreams isn't going to change that. They are just plans after all—early stage plans at that. It'll probably never happen, especially not here in Paia, so I tell myself it's nothing to worry about.

Chapter 18

Kane tags along to shop for my next tester menu. There's something so beautifully domestic about watching him push a grocery cart around. I walk beside him as he reaches for items on the highest shelf, and it just feels so normal, but I don't want to get ahead of myself. We still haven't defined the relationship, if that's even what it is. It's clear that Kane cares about me (and I care about him more than I'm comfortable admitting), but beyond that I don't know. He still insists on not being good at "the other stuff" and definitely doesn't set any expectations. From what I can tell, he's convinced that he'll disappoint me no matter what. I try not to push the issue though. It hasn't been that long and I really am having fun.

We round the produce aisle and crash into another cart. The woman on the other end looks up and smiles, like the cat that ate the canary. "Kane," she says in a husky voice. "I've been looking for you."

"I'm not interested in being found," he answers, but she just throws her head back and laughs.

"Always so stand-offish, but I guess that's what we like about you." She stops and leans one arm against her cart, giving me the chance to get a good look at her.

She's older, probably in her mid-forties, with a tan a few shades too dark for her platinum blonde hair, but she looks good for her age—too good. She's got a killer body and plenty upstairs, but from the shape and height of her breasts, I seriously doubt they're God-given. As she leans forward and wraps her long bubble-gum-pink fingernails around his forearm, I immediately see red. I push her cart aside until there's nothing between us, tearing her hand away like an animal.

"Don't touch him," I snarl.

She gives me the onceover. "And who the hell are you?"

"I'm his girlfriend." I avoid eye contact with Kane, fearing how he'll respond to my declaration, but nonetheless propelled forwards by pure adrenaline.

"Kane doesn't do girlfriends." She shakes her overly-processed head of hair in my face.

"I guess he does now."

She smirks. "We'll see."

"Stay away from him!" I spit the words at her through clenched teeth.

"And if I don't?"

"You don't want to know what happens if you don't, old lady!"

"Old lady?" She scoffs. "From where I'm standing, all of this looks better than what you're offering." She waves one bubble-gum-pink-tipped hand up and down her body.

Before my brain can catch up with my impulses, I've already slapped her across the face. It's nothing like the movies though; there's no satisfying smack of sound and my hand leaves no welting red mark. In fact, I somehow miss, catching only half of her face in a sloppy hit that leaves her howling.

"Bitch!" She screams, but before I can try for round two, Kane wraps his arms around my waist and lifts me off the floor.

"Easy, Ashley," he whispers, but that only enrages me even more.

"Your little whore assaulted me!" She holds a hand to her cheek, but it doesn't even look the slightest bit red.

"Don't call her that," he growls back. "Besides, I didn't see anything." He gives her a hard stare until she finally gives up and looks away.

"Goodbye, Monica." Kane mutters over his shoulder, abandoning the cart and carrying me to the frozen food section.

"Let me go!" I kick my legs and squirm with all my mite, but he doesn't put me down until we're far away from Monica.

I slide out of his arms and put my hands on my hips. "So is this what I have to look forward to? Running into all the shameless cougars you've slept with?"

He tilts his head and narrows his eyes. "You fought for me. You're jealous right now and it's so fucking hot." He backs me right up against the nearest freezer door.

"You have no idea how turned on I am right now. See?" He grabs my hand and slips it down the front of his low slung board shorts. He's not wearing any underwear and it feels like silk on steel.

"Kane," I moan, moving my hand up and down beneath his shorts.

"A few more strokes like that and I'll be coming right into your hand," he whispers, nipping at my chin with his perfect white teeth.

"You're feistier than I thought." He kisses along my jaw line. "I like that—loyalty—and I am loyal to you Ashley."

I meet his gaze with a pouty face. "How would you feel if we ran into some guy I was sleeping with?"

"Let me say it again, in case I wasn't clear the first time: I'm not sleeping with her. There's no one but you." He thrusts himself into my hand and levels me with a glare. "If I find out you have someone else, well, let's just say it won't be pretty for him."

"Threatening my fictional other lover now are you?" I tease, and his teeth clamp down on my earlobe hard enough that I yelp.

"You'll excuse me, *Lani*, if I don't find that very funny."

"I'm sorry. There is no one but you, I promise." I shiver when his tongue dips into the groove of my neck.

"And it better stay that way," he grinds out.

I rise onto my tip-toes and capture his mouth with mine at the same time that I wrap my fingers around his length, but he grabs my wrist and removes my hand from his shorts before pulling away from the kiss.

"As much as I'd love to empty myself into that sweet little palm of yours, I happen to like shopping at this grocery store." He murmurs the words into my ear and takes a step back.

I let my shoulders sag and lean my weight back against the cold glass door. "I'm going to run into women like that all over the island, aren't I?"

He steps forward to brace his body against mine. "Ashley…"

"Just tell me the truth. How many are there?"

He lays his palm flat against my neck and uses his thumb to lift my chin. "Ashley, look at me."

I look up into his beautiful hazel eyes, filled with a combination of amusement and sadness. "Not as many as you think."

"You promise?" I try my best to keep my voice steady, because I realize how silly it would be to cry about something like this. He can't control his past any more than I can control mine.

"That woman? It was all about release. A means to an end."

"That's romantic," I say, sarcastically, as his hand comes up to cup my chin.

"No, it's not. It was just sex. You're more than that."

"How much more?" I challenge, and I'm not at all surprised when he looks away.

"You told her you're my girlfriend."

I hear the words, but it's hard to read the tone of his voice. "What should I have told her?" I push myself off the freezer door and prepare to walk away, but only if I have no other choice. I have to be prepared for the possibility that I've scared him away.

His eyes glaze over as he focuses very hard on one spot on the ground. "That works," he says, curtly, before pivoting on his toe and heading back down the aisle, presumably in search of our cart.

"I guess that's better than nothing," I grumble. It wasn't exactly a commitment and he certainly didn't return the sentiment, but it's a start. At least that's what I start telling myself as I trail after him.

• • •

The next morning, I ask Kane to take me to a used car lot in Kahului, because I can't keep asking him, Adele, Kayla, and even Pancho to drive me around. They have lives and responsibilities, and I need to stand on my own two feet. Besides, I wanted a car in time for Jamie's visit, who called me at the last minute to let me know she was on her way. She's arriving from San Francisco tomorrow morning and I can't wait to see her.

I find a used Honda Coupe that's about ten years old but in excellent condition, decorated in the most beautiful, shimmery, metallic-gray color. The mileage on it is pretty high but it's all that I can afford without taking out a loan, which I don't want to do until the business starts making consistent money. Kane knows the owner of the dealership, of course, so he gives me a great "locals only" deal. I'm beaming with pride as I follow him home in my new ride. Pride because it's mine—all mine—and one of the first tangible things to anchor me in my new life here.

• • •

It's raining when I arrive at the airport to pick up Jamie, and it's not the indecisive San Francisco mist that I'm mostly used to either, but a torrential downpour of tropical warmth. Big fat drops of it roll down my cheeks, making it look like I'm weeping tears of joy—and I might as well be. It's been over a month since I last saw my best friend, and her coming all this way to spend time with me means more than she'll ever know.

I realize that waiting outside for her probably wasn't the best decision. My sundress is now drenched through, but there's something so undeniably sexy and earthy about the rain that I don't even mind. Pancho once told me that Hawaiians have over two hundred words for rain, plus different descriptors for it based on the colors, intensity, angles, and time of day. There are even words for rain that are tied to emotions such as the death of a loved one. I wonder absently if there's a "rain word" for the death of a relationship and then quickly shut out the thought as I run inside the terminal, shaking out my hair as I go. She's the last one to emerge, which is no surprise, and I'm not shocked to see her hauling three enormous hard-sided suitcases. She drops all three bags to the floor and throws herself into my arms.

"Ash!" She screams in my face, her arms tightening around me like a locket. It occurs to me then that no one here calls me that. The nickname is a remnant from the old life in San Francisco that I'd almost forgotten, but hearing it escape from my best friend's mouth gives me a familiar feeling of warmth.

"I've missed you!" She squeals, jumping up and down in a characteristic "Jamie" fashion.

Naturally, I squeal right back. "I've missed you too!"

"It's been a long month without you," she says, exhaling in a big gust. I give her one final squeeze before bending down to help her out with the bags.

"Jesus, Jamie, what's in these? You know you're only staying for a week, right?"

"I brought goodies from home." She wiggles her eyebrows. "And lots of different outfits. I didn't know what the nightlife was like around here and I wanted to be fully prepared."

I don't have the heart to tell her that Maui's pretty sleepy when it comes to nightlife, but if I know Jamie, she'll find a party somewhere. We climb into my new-slash-used car, and I beam when she compliments the dark gray interior and freshly Windexed sunroof.

"A car and everything? Wow, you really are serious about staying here?"

She asks the question, but I can't read the tone in her voice. I find my way out of the parking lot and back onto the highway. "I really am."

We drop her bags off at my place and then head straight to Salty's—at her insistence. I haven't told her much about the Kane situation, but she's smart enough to know that something is going on.

"I'm looking forward to meeting this prickly and terrifying yet somehow delicious landlord/boss of yours."

I roll my eyes skyward and huff out a breath. "Please behave?"

"No promises." She smirks.

We find Kane in the back kitchen, and the two of them give each other the onceover before my friend sticks out her hand. "Jamie Chen."

He stares at her fingers for a beat before clasping them in his. "Kane Keo. Ashley's... *friend*."

Her eyebrows hit the roof at the explanation. "Interesting." She turns to me. "When were you going to tell me that you guys have already smashed? I mean, it's so obvious."

I can literally feel my face turning red. "I wanted to tell you in person. It's complicated."

"It always is." Her eyes find Kane again and she gives him a shrewd look. "Are you the source of the complication? Because if you are, I feel like Ash has had enough of that to fill a lifetime."

He clears his throat in preparation to speak, but I soon interrupt. "I'm right here, Jamie. Please don't talk about me like I'm not in the room."

"I'm not going to speak for Ashley. What's between her and I is between her and I," Kane adds.

"You think you're too good for her? Is that it?" She says snidely.

I see the pain reflected in his eyes when they find mine. "That's not true at all. Ashley is way out of my league."

I swallow hard at the stare he gives me, forging forwards with his speech. "Ashley is smart and so strong. The way she's survived through all of this…I'm in awe of her."

It's the most he's ever said about me in one sentence; I can't help but be a little speechless. He gives Jamie a hard look before finishing his thought. "You may think that I'm just some big, dumb ape looking to take advantage of your friend, but I'm not." He looks at me again, and I feel like he can see right to the bottom of my soul with his gaze. "I care about Ashley more than you can understand; everything beyond that is none of your business."

Jamie tilts her head, as if considering the repercussions of this new character in my life. "Okay." She turns to me. "Now, what do you have to eat around here? I'm starving."

I lead her out to the bar with an uncomfortable looking Kane, scrounging together a late lunch for her in the back. The rain has subsided and a rainbow breaks across the sky, visible above the metal awning of the bar. The colors of it are so bright that it almost hurts my eyes to look straight into the glare.

"It's so beautiful here," Jamie says, exhaling. "I can definitely see the appeal." I serve her a plate of Kalua pork tacos with a side of pineapple coleslaw and she eats them both without coming up for air.

"More?" I ask. She crooks an eyebrow, as if to say: *What do you think?* It never ceases to amaze me how much she can fit into that tiny little body of hers.

"Do you want to try some Huli Huli chicken?"

"You already know the answer to that question, Ash."

Luckily, I have some warming on the stovetop already, so I load up another plateful and head out front to give it to Jamie. She immediately inhales the entire helping. "Yum…I miss your cooking. Dale is such a superb dick for ruining things with a kick-ass woman like you."

I laugh shortly. "Thanks, but I'm sure he doesn't miss my cooking, since he rarely ate any of it. I'm sure he doesn't think about it at all."

"Well, he's definitely thinking about you."

I don't miss how Kane's spine stiffens as he moves closer to eavesdrop.

"What do you mean?"

She just shakes her head. "It could be nothing. I just assumed he'd be all over town, man-whoring like the useless man-whore that he's always been, but it's weird."

"What's weird? Spill it, Jamie," I say, teetering on the brink of frustration.

"I ran into your old assistant, Terry."

"And?"

"And he said Dale is now trying to play it off like you're away at some rehab or something, which is *obvs* so dumb, I mean, people know what's up. When someone updates her Facebook status to single, deletes all of her Dale pics, quits her job, and moves to an island, it sends a pretty clear message to the general public."

"Rehab? He's out of hand," I mutter. "I don't get what his problem is. We sold our place, we have a separation agreement, and we're getting divorced as soon as the State of California permits it. What is he even thinking? Especially when he didn't even fight over any of it. Our relationship was over a long time ago. I think he was just as relieved as I was after all the dust settled, but you know Dale."

She snorts. "Yeah, I know Dale."

"What about him?" Kane rumbles from beside her stool.

She answers him through a mouthful of chicken. "He's a prick."

"You let your friend marry a prick?"

"I didn't let her do anything." She checks my gaze before continuing. "We met him when we were all freshmen. I knew he was a prick the moment I laid eyes on him in the auditorium of Psychology 101, but it was too late—she was already half-smitten."

I avert my eyes from Kane, trying to explain. "He was my first real boyfriend."

"In college?" Kane's eye travel over my face. "How is that even fucking possible?"

"I was a late bloomer," I mumble.

"Apparently," Jamie snickers, shifting her eyes between Kane and me. I feel my face heat up like a campfire.

"Jamie and Dale could barely stand to be in the same room as each other."

"Hate to say I told you so," she says with a shrug.

"Then don't."

"Hey, I'm sorry, Ash. You're right." She holds up her hands in a gesture of surrender. "Who am I to say anything? It's not like I make the best choices when it comes to men, and things weren't all bad between you guys. He really did love you—at least in the beginning."

Kane's mouth thins into a line, and I decide right and then there to change the subject. "So what do you want to do while you're here?" I ask Jamie.

"Don't you mean *who* do I want to do?" She answers, and I groan.

"It might be difficult to find you the scene you're looking for here, since there aren't any nightclubs in Paia," I explain.

"What about Kihei?" She asks, clearly having done some research, but I shake my head no.

"Oahu it is then. It's a short flight," she says, at the same time that Kane barks out a firm *no*.

She turns to face off with him. "Yes."

"No," he repeats. "You are not taking Ashley to Honolulu."

"Yes, I am."

"You're not." He leans forward and braces his big hands on the bar.

"Ooh, what are we fighting about?" Kayla arrives just in time to interrupt their stare down, and I shoot her a smile of relief.

"I'm taking my best friend Ashley to Honolulu tonight for a good time, and this big meathead seems to have a problem with it," Jamie explains.

Kayla shrugs. "Tell him that it's none of his business."

"I was in the middle of doing that when you interrupted. Who are you by the way?" Jamie shifts her attention to Kayla, momentarily forgetting Kane.

"Kayla. I'm Ashley's Hawaiian best friend."

Jamie's eyes narrow and sweep over her. "She already has a best friend."

"I reckon not as cool as this one though," Kayla retorts, pointing at herself.

"Oh, there's no chance that a skinny bitch like you has anything on me."

"Who are you calling a skinny bitch, munchkin? You have all the stature of a garden gnome."

They lock into a stare down so epic that I almost intervene, until Jamie finally breaks into a smile. "I think I'm going to like you, Kayla."

With the two of them distracted, Kane heads to my side of the bar and slips his arms around my waist. "You can't go to Honolulu."

"Why not?"

"Because I can't."

I sigh. "You don't need to follow me everywhere. I'm quite capable of fending for myself."

He hisses through his teeth. "You're not going."

I cock my head at him. "We'll see."

"Ashley," he grinds out, but I choose to ignore his protests and rebelliously wander over to join the girls in conversation.

Three hours later, Jamie, Kayla, and I are *in the air* on route to Oahu. As soon as we land at Honolulu International, Jamie informs us that she already booked us a place. It ends up being a hip boutique hotel with stunning views of Waikiki Beach. We drop our overnight bags in the room and make our way down to the funky outdoor pool area, which is surrounded by a large wooden deck and framed by blooming tropical trees.

The rectangular pool itself is lit from underneath, making it glow against the backdrop of fading light. We take a seat at one of the teak wood umbrella tables, and I sigh out happily as I relax into the padded chair.

"This was a great idea," I say.

"Hells yeah it was," Kayla agrees.

"Absolutely." Jamie nods. "But now that it's just us girls and *Drogo* is nowhere to be seen, I want answers." Jamie leans forward to spread her hands against the table.

"Really? Again with the *Game of Thrones* references?" I shake my head. "He doesn't look THAT much like that character."

"Changing the subject as always," Jamie says, and Kayla snorts out a laugh.

"She's good at that."

"No more stalling. What's going on with you and Kane?"

I shrug. "Nothing's going on; we're just having fun."

"You don't do fun."

"Thanks," I say, dryly.

"Not what I mean, and you know it. I guess I'm just surprised—it's only been a few months since everything with Dale and you've already jumped into bed with someone else?" Jamie tilts her head, and I don't miss the concern etched into her delicate features.

"You're going to lecture me on sex?" I laugh as she shakes out her dark mane.

"I would never lecture someone on sex. Fuck whoever you want—I certainly do, but you're my best friend and not the type to do casual."

"How do you know I'm not?"

"I know." She huffs out a breath and collapses against her chair. "If you truly were just getting your rocks off, I'd buy a bottle of Veuve and pop the cork, but I'm not about to do that. I'm worried about you."

"You shouldn't be."

"But I am. I'm worried that you're going to get hurt. What do you even really know about Kane?" She asks, glancing from me to Kayla.

"He's a good man," I argue, taking a peek at Kayla.

"Sure, he's a solid guy." She shrugs. "But in terms of relationships, I think he probably invented the term *emotionally unavailable*."

Jamie groans so loud that I jump up, right at the same time that a waiter in pressed white pants and a Hawaiian shirt rolls up to us.

"Is everything alright ladies?"

"It's fine." I smile at him, as Jamie grumbles incoherently under her breath.

"I apologize for the wait. What can I get you?"

We all order the signature cocktail and a tray of them arrive minutes later, each one complete with a skewer of tropical fruit and one of those cute little drink umbrellas.

I take a long, dragging sip as my eyes skim over the appetizer menu. "Macadamia crusted shrimp with guava glaze sounds good."

"There she goes again, changing the subject," Kayla says, right before she removes a strawberry from her glass and throws it at my face. It disappears down the front of my tank top and I gasp from the cold.

"What'd you do that for?" I shout, but she's laughing so hard that there are actual tears in her eyes. I glare at my so-called Hawaiian best friend until Jamie interjects.

"As amusing as this all is, we need to get back to the matter at hand. You, Kane Keo, and whether that's a disaster waiting to happen."

"You know what, Jamie?" I exhale a small hurricane of breath this time. "Maybe it is, but it's my disaster. I'm a big girl and I can handle my own life."

"Famous last words," Kayla grumbles, seeming to sober.

"That's exactly what you said about Dale when you knew that things were going off the rocks. I swear, from the way you used to talk about your marriage, you knew it was over years ago but didn't want to face it."

"We were knee-deep in twenty-five thousand dollars worth of baby-making treatments, so can you blame me?" I bite back.

"Dale was just another poster boy for *emotionally unavailable*," she argues. "Sure, he knew how to talk and said all the right things, but that guy was married to himself more than to you."

"Jesus, Jamie, I get it! I made a shitty choice in marrying the first man I loved, and then it all fell apart. It's not the first time in history that such a thing has happened to a woman, and I can guarantee it won't be the last, so please stop trying to draw parallels between Kane and Dale. They are nothing alike and frankly it's insulting."

I finish my tirade and Kayla clears her throat. "I think you should lay off her, old best friend."

I'm shocked into silence by her words; Kayla never defends anyone. Jamie seems to sense this because she backs right off.

"As long as you know what you're doing."

"I do," I say, firmly. At least I think I do, but I don't share the afterthought. As I throw back the rest of my blended drink, my phone chimes with a text from Kane.

Are you ok?

Followed by another.

I miss you.

Followed by one more.

Call me. Soon.

Hmm. He doesn't seem so emotionally unavailable to me, despite what both of my friends think. The lanterns around the pool flicker to life just as the sounds of Hawaiian guitar music float out from the hotel lobby. Jamie looks right at me, her shoulders slumping in defeat.

"I didn't fly you here to argue with you."

"Are you sure about that?" I tease, reaching across the table to grab her hand, ensuring that she knows I'm not serious.

"I want tonight to be fun. I want it to be about the three of us: young and free and in Hawaii for fuck's sake," she pontificates, and I decide to cut her some slack, since we came all this way.

"Cheers mate!" Kayla raises her half-empty glass.

"I'll drink to that." I lift my own glass and laugh when I see that it's empty. "That is, if someone can scrounge me up another one of these."

We head into the lobby to check out the live music, which turns into a live DJ show, and we dance the night away. Back at the room, we split a bottle of champagne and listen to party ballads from a decade ago. We slather on the charcoal face masks that Jamie brought with her, laughing and talking until the sun comes up. Somehow we manage to do it all with just two (okay, maybe three) phone calls from one very overbearing but still well-meaning Kane Keo.

• • •

Kane near tackles me when we arrive back at Salty's the next day. His bone-crushing hug is a little disarming. I mean, I knew that he'd miss me; I missed him too, but his response borders on frantic.

"Don't leave me again," he whispers, pulling me into his chest.

"Hey…" I lean back to look at him. "I'm okay, Kane, everything is okay."

"It is now." He exhales, his body sagging as he tugs me tighter against his chest.

I try not to read too much into it, even though his words throw me off kilter, because I don't know what to expect from him anyways. One minute we're hanging out and the next he's acting like we're inseparable. I'm confused—my head is spinning and I'm not even sure that he knows what he's saying—so I leave it alone for now.

• • •

The week with Jamie flies by. Before I can blink, I'm driving her back to the airport with tears in my eyes. When I turn off the engine and look towards her, she's staring out the window, but I swear her eyes look a little misty as well.

"I came prepared to try and talk you into coming back, but now that I've seen what you have here, I get it. These people, this place…it's right for you, Ash."

"You're right for me too though," I say, sniffling, leaning across the console to grab her hand.

"Oh, I'll be back, I can promise you that. But this place—Paia—it fits you like a second skin, in a way that the city never did. You never truly belonged in San Francisco, in real estate, or with Dale. I think you were meant to be here, and I think I understand now how lonely it must have been for you all these years."

"I wasn't always lonely. Besides, I had you."

She gives me a pained smile. "You will always have me, Ash—always—but it's time to focus on your two new passions: cooking and Kane."

"It isn't serious," I hedge, but she just rolls her eyes.

"Sure it isn't. He looks at you as if your existence is impossible. In his eyes, you're a treasure he didn't mean to find, and one that he doesn't believe he deserves. He's already in way deep, even if he won't admit it to himself."

"Maybe," I say.

"Oh, most definitely."

I gaze out at the rain beginning to cascade down from the sky, as if the whole world is altogether having a good cry. I wonder if there's a Hawaiian "rain-word" for saying goodbye to your friend. I help Jamie lug her ginormous bags into the terminal and hug her goodbye with every ounce of my strength. I realize in that moment how much I needed Jamie right now—to see and hear her laugh, to share our lives with each other. She's my tether to another life, a welcome bridge between past memories and the coming of my future.

"I'm lucky to have you." I whisper the words in her ear, like a perfect secret shared between kindred spirits.

"Yes, you are." She gives me a kiss on the cheek, pulling away and proceeding to rush to the gate.

I know that Jamie isn't one to cry, but as I watch her barrel toward the security line at breakneck speed, I wonder if there might be a first time for everything. When I get back to the car, the rain has let up and another brilliant rainbow arches its spine across the sky, the end of it fading into the horizon, as if beckoning me home.

Chapter 19

The following Sunday rolls around and Salty's is closed. On Kayla's recommendation, we head to Baldwin for a surf lesson. I agree to meet her at sunrise, but when I arrive she's already waiting for me with two boards stuck up in the sand.

"Hey girl." She gives me a little wave and throws something my direction. I catch the wadded fabric in my hands; it's a shorty wetsuit in bright blue and black.

"Is this one of yours?" I say, eyeing the neoprene skeptically. "It'll never fit me."

She snorts. "Wetsuits are supposed to stretch and you've got your *togs* on underneath. Besides, it'll be cold out there at this time of day. I also brought you a foam board."

I wander over to the surfboards and retrieve the one laying on top, which is bright yellow and feels pretty light. "Feels sturdy."

"Soft tops like that are good for beginners. It'll make it easier to paddle out, and we'll get you riding some of those baby waves even sooner."

I stick the board under my arm and gaze out at the surf. While the waves don't look big, I wouldn't classify them as "baby waves" either. Then again, maybe that's just my sense of pride creeping in.

"Drop the board on the sand and we'll practice standing up." She points over my shoulder, before turning her attention back to her own flashy surfboard. "And don't forget the wetsuit."

I sigh like the world just got heavier, dropping the board before shucking off my clothes. Underneath I'm wearing a bikini, but the sun hangs low in the sky and there's a bite to the morning air that covers my body in gooseflesh. As much as I don't want to try and sausage myself into Kayla's clothes, I can see her point.

I shove my feet through the leg holes, wiggling and yanking at the wetsuit until it covers me—well, sort of covers me. It's too long through the legs, too tight in the waist, and I can barely get the front zipper up over my boobs. Nonetheless, I suck in a huge breath and manage to get the teeth mostly over my chest, but it won't go up all the way, giving me some serious cleavage.

"I look ridiculous," I say, pouting.

She shoots a look in my direction. "I'd say you look warm and that's what matters most. Now quit *whingeing* and let's get on with it. Trust me, you'll be thanking me after your first few spills."

She drops her board next to mine, and we spend the next half hour practicing balance and getting up on the board. When the sun has made its full ascent and the people start to trickle onto the sand, she declares me ready.

"Okay, Ashley—let's hit the waves."

I bend down to pick up my board, fumbling with the ankle rope like a real amateur.

"Oh shit," Kayla mutters from behind me. "He does not look happy."

"Who doesn't?" I straighten up to take a look. Striding across the sand, wearing a thunderous expression, is none other than Kane. He stops directly in front of me and places his hands on his hips.

"What are you doing?"

"Kayla is giving me surfing lessons," I declare.

His eyes narrow, and he eyes Kayla over the top of my head.

"Is she now?"

Kayla seems to be shifting nervously from foot to foot. She gives me an apologetic look and shrugs. "I'll leave you two lovebirds to chat. I'm going to hit the waves."

Before I can protest, she's already knee-deep paddling out into the ocean, so I whip back around to level Kane with the meanest glare possible.

"What is your problem?"

"You're not surfing," he says, as if he has absolute power over my schedule of extra-curricular activities.

"Not currently, thanks to you."

"Not ever."

"It's Hawaii's official state sport, Kane. I'm pretty sure I saw a dog doing it with its owner the last time we were here. I think I can handle it."

He doesn't respond—he just stands there—stubborn and immoveable.

"What is your issue with surfing anyway? Tell me the real reason you don't surf anymore?"

"I just don't," he snaps, his eyebrows folding together.

"So we're back here again? Back to you evading my questions and spitting out one word answers while you continue to shut me out?" To emphasize my point, I try to slam the board into the sand, but it topples forward as soon as I let it go. Kane easily catches it, right before effortlessly digging it into the ground. I'm pissed at how easily the movement seems to come to him. It makes me want to try surfing now more than ever before.

"You can't control me!" I back up, crossing my arms around my chest.

"I'm not trying to, Lani." He sighs. "I just need you to understand how dangerous it is."

"Well, I do."

"Do you?" He mocks.

"Why don't you surf anymore, Kane? Since apparently you could've gone pro? Please tell me the truth."

His eyes darken. "Maybe I don't find joy in it anymore."

"Well, maybe I will!" I shout, letting my hands fall to my sides. His eyes follow the movement before climbing back to my chest, as his tongue steals out to wet his lips.

"I think your wetsuit is the wrong size." His mouth twitches. "Not that I'm complaining."

"Yeah, well, since I haven't even been in the water yet, I guess it doesn't matter much does it?" I shoot back.

"You're gorgeous when you're pissed."

"You will not distract me with sex, Kane!"

He cocks an eyebrow in challenge. "We will see about that." He moves across the sand in three long strides and pulls me into his arms. He lifts me up, grabs my ankles one by one, and wraps them around his strong waist, at the same time that his mouth meets mine. His tongue easily gains entrance and swipes gently at the inside of my mouth, coaxing and teasing me into submission.

"We didn't finish our conversation," I say, fighting the urge to melt against him. I'm shivering despite the warmth of his arms nestled around me.

"I think we did." His hands slide down my back and cup my ass. "Besides, you're freezing. Come back home with me and I'll warm you up."

"What about the board?" I wiggle against him, eliciting a deep groan in response.

"Leave it. Kayla can get it." He rocks against me, and this time I'm shivering for a different reason.

"I guess I can try surfing another day," I gasp out.

"Mmmhmm…" He hums. Even though he's patronizing me, I can't summon the energy to care, especially not when his wide palms are mercilessly gripping and kneading my ass cheeks.

"I love this ass." He whispers. "I think it's time that we had some fun with it."

Without waiting for an answer, he walks us to the parking lot and his ever present Jeep. Part of me is disappointed that I didn't get to try surfing, while another part of me stubbornly chides myself for letting him win, but it's hard to listen to those rational parts when my less rational ones are pressed up against the hard, strong body of Kane Keo.

Chapter 20

After much begging and cajoling on my part, Kane finally agrees to take me to a luau. I've never been to one before, my only reference being what I've seen in the movies. Kane assures me that they're mostly designed to rip off the tourists, but he still drives me halfway across the island to see one that he deems "the best." We arrive at dusk, the sun beginning to chase the horizon and leaving a vivid rainbow in its wake. We walk through the lobby of the hotel and onto a patio with a panoramic view of the sea. There's a light breeze in the air, just enough to set the palms trees swaying back and forth, but not quite enough to make me regret my chosen outfit of a light blue sundress.

I head toward the ticket booth, but Kane grabs my elbow and leads me off to the left. "Where are we going?" I say, glancing over my shoulder at the line now forming.

"A friend of mine works here."

"So?" I give him a look.

"So we're going to see the luau my way, without forking over a hundred bucks a head."

"Isn't that cheating the system?"

He just shrugs. "*Kama'aina* discount."

"What does that mean?"

He gives me a secretive smile. "People of the land."

I follow him back inside, venturing to the end of a narrow hall, where a dancer with a big smile awaits us in full gear.

"Keo!" The man shouts, and I'm shocked when Kane leans into hug him. I mean, it's really one of those man-back-slapping affairs, but even so, it's still a hug. When Kane pulls away, he turns to introduce me.

"Niko, this is Ashley; Ashley, Niko. He's one of the Polynesian drummers for tonight."

I take in Niko's broad tanned chest, his chiseled abs visible beneath the palm frond of his necklace. Other than the palm leaf legwear extending from below his knees, or the tiny green and black wrap around his waist, it's the only clothing he wears. He looks exotic with the intricate black lines painted on his face, and more than a little scary.

"Keo and I go all the way back to primary school. Nice to meet you, Ashley." His eyes sweep me from head to toe. "Your girl?" He asks Kane, still gazing at my face. Kane gives the slightest of nods before answering.

"Yes." His answer causes butterflies to take up residence in my tummy. I don't think I'll ever tire of hearing Kane claim me.

"Nice."

"Careful," Kane hisses.

"I'm a man that appreciates beauty, *bruddah*," Niko says, 100% nonplussed. "Why don't both of you come backstage to meet the rest of the crew?

He leads us outside and down a cobblestone path, revealing the private area behind the stage. The strong scent of propane Tiki torches fills my nose, along with the tang of salt from the waves crashing like lucid dreams against the shoreline. Backstage, I'm treated to the once in a lifetime experience of witnessing an entire ensemble cast prepare for their performance. The women are drop-dead stunning in their brightly colored tops and hula skirts, serving as the perfect complement to their shiny black hair and plump red lips. Fresh leis adorn their necks and wrists, and the smell of Hibiscus invades my senses as I pass by each of them. Some wear long grass skirts, with shell bras and flower crowns dyed all shades of pink, beige, and red, while others wear shorter green skirts sitting low on the hips and undulating always with a life of their own. I feel more starkly out of place by the minute.

Niko stops before yet another handsome performer and pauses to introduce us. "Guys, this is Harry. He's our main fire-performer for tonight."

Harry is about my height and doesn't have an ounce of body-fat. His torso and arms are completely covered by Samoan-looking tattoos.

"Harry, do you mind if Ashley waits with you for a minute, so that I can set Kane up with a spot for them to watch the show?"

Harry flashes me his pearly whites and penetrating gaze. "It would be my pleasure."

I glance at Kane, whose jaw is set in hard line; for a moment, I think he's going to argue, but instead he steps forward and gives me a quick but searing kiss.

"I'll be right back." He directs the comment to Harry, who simply shrugs and waves him off.

Harry fills the time by showing off his spinning poi, which basically consists of two wire chicken cages sitting atop metal chains, their thick rope wicks set to burn at either end. I ask him if it's dangerous, but he just laughs and tells me that that's the fun. "*Poi* is a Maori word that literally means ball on a string," he explains.

I laugh, imagining my grandmother's knitting. "Pretty accurate."

"It was originally used as a form of battle training. You want to hold it?" He steps closer to place the thick chain in my hand, at the same time that Kane rounds the bend. When he sees us standing shoulder-to-shoulder, his facial expression is less than impressed. Kane not-so-subtly steps between us and bumps Harry aside.

"We're going," he says, his voice leaving no room for argument.

I wave goodbye to poor ol' Harry over my shoulder, and Kane drags me away by the fingers. Once we've walked a few feet, I dig my heels into the ground and yank my hand from his grasp.

"What was that?"

"What?" He shrugs, stopping for the briefest of moments before plowing ahead so fast that I have no choice but to keep up with him.

"Harry seems nice," I pant out.

"He's really not."

"He was nothing but polite, and he even showed me a picture of his daughter," I argue, but Kane just scoffs.

We walk in silence for a beat before I stop again, this time placing my hands on my hips. "Is there anyone that you *do* like?"

His lips twitch before he answers. "I like you."

"Sweet relief," I say, rolling my eyes.

"Smart ass," he cracks back. "Careful, or I'll have no choice but to spank that smirk right off your beautiful face."

I squeeze my legs together at the threat. It's the second time that he has mentioned spanking me, and the suggestion does surprising things to the pit of my stomach. He leads me over to a patch of pristine grass alongside the stage, where a small blanket awaits us. I kick off my sandals and flop myself down. We're set back from the rest of the crowd, where the other guests are seated in modern civility at their own tables.

"I guess the chairs are for the paying guests?" I say, although I do appreciate our Shakespearean blanket in the grass.

"I promise that the view is better from here. Besides, now I have you all to myself." He settles in behind me on the blanket.

I'm just messing with him, and he knows it. In truth, it's quite literally the perfect spot. I love how the long blades of grass feel between my toes. Kane wraps his arms around my waist and nudges me closer into his chest, where I relax and melt right into him.

A few minutes later, Niko arrives to give Kane a couple of ticket stubs. "They're staff meals—this way you guys can hit the buffet."

We wait until it appears as if the other guests are fed before getting to our feet. At the buffet, I load up my plate with pig, poke, Lomi Lomi salmon, mahi-mahi, beef teriyaki, and char siu. The food looks amazing, but there are so many choices, so I prepare a small bite of the purple sweet potatoes and macaroni salad.

"Take some of the haupia." Kane slides a few white squares onto a separate dessert plate.

"What is it?"

"Basically hard coconut pudding, but you'll love it."

I know it's just pudding, but it makes my eyes blister with dormant tears. They cluster together, waiting for the force of gravity to pull them down my cheeks. He just gets me—from my love of food to my willingness to try new things. This one small gesture speaks volumes, and I can't help but think about my ex-husband, who never would've filled a dessert plate for me, let alone encouraged me to try anything new. In fact, he probably would've launched into a passive-aggressive lecture about the evil effects of sugar on my waistline.

I look up at Kane, who's watching me like a hawk. I don't know how to explain my gratitude towards him, so I just give him a wide smile.

"Thank you," I whisper.

His mouth goes slack. "I'd fill the back of a dump truck with haupia, if it earned me one minute of seeing you smile that way."

We carry our plates back to the blanket and dig into the food. "How do they manage to cut up the pig so quickly?" I say, through a mouthful of Kalua pork.

He just snorts. "I doubt it's the same one that's turning above the fire. The *haole* might be eating day old *pua*."

Kane gets up and disappears, only to reappear with a glass of white wine for me and a bottle of water for him. As the sky fades from crimson to the deepest of navy blues, the drums sound with a base that I feel deep down in my bones. I lean forward and place my chin on my knees, enraptured by the show unfolding before us. The swaying hips of the hula dancers and the sweet melodies of their voices, at times mournful and haunting. When the fire-knife dancers come out for the finale, I'm so enthralled that I barely notice when Kane pulls me into the V of his legs. He's wearing board shorts and the heat of his bare skin sparks against my thighs, caging me inside his legs. He guides my head back until I'm resting gently against his chest. A shudder moves through my entire body as he presses his warm lips into the shell of my ear.

"In ancient Hawaii, Hula was used as a form of religious storytelling. Each movement, gesture, touch, sway, and tilt of the hips holds a special meaning."

As he speaks, his hands roam all over my body, skimming down my sides and across my stomach. He slides one hand across my chest and cups my throat with the other, ravaging my neck with kisses. When he finally tears his panting mouth away, my skin pebbles and burns in response to the loss. "There's something so primal about it, don't you think?" His voice is hoarse as he speaks into the curve between my neck and shoulder.

"Kane," I moan out, causing his fingers to tighten around my throat. It's not uncomfortable, but firm enough to let me know who is in control.

"Tell me." He flexes his hand. "Tell me what you need."

"I need you," I keen out.

"Need me to what?"

"I need you to be inside of me right now."

He pulls me even closer and digs his hard length into my back. "Just remember that you asked for it," he growls, getting to his feet and taking me with him. I accidentally kick over my glass of wine in the process, sending it into my half-eaten dinner plate with a crash and pursuant shatter.

"Stay in front of me," he demands, bending down to thrust against my ass once more. I'm guessing he wants me in front to cover the state of his arousal, but I probably couldn't pull myself away from him even if I tried. He maneuvers me back into the interior of the hotel and down another narrow hall to a set of doors. One of the doors is marked **Change Room**, and he leans forward to try the handle. "I noticed this when we were back here earlier with Niko."

The door pushes open and he guides us both inside. When the lock clicks behind us, he shoves me up against the doorframe and ravages my mouth. It's dark inside, with only the light from the hall filtering through the door. We fumble around, panting heavily, until we both crash into something that makes a loud clang.

"It's a chair," I say, pulling my mouth away long enough to inhale a breath of air.

"Sit on me," he barks out, collapsing onto the hard, cold metal.

I slip off my underwear and hike up my dress before straddling his lap. He yanks down the thin straps of my sundress, bringing his hands up to palm my breasts. They're sun-kissed and heavy with need.

"No bra," he whispers, craning his head to feast on them. I start moving on his lap, slowly at first but picking up speed as the friction of my bareness against his board shorts starts to drive me wild. I can feel the pressure building as his hands clamp down on my waist, holding me in place.

"You are drenched," he pants out, scraping his teeth against my ear. "I love having you on top of me, feeling you soak through my clothes. Come for me."

It's too much. I throw back my head and scream, riding crest after crest before collapsing into his shoulder. His hands rub circles on my bare back, and I work to bring my breathing back to normal. "Thank you." I whisper into his neck, feeling his hands slip under my dress to squeeze the backs of my bare legs.

"You just came in my lap, with barely any prodding at all, and you're thanking *me*? I think you truly are a gift from heaven, but I'm not even close to done with you." I can just make out his smug smile in the darkness.

"Let me have some fun with you first." I slide off his lap and onto my knees. He doesn't even try to hide his tented board shorts. There's no embarrassment or hesitation as he unties the strings and pushes the shorts down his powerful thighs. He strokes himself lazily, his beautiful eyes never leaving mine.

"What kind of fun did you have in mind?" He rasps, and I answer by scooting forward to wrap a hand around the top of his impressive length. He hisses out a breath as my thumb circles the tip. I take as much of him as I can in my hand and proceed to stroke him up and down. When I finally wrap my lips around his hardness, he yells out my name. He runs his hands down the front of his thighs as his muscles shake, barely restrained. I relax my throat to take him deeper into my mouth, and he releases a guttural moan. "Ashley, if you keep doing that, I'm not going to last long."

I hum against his warm skin, feeling the vibrations in my teeth as I suck even harder. "Fuck, woman!" He shouts, almost as if in pain. "You have to stop, or I'm going to come in your mouth."

He starts to push me away, but I shake my head *no* and join my mouth and hand together, coaxing him to the brink. I look into his eyes, loving that I have the power to make him feel this unhinged. He grabs a handful of my hair and thrusts harder into my mouth, and I know it won't be long. He yanks on my hair hard enough to bring tears to my eyes and cries out my name. I swallow his release and sit back on my heels.

He lays boneless against the chair, his breathing ragged. "You." He cups my head with both hands and tilts up my chin. "That was amazing, but I'm still not done with you—and I'm not going to be gentle, not when I'm this riled up. You understand?"

I nod briskly, unable to speak as the words catch in my throat. He bends down to lift me up and guides my legs around his waist, backing me against the wall once more. His shirt is still on and my dress bunches around my hips, but I don't care—I can't be bothered to care with the way he's looking at me right now—a combination of lust, possession, and something else entirely. He flattens his palms against the wall, and when my back hits the rough plaster, he drives into me in one powerful thrust. He keeps his promise to me, because he isn't gentle at all. Not one bit. I like men who are good at keeping their promises.

Chapter 21

It's a gorgeous Monday morning beneath a cloudless blue sky with all the birds chirping in harmony. You'd think that working six days a week would have me run off my feet, but I've never felt more alive than I do working at Salty's. I love it, despite that my feet ache constantly and I smell like fryer grease most nights. The bar has been open only about an hour, and it's already slammed with tourists and surfers fresh off their morning sets.

I'm back in the kitchen when Vampire Weekend's song "A Punk" comes on the radio. I crank the volume up and dance over to the stove while waving my spatula high in the air. *"Look outside at the raincoats coming, say oh, eh, eh, hey, hey!"* I'm singing at the top of my lungs, so when Kane comes up behind me, brushing the hair from my shoulder to kiss my neck, I let out a squeal of surprise.

"You are so damn cute." His hands circle my waist and slide down the front of my cutoffs to play with the hem. "But still so damn sexy," he whispers in my ear.

His fingers maneuver my panties out of the way as he slips two of them inside me, causing me to buck against his hand.

"Kane! I'm cooking!" I hiss.

"I don't fucking care."

"This isn't food safe. My skewers are ruined now."

"So make another batch." He moves his fingers ever-so-slowly in circles. "It's your fault for being so irresistible."

The new guy, who Kane hired to help with the hungry crowds, chooses that exact moment to stick his head inside the kitchen.

"Ashley, someone is here for you."

"Thanks, Ben," I manage to croak out, thanking God that Kane's back is towards him.

Kane removes his hand. "You expecting someone?"

"No one that I can think of." I head to the sink to wash my hands and wipe them off before heading out. I look at Kane before I leave, laughing when I see what condition he's in below the belt. "I guess you'll have to stay back here for awhile." I gesture to the monument in his shorts.

"You're a tease, Lani." He shakes his head, smirking. "But I'll make you pay for it later."

"I look forward to it," I say, biting my lip. He groans, and I rush from the back room into the car, coming up short when I see who's waiting for me.

"Hello, Ashley." Despite all the years that we spent together, the sound of Dale's voice suddenly makes my skin crawl.

"Dale." I spit out his name, not giving anything away.

"And how exactly is my little runaway wife doing these days?"

"Ex-wife, Dale, emphasis on the ex." I glare at him, crossing my arms over my chest.

"Semantics, sweetheart, and the ink isn't dry on anything yet."

"You don't ever get to call me sweetheart again." I speak through clenched teeth. When I glance over Dale's shoulder, I notice that we've started to attract a crowd. Pancho and Kayla openly gape at us from the bar. "Not here," I snap, stomping over to one of the available tables.

Dale follows and takes the seat directly across from me. He's wearing a suit, of course, but he's forgone the tie and left his collared shirt unbuttoned at the neck, which is Dale's version of holiday-wear, if I remember correctly. He has the same lean frame and stereotypically handsome features, and his neat blond hair is slicked back from his face. Still, I struggle to remember what I saw in him in the first place. All I see now is a soft jaw, thin lips, and arms that proved too weak to hold me, even when it mattered most.

"What a charming spot you've found for yourself," he deadpans. "Are you an actual waitress now?"

"I'm a chef," I shoot back, but he just chuckles.

"And how long, pray tell, do you think that is going to last?" He crosses his legs and leans back in his chair, in that annoyingly patronizing kind of way, and I bristle at the thought of him staying a while.

"You look good." He gives me the once over. "A little feral, maybe, and you've had too much sun, but otherwise good."

"I like the sun," I snap.

"Tans are for field workers and white trash, Ashley. You looked better the way you were."

I sigh in frustration. "What do you want, Dale?"

"Look, I get it. I made a mistake with Erin, and you've made mistakes, too, but it's time for this charade to end. I want you to come home."

I choke out a laugh. "Are you crazy? I'm not moving back to San Francisco. I quit my job, we sold our place, and in four months, we'll sign on the dotted line and be rid of each other for good."

Dale gives me a pointed look. "What makes you think I'll sign anything?"

"Don't be a child, Dale, we've talked ourselves to death about this. You know exactly how it ends."

He snorts. "You're calling me a child? That's rich—you're a twenty-seven year old woman who just shirked all her responsibilities for a Hawaiian holiday, simply because her feelings got hurt. You sold your belongings, cut ties with everyone you knew, and then left me behind, all within a month. I mean, how selfish can you be?"

"Selfish?" I scream—I don't even care about the audience anymore, now that Dale has me all fired up. "Having my body poked and prodded for the last two years—being swollen, nauseous, sore all over, tired and anxious, all while you were putting your thin dick inside someone else—and I'm SELFISH?"

"Look, I realize that I carry some of the fault in this situation, but you really need to take some ownership as well."

"Excuse me?" I can feel my eyebrows shoot up into my hairline.

"You were so obsessed with having a baby! All those treatments made you moody, and it became more about you than me." He shrugs.

I can actually feel my blood boiling inside my veins. It takes everything I have not to scratch his eyes out. "I'm sorry, let me get this straight. You mean to say that, in a failed attempt to conceive the child for whom you begged me, I was regularly injected with hormones that made me feel half crazy, and that it's *my* fault for not paying attention? Is that about right, you selfish prick?"

"Alright, Ashley, you've made your point. There's no need to cause a scene." He leans forward in his chair. "Have your tantrum if you like, but one way or another, you're coming home with me."

"She isn't going anywhere." I look up to see a furious Kane eclipsing the sun. Kane braces his big hands on either side of Dale's chair. His eyes are wild, and for a split-second, I'm actually worried for Dale.

Dale whips around so fast, I'm surprised that he doesn't pull a muscle. He's still wearing his usual air of confidence, but his smile seems uncertain. "And who the hell are you, exactly?"

"This is Kane Keo, the owner," I croak out.

"I'm her boyfriend," Kane declares.

Boyfriend? It sounds so juvenile. Kane Keo is no boy, but him officially claiming the title makes me tingle all over. Dale turns back around slowly and narrows his eyes at me.

"I see what this is. You're angry with me, so you let this Neanderthal fuck you to get back at me. I have to say, I'm sort of proud of you, sweetheart. Who knew my wife could be such a little slut?"

Kane releases an actual animalistic growl, yanking Dale up by the armpits and dragging him from his chair. The bar erupts with excited chatter as a number of patrons crowd around the men. Lance takes Kane's side, more than ready for a fight and meanwhile glaring daggers at Dale. Kane tosses Dale to the ground, towering over him like a noble savage. "Don't ever call her that."

"Call her what? Sweetheart, or slut?" Dale spits back, struggling to stand on two feet.

"Either."

Dale manages to stand up and straighten himself into a totem pole, but Kane still has a good half a foot on him. He adjusts his shirt sleeves and straightens his collar. "Wow, she really has you fooled with that magic pussy of hers—and believe me, it *is* magic." Dale looks my way and flashes me a lazy grin, perusing my body like I'm naked.

I know he's baiting Kane, and it works. Before I can even blink, Kane cracks him across the jaw with a powerful right hook. Dale's head whips to the side, and he falls to the ground. The crowd goes wild. I hear one of the regular surfer dudes chant: *fight, fight, fight.* Kane breathes heavily with his fists clenched at either side, but he doesn't make another move toward Dale. He starts getting to his feet, a river of blood leaking from his nose and onto his pristine white dress shirt.

"You people are all animals." He wipes the blood from his nose and turns toward me. "You don't seriously think you'll last here, do you, Ashley?"

"Of course I will. This place fits me better than my old life ever did."

"But doesn't that old life mean anything to you anymore?" For a moment, I feel bad for him, but it doesn't take long to remember what brought us here.

"Did you ever even love me, Dale?"

He looks at me like I'm crazy. "Of course I did, *Leelee*." He uses the nickname he gave me in college, and it pinches my heart.

"Just not more than you love yourself." It feels freeing to say the words aloud—the same words I've been thinking for years—like a weight off my chest. I'm about to say more, but Pancho beats me to it.

"Hey, *haole*, Ashley is one of us now!" He shouts, hiding himself behind Kane. "Go back to the fucking mainland and leave us alone!" The bar erupts in a round of applause.

Dale looks between me and Kane, weighing his words against the atmosphere of the bar. "You people don't actually believe that she's one of you, do you?" He runs a hand through his wispy blond hair. "I bet you don't know that Ashley is one of the best commercial real estate brokers on the West Coast. She works for me, at Silverdale Developments."

"Worked," I say, correcting him.

"Oh, is it past tense? Then you won't mind me telling these lovely people about the plans we sent you weeks ago—you know, for the construction of a full-scale five-star resort in Paia?"

"It's not like that—" I start, but he cuts me off.

"You see? She isn't even denying it, and why would Ashley Silver deny her affiliation with the company that shares her name?"

"Ashley Walsh," I shout at him.

"Ashley Silver," he stresses, "is one of the best in the game. I've seen this woman drink tea with little old ladies just moments before they sign their property rights away at below market value, never without smiles on their wrinkled faces. Don't even get me started on the men, either—one look at her rack and the male clients were eating from her hands. I used to get so hard watching her work." He looks at me one last time, before finally stepping back from the crowd.

"So enjoy your shithole town as long as possible, because once my wife is done with Paia, this place will be unrecognizable. See you at home, *Leelee*." Dale blows me a kiss, elbowing his way past the lingering patrons and straight through the front door.

The bar is quiet after Dale leaves. No one moves but to return to their seats. Pancho finally steps forward, but the look on his weathered, tanned face reminds me of an abandoned bear cub. "Is it true? Is that why you're here?"

His expression makes wetness pool behind my eyes. "It's not how he made it sound, Pancho. I don't work for him—for them."

"But there are plans?"

I can't help but sigh. "There are, but I'm not part of them." Before I can explain, he shakes his head and turns away.

"I really thought you were one of us, Red."

"I am!" I protest, and my eyes find Lance in the crowd. "You believe me, right Lance?" I plead for him to understand, but he just shifts his weight from foot-to-foot.

"Jeez, Ashley, a resort? You know what that'll do to my beach—it'll get jammed. Old minty and I will never see any surf. I like Paia the way it is. I thought you did too."

"I do! I love it!" I cry out, but I don't know how to explain without making the situation worse.

I push through the crowd until I find Kayla, who's wearing a look of pure disgust. "Wait until Adele hears about this. It's like I always say: you really can't trust anyone but yourself."

No, no, no this can't be happening, I tell myself. It's all wrong. I didn't mention the plans earlier because I didn't want anyone to freak out. I wanted to dig around first and see how concrete they were, or find a viable way to stop the developers from pursuing the project. I want to explain all of this to my friends, and more importantly, to Kane, but he storms out of the bar long before I have a chance. I forget about the kitchen for now and proceed to chase after Kane, but his jeep is already tearing away from the parking lot. I head for my new beater-of-a-car and jump inside, but the ignition won't start—screw Murphy and all of his Laws. It just keeps turning over and over.

I scream in anger before heaving the door open and leaping onto the pavement. My only option is to run back to the house, so I set off on foot and by the time I reach the driveway, my tank top is drenched in sweat. I jog down to my suite with a plan to change my shirt before setting out to find Kane, but instead I find him inside, standing at the small kitchen table with the resort plans clutched in his hands. He's obviously deep in concentration, and I figure he must have rummaged through every drawer to find the plans, given the chaos with which they're strewn across the table.

"Does part of the rental agreement including snooping?" I ask.

His eyes snap up to me. "These plans are ridiculous."

I take a deep breath. "I know."

"They'll never be able to build this close to the water line, never mind that none of this is energy efficient and the proposed amenities contravene about fifty different land use policies," he continues, but I cut him off.

"I know," I speak louder this time, leaning into the wall for support. The run really knocked the wind from me and I have yet to recover. Spinning I can manage, but I'm definitely not a long distance runner.

"You kept these from me," he accuses.

"Yes, I did." I feel my shoulders sag. "I kept them from everyone, because I know how seeing plans like these would hurt this community. I don't work for Silverdale and I never will again. This development is an insult to Paia Town and all of Hawaii, and I will do everything in my power to see that it doesn't happen. That's the real reason that I kept them;

what you're holding right now is insider information, enabling us to stop the development altogether. Please, Kane, you have to believe me."

He runs a ragged hand through his hair before tossing the plans down on the table. "I do."

"Wait…what? You do?"

"I never doubted you, Lani, not for one minute."

"Then why did you race out of the bar in such a state?"

He just shakes his head. "Because he talked about you intimately…about touching you…and the way he looked at you…" He laughs without any humor.

"I was married to him, Kane," I say, throwing my hands up in the air.

"Yeah, about that…" His voice is gruff, but there's a smile playing across his lips.

"I know. I concede that it wasn't one of my better life choices."

"The truth is…" He says, pacing like a cougar. "I don't like picturing you in anyone else's arms. It seems unnatural to me."

Between his earlier declaration of coupledom and now these words, my heart pounds staccato. "It seems unnatural to me as well." My voice is soft, but he's so busy pacing that I don't think he hears.

"He called you sweetheart. He called you his wife. He's seen you naked. It makes me see nothing but red."

"I can't change the past, Kane, no more than you can."

He flinches at my words. "Understatement. But I hate that he had you first. I hate that he had you at all."

I grab his arm like someone under arrest. "He never had me, Kane. Not like you do."

Kane sweeps his thumb across my bottom lip. He doesn't say anything, but his eyes tell me everything that I need to know.

"Are you mad at me then?" I whisper.

He sighs and gazes at me with full eyes. "I'm insanely jealous, Lani. I'd love to know where he's staying, so that I could drive over there tonight and beat the shit out of him for disrespecting you, but no, I'm not mad."

"That's good, I guess, but everyone else in town is mad at me, even my friends. What am I going to do?"

"You'll figure it out."

"That's helpful."

"I thought you wanted to take care of yourself." He raises one eyebrow at me.

"Now you choose to listen to me? *Now?*" My voice goes up a whole octave, but he just chuckles and pulls me against his chest.

"Don't hug me, I'm sweaty." I try to pull away, but Kane doesn't budge.

Instead he just murmurs into my hair. "I don't care."

"And this whole development business…I'm going to pay a visit to the county tomorrow and get details on Paia's community plan and zoning regulations. Dale was exaggerating when he talked about my old job, but he wasn't totally wrong. I did things that I'm not proud of back then—real estate, especially development, is pretty cutthroat. I got so caught up while I was trying to grow my career; it felt like the right thing to do at the time. You know what I mean?"

Kane kisses my forehead. "I love that you want to help, but don't waste your time. Trust me when I tell you that this development thing is dead in the water."

"What makes you so confident?"

"Well, for starters, I own a lot of the private waterfront land already, along with a few commercial spaces in town."

I narrow my eyes at this mysterious man. "How many is a few?"

He clears his throat. "Maybe more than a few."

Kane snuggles me into his chest, and I do the quick math in my head. Water frontage in Hawaii, times commercial space, times land, equals—holy hell—Kane Keo is loaded.

"So you're, like, a real estate baron?"

He laughs and shakes his head. "I'll show you my bank account statement. I assure you it's not very impressive, but I started buying land when I was twenty-one—made a few good decisions, got lucky more than a few times. There was never much for me to fall back on financially, and I didn't go to college after high school, but my grandpa gave me a good start. He lived his whole life in Hana, raising me after my mom died, and when he passed, he left me his land. It's for agricultural use and cannot be developed, but that wouldn't be my game anyways—this town means too much to me."

"I'm sure your bank account is still more impressive than mine." I think about my student loans, and that stupid pair of embellished Jimmy Choo shoes, which I bought with a Sax card during a fit of emotional holiday shopping last year. "But even if you *are* the King of Paia..." I tease, watching him roll his eyes. "I still want to go to Oahu and gather the information. I want to tell my friends exactly what happened and how I'm going to make it right—as soon as I figure that out myself."

"Then go," he says. "And trust me when I say that everything will be fine."

"Wow. I think that's the most positive thing I've ever heard you say."

He smiles crookedly. "I'm not that bad, Ashley."

"Uh-huh."

"Why don't I show you just how good I can be?" He lifts me up, resting my bellybutton against his erection.

I let out a little gasp. "Yes, I'm definitely more of a visual learner." I feel myself losing oxygen as he tugs off my tank top.

"Then prepare yourself for lesson number one, Lani."

He carries me past the wicker divider and into the bedroom, before throwing me down against the sheets like a prize.

Chapter 22

It's takes all of my courage to face the crowd at Salty's the next day. I hope things will be business as usual, but apparently no one's hungry today. By one o'clock in the afternoon, two hours have passed without anyone placing a single order, but I keep my head high and ignore the whispering glares cast my way. I'll do whatever I must to show these people how sorry I am for not being upfront with them. Since there's no cooking to be done, I offer to help Kane re-stock the bar. The only two patrons here are Pancho (who hasn't looked my direction once), and a young local who I've seen around a few times.

"Hey shark bait," he calls to me. I look around before making eye contact with him. "Yeah, *you*. No wonder your husband fucked around on you, ice-queen. Sounds like you're a real cold-hearted bitch."

My throat closes up and my nose tingles with the beginnings of tears. I glance over at Pancho, but his face is impassive.

Kane, on the other hand, is listening like a hawk. "Get out of my bar," he says.

"But…"

"Now."

The guy mutters a string of curses but hops off his stool and heads for the door.

"Please don't," I whisper. "I've already affected your business enough. I don't want you to lose more customers because of me."

He gives me a look. "No one calls you that." He resumes stocking the back bar, so I wander over to Pancho, who's nursing a beer with a sad look on his face.

"Pancho?" I say quietly, but he doesn't speak a word. "I know that you're angry with me right now, but I'm hoping you'll come to my place this evening. I'm inviting everyone over to explain. Please let me explain."

He doesn't look at me when he answers. "I don't know, Red. What you did was pretty *lolo*, but I'll think about it." I nod my head and even though it's hard, I leave him be.

When Lance arrives, he reluctantly agrees to come over later, and I leave messages for Kayla and Adele. The rest of the afternoon is more of the same. As hard as I try not to let it affect me, every nasty comment and dirty look digs deeper every time. Then, as if my day couldn't get any worse, Dale saunters into the bar later that afternoon. I cringe upon seeing that he's traded his suit for pink oxford shorts and docksiders. He looks so out of place in Salty's; it's almost comical, with emphasis on the *almost*. Kane shoves me behind his big body and plants his hands on the bar, but Dale ignores him, sliding onto one of the bar stools.

"Relax, mouth breather. I'm here for Ashley."

"Like hell you are," he growls.

"I only came to tell my *wife* that I'm leaving today." He turns his gaze on me. "I wanted to give you one more chance to change your mind."

I step past Kane and dart around the bar until I'm face-to-face with Dale. "I think I made myself pretty clear. We are done. I'm never changing my mind. This is my home now."

Dale looks around the bar and snorts. "Why stay? These people clearly hate you. Besides, you belong working at Silverdale. You belong in San Francisco and you belong in my bed."

"I'm going to fucking kill this guy," I hear Kane say behind me.

"That's right, big guy, keep muttering threats. You'll be hearing from my lawyer over last night's fiasco," Dale shoots back.

I have no doubt that he's serious. Being the son of one of the city's most prominent developers gives you unlimited access to legal advice.

"Please leave Kane alone." My voice betrays me with quiet shaking. "This is where I belong, and these people, they may hate me right now, but I love them. I'll earn back their trust no matter how long it takes. They are my *ohana*." My eyes start to burn with unshed tears.

"I hope you realize how ridiculous you sound," he scoffs, glancing at Kane, who hovers so close that I can feel his buttons pressing into my back. "Most of these people won't even look at you right now, and you're spouting off nonsense in Hawaiian like you belong here."

"She does," Kane states, looping an arm around my shoulder. "Did everyone hear me clearly?" He shouts out, looking around the bar.

Dale's face knots into a grimace at the sight of Kane's strong arm encasing me. "Right, well, you can kiss that job at Silverdale goodbye forever."

"With pleasure," I say.

"I guess now would probably be the right moment to tell you that it wasn't just Erin Perry I got off with." Dale clicks his tongue. "I fucked around on you a lot. It was almost too easy, but I won't lie…I am going to miss that gorgeous ass of yours. Good thing I have so much other ass on the side to keep me going."

I hear Kane mutter "fuck." His arm drops from my shoulders but I reach back and grab hold of his wrists to steady him. I don't want him hitting Dale again, and I can already see where this is going. Dale slips off the stool and starts to leave before making a quick pivot in the other direction. "Oh, and I've been thinking about the townhouse—I may have had a change of heart."

"But we both put down money," I say, but Dale releases a cynical chuckle.

"I put down more though, which is what really counts." Dale mimes a mic drop and spins on his heel like a teenage boy.

I look over at Kane, pleading with my eyes for him not to chase after Dale. "It won't help anything," I whisper, shaking my head.

"If he's already going to sue me, what does it matter?" Kane says flatly.

"Don't say that please!" I spin around to face him and see that he's laughing.

"I'm not worried about it, Lani. I own a bar and lots of real estate; I know a thing or two about people threatening to sue."

"God! He is such an asshole!" I scream, balling my fists together as Kane raises his eyebrows. "What?"

"I don't think I've ever heard that cute little mouth of yours swear."

"Asshole isn't a swearword," I argue, "I mean, not really. Whatever, I'm just glad he's gone for now."

Kane stares at the door with a dark look in his eyes. "If he knows what's good for him, *for now* will become forever."

• • •

Around dinner time, Kane tells me to go home. I give up and head out to my new-used car, but someone has smashed out the driver and passenger side windows. There's broken glass all over the seats, but I'm far too worn out to care. I sit on top of the debris, letting them cut into the back of my legs. I rest my head on the steering wheel and finally let everything go. I cry so hard that I'm practically hyperventilating by the time Kane finds me.

In silence, he gently removes me from the car and dusts the broken glass from my back, handing me to Taylor. "Taylor's going to drive you home." He kisses my cheek. "And I'm going to take care of this." His voice sounds raw and hoarse.

I want to tell him that I don't care about the car—that I'm just overwhelmed—but all I can do is sob. I climb into Taylor's idling BMW and we drive the short distance in silence, giving me time to calm down and reflect.

"He cares about you a lot," Taylor says, his car rolling to a stop before my place.

I swallow a big hiccup. "I know."

"You better feel the same way, because the Kane I know doesn't have the capacity to just turn it on and off."

"And you think I can?" It's on the tip of my tongue to tell Taylor the truth—that I love Kane and feel terrible for putting him in this position.

"Kane Keo doesn't care what other people think, but clearly he cares about you. Just be careful with his heart, please?"

"Is he going to be careful with mine?" I whisper.

Taylor sighs. "He'll have no choice but to be careful. When Kane loves something, his love is fierce and constant, like the surf. He had love, great love, with his son, but losing Kaiden broke him. I came here every day for three months—did you know that? I came and opened the blinds, put the dishes in the dishwasher, got him out of bed, made him stand in the shower, forced him to eat. Even still, almost seven years later, it feels like he just gets up out of habit—not because he wants to, because he has to. He lives life by going through the motions. At least, that's how it felt until you came along."

"Isn't that a good thing then?"

Taylor leans back in his seat and really looks at me. "That depends. I don't think he can survive another heartbreak, and I don't mean that figuratively. So you need to be sure—about him, and about Paia."

"I appreciate what you're saying, Taylor, I do, but there are no certainties in life. I've learned that the hard way. I love Kane and I want to be with him, but it takes two people to make that decision. I can't force things if he's not ready to open up for me."

"You love him?" He says, the ghost of a smile on his face.

"I really do."

"Fair enough, but just so we're clear—I don't think it counts as forcing someone if the other person needs a little nudge, even if they don't know it themselves."

Chapter 23

By ten in the evening, no one has arrived and I can't help but feel nervous. I've made a huge batch of mea culpa mojitos and plenty of appetizers, not to mention spending the last hour practicing my apology at the table. When there's finally a knock at the door, the first to arrive is Adele. She takes one look at me before kissing my cheek and running her papery-skinned hands up and down my arms. I almost lose it right there.

"Everything will be fine, darling. This too shall pass." She may not have witnessed last night's drama at the bar, but I'm sure Kayla brought her up to speed.

"You're not mad at me then?"

"Of course not. I know your heart. I don't doubt that it's in the right place." She skirts around me on her way to the snacks, leaving me with my feet glued to the floor.

Kayla is next. She gives me a curt nod, but still she looks pissed—really pissed. A suspicious looking Lance arrives, and the last through the door is Kane with Pancho in tow.

"I found him out by the road walking in circles," Kane explains.

"I wasn't sure if I was ready to listen to this *kolohe* talk stink." He stuffs his hands deep into his pockets. I don't know what a *kolohe* is, and I can never tell if it's good or bad when Pancho starts using Hawaiian words. "I'm sorry your car got all busted up like that though—that wasn't right."

"I don't care about the car. Just hear me out, please." I get everyone set up with drinks and small plates, letting them congregate on the little furniture that I have available.

"There's no better place to start than the beginning." I tell them all about my old life, about Silverdale and everything of which I'm not proud. I fill them in on the less-than-savory tactics often employed by my old company, with its high pressure deals and false promises. "I'd go door-to-door instilling excitement across entire neighborhoods about new development projects. There were always carrots to dangle alongside the development—new turf for the soccer fields, an addition to the school, a state-of-the-art playground, or maybe a community dog park—but more often than not, those promises didn't come to life and people were left disappointed. I am, in part, responsible for that."

I take a deep breath before continuing. "Maybe at first, I didn't know what I was getting into myself, but after awhile it became the norm. I took the salary, bonuses, and promotions, and as time went on, I started to feel sick to my stomach. I'd stare out my office window wondering how I got there and how I could get out. It never felt right, and in a way, my marriage ending was a blessing, because it was the catalyst for me to be myself. I promise you that I was never going to take my job back at Silverdale, and I never would. When Dale Sr. sent over the plans, I thought it was an opportunity to see what he'd proposed and how it could be prevented, but I was wrong to keep them to myself. I should've told you from the beginning."

I glance at Kane, who gives me an encouraging nod to continue. "Whether you forgive me or not, I want you to know that I'm committed to fighting this. I know it's unlikely to get anywhere regardless, given the protections that Paia has in place, but I do have a few ideas of my own to discourage the developer himself. I've seen almost every trick in the book when it comes to that man, but what's most important is that you believe me. Do you believe me?"

Kayla is the first to answer. "I reckon that it all looks pretty bad on your part."

"I know it does." I hang my head. "All I'm asking for is another chance. What do you say…will you give me another chance?"

Everyone's eyes turn to watch Pancho. He looks up, wondering why he's suddenly the center of attention. "Oh, okay."

"Okay? That's it?"

"Yeah, that's it. You're still one of us, Red. Now let's put our heads together to figure out how we can kick some *haole* ass." The snacks run out, but I make a new batch of mojitos as we brainstorm.

"Why does this company think they stand a chance at developing Paia? You can't even legally hang a billboard in Maui, so what makes them think they'll have any success with this eyesore of a resort?" Lance asks.

I shake my head. "I can't help but feel like this is my fault—that it's personal, but I might be giving myself too much credit. If the Silver's are known for anything, it's their love of challenge."

Kane smiles. "Well, I say we give them a challenge then."

Pancho agrees to start a petition and Lance volunteers his buddies to hang anti-development signage. I offer to attend the next city hall meeting, and Kane says he'll talk to his contacts at the land preservation society. Since Kayla is stunningly gorgeous and already looks like a spokeswoman, I put her in charge of talking to the local paper and news stations. Last but not least is Adele—when I ask her what part she'd like to play, she just laughs.

"Well, that's easy, darling. I'm the money. I have oodles of it to contribute to the cause in whatever way might be necessary."

Chapter 24

Sometimes it takes a village—one village of super passionate, super smart, kick-ass people who value family and community above all else, people like my beautiful friends and Kane Keo. I mean, who could possibly say no to the sea-blue eyes of semi-pro surfer, Kayla Lee, as she conjured up tears on live TV over the development plans themselves. Pancho was instrumental in rallying the town to affix signage, flyers, and posters. He even managed to procure a petition that must have been signed by three quarters of the island's residents.

I never ended up seeing either of the Dale's—Junior or Senior. They sent along some Silverdale-nobody to oversee the city's discussions instead. The reputational pressure alone was enough to cause the corporation to back down from their plans, which they deemed too expensive in the end. After consulting with the Maui Economic Development Board and the Paia Town Association though, it did seem that the development was likely dead in the water from the start. Maui has seen its share of urbanization over the last decade—with multi-family housing projects and the creation of master-planned communities—and those have resulted in new congestion and infrastructure challenges. Add offshore investing and inflated housing prices to that equation, and it amounts to a lack of affordability for the locals. The county made it very clear to Silverdale, and to the *kama'aina,* that their goal is to preserve the unique culture of the island by ensuring resident access to housing, health services, and local jobs. However, regardless of the deciding factors, the end conclusion was a loss for Silverdale Developments and a win for the people of Paia.

• • •

In celebration of our win, Kayla and Adele have planned an evening beach barbecue at Baldwin. The sun is just starting to set over the skinny palms as I make my way through the butterscotch colored sand, carrying Hawaiian sweet rolls and lomi salmon salad. It's a balmy 87 degrees outside, and across the beach, I see that Lance and Taylor have already arrived. They're manning the grill, as Kayla sets up a table spread of green salad, cut up vegetables, and a mess of different condiments.

A cooler stuffed full of Maui brew gapes open, and the chairs are scattered everywhere. Adele is opening up a package of paper plates while her date, Maui Maude, helps with the utensils and cups. Pancho and his family arrive in my wake, and it's the first time I've met their little girl in person. She's stunning with her long black hair, light eyes, and naturally red lips. The pride shining in Pancho's eyes is hard to miss.

"Melia, this is Ashley. Say hello."

"Hello," she says shyly, tucking her hair behind her ears in a gesture so sweet and innocent that my heart nearly bursts.

"It's so nice to finally meet you! I've heard a lot about you from your dad."

She gives him a look, as if to say, "What have you been telling people?" before politely excusing herself to play in the waves.

"The little grommet has the right idea." Kayla comes over to hug Pancho and Keiko. "Nice swell today."

"Winter swell," Pancho adds, nodding. The waves don't look particularly high, but this spot is usually referred to as the baby beach. I guess any amount of waves is cause for excitement.

"Perfect swell for beginners." Kayla waggles her eyebrows at me. "The surf along the east shore will be three to six feet today, with occasional higher sets in between."

I bite my lip and gaze out at the ocean. I've been dying to try, but Kane is so adamant that I shouldn't. Still, I wonder if surfing will bring me closer to him. Surfing is something he once loved and thought about all the time. While I appreciate his concern, I know he's overprotective. Kayla is a bonafide professional surfer and I'd be in good hands. Besides, he'll probably be stuck at the bar late tonight. He told me not to expect him anyway, and what he doesn't know won't hurt him.

"Okay, after we eat, I'll give it a try."

Kayla hoots and claps her hands together. "I'll be with you the whole time."

I laugh. "You better be!"

Lance shouts happily at us from the grill. "Get those beautiful butts over here for some burgers and dogs!"

We load up our plates and make a semi-circle with our beach chairs and blankets, eating and chatting together. Lance puts on the Maytals song "Pressure Drop."

"Turn it up loud!" Pancho shouts through a mouthful of burger and everyone laughs.

Adele stands up and taps her plastic wine glass with a plastic fork. "I'd like to make a toast—to my darling Ashley, for her work in ensuring that Paia remains a slice of heaven for years to come. Ashley, you may have started out as a mainlander, as many of us do, but you were never an outsider to me. You are one of us—you're family—and we love you. To Ashley!" She raises her glass to the echo of cheers.

Happy tears well in my eyes, beginning to roll down my cheeks. "Thank you," I manage to squeak.

Kayla rolls her eyes, but she's smiling. "You *would* cry. You're such a *sook*."

"Also," Adele interjects, "on an equally happy note, I'd also like to toast to my darling, Kayla Lee, who has been featured in this year's Hawaiian Surf Babe Calendar." Adele unearths a package from her beach bag and waves it haughtily over her head. "I just got my hands on one of the first copies, so raise your glasses for Miss July!"

Almost everybody cheers, except Taylor, who stands to the side with a scowl on his face. Adele passes around the calendar and we all peek at Kayla's page. She looks stunning in her cropped Roxy rash guard and white string-bikini bottoms. She balances a surfboard on one arm while gazing over her shoulder, her best asset jutting out on display. Man, Kayla is lucky to have a perfectly sculpted butt. I'd die for such a high and tight toosh like hers, though I'm sure surfing has helped it along. Lance whistles at Miss July while Keiko compliments her beauty, but when the calendar lands in Taylor's hands, he folds it closed with a sour look on his face.

"Something about my ass cheeks offend you, Akana?" Kayla says.

"No, there's just a lot of ass cheek to see."

The group quiets down, and it's Pancho that gives him a hard look. "What of it, *bruddah*? Our girl here is a beauty. She should be proud of who she is."

"And if it was Melia?" Taylor challenges, but Pancho just huffs out a laugh.

"I'd be proud of her, too. Melia is a beautiful spirit, and I always want her to feel proud and comfortable in her body. Her beauty shouldn't be defined by other people."

It's one of the sincerest and wisest things I've ever heard from Pancho, and naturally it makes me love him all the more. However, Taylor's response is to stuff the calendar in his bag and mutter something unintelligible under his breath.

"Excuse me, but that's my copy," Adele says.

"I'll buy you another," Taylor growls, getting to his feet and stalking off down the beach.

I look at Kayla, who just shrugs, so we carry on with our meals. When it comes time to pack up though, Kayla is all over me again.

"Ready to give Maui surf a try, city girl?"

Lance sidles up behind us. "I'll paddle out with you for support, but these are baby waves anyways. You'll be fine."

Kayla lends me her board and rash guard, but the top is far from fitting over my generous boobs. We practice balancing on dry land for a while, and I get pretty good at standing up. Since I have her treasured board, Kayla wades waist deep into the water once it's finally time to paddle out. Lance goes ahead of me, and I study his movements as he watches a wave approach and gets up on it with ease. I watch him a few more times until I feel ready, waving my arms above my head to let Kayla know that I'm about to give it a try.

I fail spectacularly on my first go, wind-milling my arms around as the board flies into the air and sends me crashing back into the waves. I grab ahold of it again and paddle out beyond the break, but the second time isn't much better. I manage to stay upright on the board for about ten seconds, stumbling at the last minute and pitching forward. I'm laughing so hard that my sides still ache when Kayla high-fives me.

"Good on ya! I have to say, San Fran, that was a pretty decent first effort." It's the highest compliment she could've paid me, and I bask in it for a moment. "You done girl?"

I shake my head. "Not even close. A few more please?"

We head back out, and next time I manage to stay up until the wave fizzles out beneath me. It's such a rush, as if I'm walking on air. Lance gives me a wave of approval and paddles out further. I notice the sun making its descent in the sky, leaving only the burnt orange-pink streaks of another Maui evening across the landscape. On the beach, I think I see Kane emerge from the parking lot, no doubt having caught wind of my big moment.

"One more!" I shout toward Kayla, waving my arms like a madwoman.

I paddle out further and the biggest wave I've seen all day rolls towards the shore. I paddle forward as hard as possible as the wave begins to crest, but I don't make it in time. Instead the wave crashes into me, yanking the board from my hands and sending it vertically into the air. I inhale a mouthful of water as I go down, sputtering to the surface just in time to see the board slam into me. It smacks me in the head so hard that I see actual stars for a split second, and then everything goes black.

When I come to, I'm underwater and sinking fast. I try to move my arms but they feel sluggish, as if they're made of stone. My lungs are burning and my eyelids feel heavy. Just then, I see a flash of black above me, followed by a hot flash of white, before two strong arms appear before my eyes. One clamps over my mouth and nose, and the other encircles my chest and pulls me up by the armpits. It feels like an out-of-body experience. His arms pull me from the water and onto the beach. Familiar warm lips connect with mine in what feels like a kiss, at first, but it's too brief. The next thing I know, I'm choking up a mouthful of water, gagging as the saltiness pours from my lungs and onto the sand.

My vision is blurry and I close my eyes. When I open them again, I see Kane's face hovering above mine. I try to smile but my lips are stiff. "Kane," I croak out, taking in his dripping wet hair, all slicked back from his face. His white t-shirt clings to his massive chest like a second skin. In that moment, I think he's too beautiful—for me or for anyone—like a hero in one of those romance novels I devoured on the plane ride from San Fran. His eyes look all wrong though: wild, horrified, and drilling holes into my forehead. He repeats my name like a broken record while I struggle to sit up.

"Kane." I say his name again, but his face is deathly pale. He gets up from his knees and runs a pair of shaking hands through his wet volcanic hair, flitting his eyes frantically around the beach. I scan the beach and see my friends staring at us with similar expressions of worry on their faces, none of which I understand. Kayla is on the phone beside a stricken Adele, who waits with a mountain of towels in her arms.

"Kane?" His name comes out like a question this time, as his troubled but lovely hazel eyes lock into mine.

He opens and closes his mouth without speaking, reminding me of a fish out of water. Finally he speaks. "I'm sorry, I can't, Ashley. I just…I can't."

He stumbles backwards and turns to walk away from me. His wet jeans are molded against his legs as he runs at full speed toward the parking lot. Adele wraps a towel around my shoulders while Lance holds a bottle of water up to my lips.

"Ambulance is on its way," Kayla says quietly, kneeling down to rub my back. I look at Pancho with Melia in his arms. She appears to be crying from the way her back trembles.

"You were under a long time before he got to you. You gave us a big scare," Lance explains, but his voice sounds shaky and unsure.

"I was?" My own voice is ripe with confusion—disoriented beyond belief—and it frightens me to my core.

"I tried to find you," Lance adds. "Kayla swam out, too, but Kane saw right away; he knew. He found the exact spot you went down, almost as if you were wearing a beacon."

"But where did he go? Where's Kane?"

"I don't know, but you're safe now. We're here and we've got you," he says.

I should be comforted by my friends rallying to help me, but the only thought running through my mind is that Kane left me. I almost drowned; he saved me and then ran away as if he couldn't face the rest. When the ambulance arrives to take my vitals, I refuse their offer to escort me to the hospital. They make me sign a waiver releasing myself instead. Kane doesn't return and Taylor is nowhere to be found, but everyone else sticks around to see if I'm alright.

Adele and Kayla offer to take me back to their place, but I insist that I'm fine to drive. Other than a small cut on my forehead and a sore throat, I feel fine—and very lucky. I drive around for awhile until the navy blue sky fades to black, and when I finally feel ready to head back home, the first thing I see is Kane's Jeep parked at a forty five degree angle in the driveway. I don't know why I'm nervous to see him now, but his reaction has me reeling. I don't know whether to be angry or scared or both. I park and walk straight over to Kane's place with my head held high, but it's Taylor who intercepts me when he answers the door.

"He doesn't want to see you, Ashley." Exhaustion spills from his voice.

"I don't care what he wants. He doesn't get to make that decision."

"It isn't pretty right now." He says, kind of cryptically, but I ignore the comment and press onwards.

"What gives him the right to up and leave me like that?"

"It's not about entitlement, Ashley, you know that. It's just a reaction. I haven't seen him this bad since…" He trails off.

"Since the big thing that he refuses to talk about happened, yeah, I get it. But I'm coming in whether you like it or not."

Taylor sags his weight against the door. "No point in coming inside. He's out back."

I don't even say goodbye before marching straight through the garden and onto the back lawn. There are no lights on inside, so I don't see him hunched over on the ground at first, but when the moonlight hits him, I get the full effect. He's on his knees, collapsed in the middle of the concrete filled pool. I can hear him softly crying. I approach him one step at a time, moving across the uneven stone until I'm close enough to sink down onto my knees beside him.

"Go away," he mumbles, swinging a half empty bottle of Grey Goose around in a circle.

"No."

"I said go away!" He screams, louder than I've heard him yell before, but his words are slurred, no doubt from the vodka.

"I won't, not until you give me some answers."

"You want answers?" He laughs before taking a swig from the bottle. "I got answers. They were right."

"Who was right?"

"All of them." He answers with a riddle again. "When they said it."

"Right about what? Said what?"

"That I killed my family. It's true." He hiccups back a sob. "It's true that I killed them. They are dead because of me."

Chapter 25

For a brief moment, I'm struck speechless, a thousand thoughts swirling around inside my head. I mean, logically, I know that he can't mean what he's saying. I remind myself that he's distraught and drunk and his words can't be trusted. I'm about to ask him more, but he saves me the trouble.

"We were always fighting about something—his mother and I. One thing or another. We were so wrong for each other from the beginning, but we were both too stubborn and loyal to do anything about it. Maybe if we had…" He stares into the distance, lost in thought.

"Your wife you mean?"

"Anna." He nods his head. "That time, we were fighting about money. She wanted to renovate the kitchen again. She was always so bored, always looking for the next thing to fill her up. I swear he was right at her side when we were in the kitchen. Kaiden grew up at the beach. I had him on a surfboard when he was one-year-old; he knew the water."

My stomach drops, and I immediately know where this is going. I make a move to touch and comfort him, but he just shrugs me off.

"Somehow he managed to slip under the pool cover, and because of that, it took time to find him—longer than it should have. There was no screaming, no splashing, no noise. He was just there and then he wasn't…and it's all my fault." With those last words, he cries so hard that I struggle to understand what he's saying.

"What kind of father lets that happen right under his nose?"

"I don't think that's a fair question to ask."

He holds up a hand to silence me. "Do you know, Ashley Walsh, that it only takes about four minutes for irreversible brain damage to happen when you're underwater?" He falls back against the rough concrete, breathing in tune with the heavy rhythm of the crashing sea. "And drowning, let me tell you, that's not something you want to Google. It's supposed to be the worst kind of death. I read one article that called it intolerable anguish. When I close my eyes, I try to imagine how he felt under that pool cover, how scared he must have been while his tiny lungs filled with water and his body slowly started to shut down. The whole time, his mom and I were upstairs bitching about granite countertops."

"They say you have a rescue window of sixty seconds. One fucking minute to save a life!" He roars, sitting up in a flash. "I know what you're thinking…" He points a finger at me. "You're thinking that sixty seconds sounds short, but it's not short. Day after day, I watch the clock and reflect on the number of seconds in one minute, and every single day I'm reminded of what a fucking failure I am as a man—as a human being—for not being able to save my son."

I let the silence stretch between us; his labored breathing is the only sound filling the space. "So you plan on torturing yourself forever? This eternal purgatory where you count down the seconds and push people away?" He ignores me entirely, fixating his gaze on the ocean.

"I remember that day like it was yesterday. The temperature outside, the smell of the ocean, the dirty streaks on the windows from his sweaty little palms, the red shirt he was wearing when I fished him out of the pool. I am forever a prisoner of that day. You don't understand; I'll never really be here, not fully, because I'm always there. It's where I deserve to be."

"But your son isn't there anymore, he's not a prisoner to that day, and your wife isn't either," I say, softly. "I don't know what you believe when it comes to the afterlife—most days I don't even know what I believe—but I do believe that they would've moved on from that horrible day. Wouldn't they want you to live in the present, learning day-by-day to watch the clock a little less?"

"No one should ever have to bury their child."

I don't respond, because he's right; I don't know what it feels like. What I do know is that he stands before me in absolute agony, and I'll do anything to help him.

"Thank you for telling me," I whisper.

"Now that you know what kind of monster I am, it's time to run back home." He laughs harshly, and I don't miss the crazed look in his eyes—it's wild and unleashed, like a man spiraling out of control.

"I'm not going anywhere." I say, jutting out my chin. "This is my home now."

"No, it's not," he snaps. "Don't you understand? I can't be with you—not now, not ever. I can't even look at you anymore. When I pulled you from the water today, blue-lipped and barely breathing, I realized something."

"Realized what?" I ask, though I'm afraid of his answer.

"That I'm going to end up killing you too."

"That's ridiculous, Kane. You can't put today on yourself. It was an accident! I went surfing—"

"Exactly!" He shouts. "You did something dangerous that I didn't want for you, putting your whole life in jeopardy."

"It was just surfing! Everybody surfs here, and if I'm not mistaken, you used to surf as well."

"You're missing the point." He moans and rubs a big hand across his tear-stained face. "I can't stop you from doing any of that stuff, not any more than I can control the waves, but there are too few seconds in a minute. I will always worry about you.

"Let me worry about me, Kane, but let's figure this out together."

"Don't you get it, Ashley? I don't want to figure it out!" He shouts. "I can't love you. Being with you gives me constant anxiety, and I don't want to live like that. Caring about you makes the fear so much worse."

I reach forwards and place my hand on his arm. "You don't know what you're saying, Kane. Look at me, please. I love you." The words rush out of my mouth, and he yanks his arm away like my hand is on fire.

"Go home, Ashley."

"Please, Kane," I beg, as my own tears filter down my cheeks. "Please listen to me. I love you."

He slowly gets to his feet, swaying upright and holding the now empty bottle of vodka over his head. "Go home!" He screams, almost frantic. "Get away from me!" He slams the bottle onto the concrete, where it explodes and shatters in time with my heart.

His chest rises and falls as he stares at the fragments all over the rough concrete. I let my tears fall freely now. I need to get to my feet, but I feel paralyzed. He glances over to catch me crying and winces.

"Just go. I'm done. This is done." He sounds completely broken, as if every ounce of fight already left his body.

I rise onto my wobbly legs and carry myself with as much dignity as possible back over the grass, heading in the direction of my suite. The porch light is still on, casting a welcoming light to guide me home. As I step inside, I fight the overwhelming urge to break down. I fight the urge to yell and scream and cry and throw things until there's nothing left of the little cottage but remnants of my once-upon-a-time life here. As much as I want to fall apart, I know I can't do that right now. Instead, I take a deep breath and do the next best thing possible right then.

I start to pack.

Chapter 26

I putter around my tiny apartment in my best attempt at cleaning up before the ladies arrive. I toss the built-up pile of shoes into the closet by the front door. I remove a stack of bills and magazines from the hallway table. I don't have much furniture—let's face it, the space isn't large—but the small sofa and vintage wooden coffee table that I acquired at a garage sale are decent enough. I light my coconut-milk-mango candles, putting out some wine glasses and side plates for my homemade pupus. The kitchen in my Kahului condo is almost non-existent, but as with a lot of things lately, I've learned to make it work.

The one-bedroom space isn't all that bad; in fact, it's cute, cozy, and conveniently close to everything, including the beach. It's also near the university and seems to be priced for students. Every time I run into a new neighbor, I feel a hundred years old. I would've preferred to stay in Paia, but there were very few rentals available and even fewer jobs. With everything that went down between Kane and me, it just felt a little too close. I miss Salty's—I miss cooking there and I miss my friends—but if I'm honest with myself, mostly I just miss Kane.

He hasn't called, texted, or visited, and I know he won't. One thing I learned about Kane very early on is that he doesn't operate ambiguously. He always made his feelings crystal clear. When Pancho visited me with his wife and daughter, at the restaurant where I'm working in Lahaina, he hinted that Kane was in really rough shape, but there's nothing I can do if he doesn't want me around. I hear a knock at the door just as I'm setting out the sea salt caramel popcorn. Adele doesn't wait for me to answer; she just lets herself in, making me wonder why she bothers to knock at all.

"Kayla is parking." She breezes inside and kisses both of my cheeks.

By some miracle, we've actually managed to stick with our weekly wine and movie dates. Maui Maude joined us for the first one, but Adele later announced that they were no longer together. She decided that she liked penis infinitely more.

"Really?" That was my response, after spitting a mouthful of California Chardonnay all over the floor.

"Really." She'd nodded sagely. "Even shriveled old ones. Turns out, I'm still a fan."

Ever since, we've kept movie night to just us three. We rotate our viewing selection every week. Tonight is my pick, and I've chosen *Blue Hawaii* because I've never seen it. Kayla bursts in with her surfboard under her arm, banging it against the hall table within two seconds of walking inside.

"What?" She says, innocently, as I give her a look. "I'm not leaving it down there with all that riffraff running around."

"What took you so long?" Adele scolds.

She snorts. "Have you seen all the frat boys around here? I got asked for my number twice on the walk up." She rolls her eyes, but I'm not surprised. Her catalogue-looks, combined with that piss-right-off attitude, send guys after her like lost little puppies. "You need to move." She places her board against the wall, slamming the door on her own perfect ass.

"And go where?" I shrug. "Besides, it's close to my new job."

Kayla shakes her head. "You got another job?"

"What job?" Adele ventures.

"It's just a temp job, mostly office administration and general reception, but it'll pay the bills.

For some reason, Adele seems relieved by this news. "Nothing serious then." She nods her approval—weird.

Kayla collapses onto the sofa, snagging the DVD case from my hands. "Blue Hawaii? Really?"

"Come on, musical interludes and Technicolor—it's got to be great, right? What's not to love?"

"How about the fakest surfing scenes ever made," she grumbles. "You do realize that Elvis sings about cheating on his girlfriend like five minutes into the movie?"

I snatch the DVD case back from her and flip it over in my hands. "Well...hell."

"He also spanks a teenage girl, who he's supposed to be chaperoning."

"Okay, forget it. I don't even want to know." I drop the case on the coffee table, recalling my last one-night-stand in San Fran. It was the Blue Hawaii poster that inspired my move to Hawaii.

Her voice is smug as she dips into the popcorn. "You're the one that picked it."

Adele takes the seat beside the window, but only after pouring herself a sizable glass of white wine. She holds her glass by the stem and raises it in the air.

"To friendship, family, and my two girls—the daughters I always wanted."

I feel a lump forming in my throat, threatening to bring me to tears. I've shed too many tears over the last while, so I chase away the feeling with a big swig of wine.

"Are you happy here?" Kayla asks.

I'm surprised by the question, as Kayla isn't typically one to prod. "As happy as I can be, I guess." I mumble and fiddle with a lock of my hair.

"You look thinner than last week." Adele gives me the once-over. "Are you eating well?"

I huff out a dramatic sigh. "Can we not talk about me, please? You guys walk on the same egg shells every week, and I get it—I'm sad and lonely. I don't sleep or have an appetite. I'm a goddamn mess and I get it, so can we please just watch the movie?" I pick up the remote to hit play, but Kayla pries it from my hand.

"Are you going to tell her, or do I have to?" She gives Adele a dark look.

"Tell me what?" I say, exasperated.

"I was going to ease into it, but Kayla here is no more tactful than an elephant, so I have no choice anymore. Ashley, my dear, we're not here to watch a movie tonight."

"You're not?" I say, obviously confused.

"We're here to bring you home."

"Home?"

"Kane wants to see you." She mutters under her breath.

"No."

"He said you'd say that," Adele says with a chuckle.

"No shit," I bark back.

"My stubborn girl." Adele smiles.

"I love it when you swear," Kayla adds, nodding her approval.

"I'm not going back there. Kane made it very clear that he doesn't want anything to do with me."

Adele stands and places her hands on her hips. "Now you listen up, darling, the only thing Kane Keo made clear is that he's scared, vulnerable, and so deeply in love with you that he doesn't know what to do with his feelings."

"He never said he loved me," I challenge. "Not once."

"Does he really need to? Be honest with yourself. You know he loves you because you saw it in every look and gesture."

"If that's true, why not just say it?" I bark back, letting my voice crescendo.

Kayla clears her throat. "Because he's terrified of losing you, too, and being right back where he started—gutted and alone." Her words surprise me, because I don't think I've ever heard her defend Kane.

"So just like that, he told you to come and collect me like some kind of object? He didn't even bother to show up here himself?" The mere mention of Kane has my heart pounding, but I'm positively seething from the highhandedness of it all.

"It isn't at all like that, darling. He didn't come because he needed to prepare. He has something he wants to show you, so please do give him a chance."

After a brief standoff, I begrudgingly agree to go, but I draw the line at changing my clothes or doing my hair. I stay in my baggy Peter Tosh t-shirt and sweat-shorts, not even bothering to put on a bra. I throw a baseball cap over my messy hair, causing Adele to shake her head in disapproval as I reach the door.

"What?" I snap, and she rolls her eyes. Sometimes it feels like she's mothering me, and not in a good way.

"Men are visual creatures, darling."

"They're creatures alright," Kayla says under her breath. At that, I can't help but laugh.

"Trust me, Adele, the only visual I want to bestow upon Kane Keo is me giving him the middle finger for dragging me back to Paia for some demonstration. If he doesn't like how I look, well, he can go ahead and eat my sweat-shorts."

She sighs heavily, but I see a flicker of amusement on her face. "Come on then," Adele says, shooing us both out the door.

I sit in the backseat with my arms crossed the whole ride there. As the familiar streets of Paia Town come into view, my stomach starts to churn. It's a strange mixture of longing and fear; it feels simultaneously wrong and right to be back, but even with the anxiety building in my chest, I can't deny that it feels like home. It's crazy how quickly this place became a part of me—and even if it's the last time I'm here, I know that Paia played a big part in helping me heal. Adele pulls her Land Rover to a stop in front of Salty's. It looks the same as always, with its hanging bamboo sign and vibrant green paint, but why wouldn't it? It's only been a month, even if it felt like years.

What I'm not prepared for is the new storefront just adjacent to Salty's. It looks like a different business, lit up and glowing on the inside, has recently taken over the space. I undo my seatbelt and slide from the car, as if somehow magnetically pulled towards the vibrant interior. I don't even glance back at Kayla or Adele as I peer though that big front window. There's no one inside right now, but it looks like a small restaurant with about a dozen tables. The décor is what I'd called *west coast chic*, all white and chrome with red accents, and big brushed stainless steel pendant lights decorating the ceiling. There's a big chalkboard menu above the open counter with only two words scrawled across the center: *Laki Maika'i.*

I read the words aloud as Adele approaches from behind. "It means *good luck*," she says.

"Why?"

"Why does it mean good luck?"

"No, why is this place even here?"

Adele's gaze shifts over my shoulder. "You'll have to ask him that."

I turn around slowly, only to see Kane watching me through the window, his big hulking frame filling most of the cozy space. As I watch him through the glass, it feels like my feet are frozen to the ground. Do I go in? I know that I don't have to; I could drive off in Adele's car and never look back at this place again, but the last time a man hurt me, I ran. It might have been the right move with Dale, but I'm stronger than that now. I have no choice but to face whatever this is, and to face him, even if that simply means goodbye.

A quaint-sounding bell jingles as I open the door to the restaurant. He doesn't move an inch from where he's standing, but his eyes follow my every move. I take it all in. Everything is more incredible up close. The walls are lined with red-framed black and white photos of various landmarks, and I do a double take when I notice they're all of San Francisco: The Golden Gate Bridge, The Palace of Fine Arts, Fisherman's Wharf, Chinatown. I take a quick inventory of the space before coming to a complete halt before Kane.

"You summoned me?"

He speaks with a familiar huskiness. "You're so beautiful."

I snort in response. "Hardly."

He lifts his arms and pulls the baseball cap off my head, tossing it onto the nearby table. I can only imagine how my hair looks right now. He tries to smooth his hands over my red locks, but I slap him away.

"Why am I here, Kane?" His golden skin looks paler than usual, and I notice black circles under his eyes.

"Because I love you."

My jaw drops. It seldom happens that I can't find the words to express my thoughts, but this is one such moment.

"I'm sorry, I should have told you sooner. I was so cruel to you that night. You deserve more. I told you from the beginning: I'm not good at the other stuff, and that hasn't changed. Look at me, Ashley, I'm a mess, but I know that I love you. I have loved you for awhile."

"You're not a mess."

"I am." He laughs without any humor. "I let go of the only person who made me feel happy in the last seven years, who made me feel alive again. I let go of you and me."

I tilt my head. "Why did you let me go, Kane?"

"As much as I love you—and I do, Ashley—I don't even know what that means anymore. I don't know how to love anymore, at least not in the right way."

"I don't think there's supposed to be a right way, Kane."

He shakes his head. "My past will always be there. My guilt is ugly and permanent; even if it lessens, it won't go away. I'll never be casual with you. If you're mine, you're mine, and I know how I am sometimes. If you think me telling you to put on sunscreen and stay out of the water is bad, that's just the tip of iceberg, Ashley. Protecting you—keeping you safe and knowing you're going to be okay—is everything to me. The way I feel…I guess I'm worried it will just get more intense with you."

His shoulders sag as he finishes, and I take a deep breath. "I understand."

"Do you?"

"I do, and I'm okay with it."

He shakes his head. "You can't be."

"But I am." I wrap my hand around his wrist and give it a little tug. It's so large that my fingers hardly make it all the way around.

"So you love me?" I say, feeling a little lightheaded. "Kane Keo loves me…but I repeat, why did you bring me here?"

He looks down at the hand around his wrist, then up at me. "This place is for you. It's all for you. Even if you don't want to be with me, you belong in Paia. You're one of us now and whatever's happening between us doesn't change that. This restaurant is yours."

"You can't give me a restaurant!" I shout, stumbling backwards.

"I just did. You make beautiful food—food that makes people happy—so keep doing that. It's good for Salty's."

"But is it good for you?" I say, my grip tightening on his wrist. He steps closer and brings my arms around his neck, until I'm stretching up on my tiptoes. His answer is a deep, unrelenting kiss. The soft lips that I've missed so much work in rhythm against mine, searing this moment into my brain for eternity. His tongue gains entrance into my mouth and I moan in response, but when I try to deepen the kiss, he pulls back and staggers for breath.

"You *are* good for me, Ashley, even if the opposite isn't true. I promise I'll try every damn day to be better for you."

"Kane..." I start, but he silences me with a kiss before pressing onwards with his speech.

"I am trying. I'm seeing someone that Taylor recommended—a head-shrinker. I wasn't too sure about the idea. He's this long-haired, draft-dodging hippie, but it's not all that butterflies and rainbow shit—he tells it like it is."

"So you like him then?" I say, grinning.

"I like him." He chuckles, but the laughter dies in his throat. He skims his hands up my sides and around my back.

"Are you not wearing a bra?" He groans out.

I shrug. "I didn't exactly have time to prepare for this little meeting."

Before I can say anything more, he whips off my t-shirt and throws it onto the floor. The cool breeze from the air conditioning hits my bare breasts and my nipples instantly pebble.

"Kane!" I shout, but he doesn't hesitate, dropping his head and capturing one of my ready nipples in his mouth. My hips jerk forward as I try to form words.

"Everyone can see inside." I moan as he switches his attention to my other nipple.

"Fuck them," he whispers, licking a path down the valley of my breasts. "No one's out there anyways. I need to have you right now. It's been over a month since I've been inside of you and I'm losing my mind."

He licks around my navel and starts tugging down my sweat-shorts. "I am going to fuck you so hard, Ashley."

"That's romantic," I tease, but his words make me melt.

"Today isn't about romance, *Lani*, I can promise you that. Today is about being so deep inside of you that I become part of you. I want you screaming my name over and over, until you remember where you belong."

Warmth floods through my veins with every word he speaks, making me dizzy on my feet. "I won't forget," I say, shakily.

"Let me remind you anyway—just to be sure." He smiles at me in a predatory way and tugs off my shorts, swearing when he notices that I'm not wearing anything underneath them.

"No underwear either? Fuck woman." Then his mouth is on mine, working its magic. I don't stifle the cries escaping from my lips, despite that my legs are going to give out at any moment.

I come so intensely that I actually see black spots along the edges of my vision. I have to grab onto his silky brown hair for support, as his tongue continues to probe my sensitive flesh. I ride out the aftershocks and once he seems satisfied, he pulls me down to the floor. He doesn't speak as he sheds his clothing and enters me, stretching me to the brink again.

"Are you okay?" His voice strains, but I can only nod.

"I love you, Ashley Walsh. I'm sorry for everything that I put you through, and I'm never letting you go."

He pulls out halfway and slams back inside me, tearing a scream from my throat. He rocks into me with a kind of reckless abandon, his eyes heavy-lidded and his big hands curling around my thighs to keep me in place. He looks so fierce, wild, and beautiful that I'm speechless. His deep hazel eyes alight with passion, and I watch the pectoral muscles of his wide tanned chest jump up every time he drives into me. When he nears release, he lets out an animalistic roar and collapses on the floor beside me. The restaurant is quiet, apart from the mingled sound of our overlapping breath.

Kane props himself up on one elbow and looks into my eyes. "I am sorry."

"Sex like that isn't something to apologize for…" I answer with my eyes shut, stretching my arms above my head.

"Ashley, look at me." I open my eyes and give him my complete attention. "I'm sorry for everything I said to you.

I'm sorry for what you saw. It's been a long time since I've gone to that place in my head."

"Don't be sorry. Your pain is part of you, but so are your memories. That life—it's still your life. It's not about forgetting or apologizing; it's about learning to live with what happened, and to keep on living. I think, in a completely different way, I finally understand that for myself as well. What I had with Dale, my life in San Francisco, it's not something I can erase or forget about, because whatever I endured brought me to here and now."

He lies back against the floor and drapes me over his chest. "When did you get so wise?"

I'm not sure if he's teasing me, so I ignore his comment and feather a trail of kisses down his chest. "I love you, Kane, more than you'll ever know—but I do have one more question."

"Anything. Ask me anything you want."

"How did you get a whole restaurant built in one month…in Paia, at that?" This obviously isn't the question he was expecting, because he looks relieved and laughs out loud.

"Honestly? I had to call in every damn favor I had left on this island, and I still didn't get it all done. The sign out front isn't up yet, but it will be soon."

"The sign?" I say, my mind going to the words on the chalkboard.

"*Laki maikaʻi.*" He looks uncharacteristically shy as he translates the phrase. "It means good luck."

"Adele told me, but why good luck?" I ask.

He rubs his stubby cheek against mine, and I feel the beginnings of a new beard covering his chin. "Because that's exactly what you are to me."

There are no words to convey how much this gesture means, so I simply seal my lips over Kane's. His jaw goes slack as I pull away, and once again, I feel his length twitching against my stomach. "But we've already christened the floor," I say, wriggling against his hardness.

"Oh, that was just a little *pupu*, and the main course is yet to come. I'm going to feast on you all night." He inhales a deep breath and surprises me with his next words.

"I want you to live, work, and be with me forever."

I suck in a breath of fresh air. "You want me to move in with you?"

He gives me a sidelong look. "There is no other option."

"I have a place in town," I argue. "Maybe it's too soon. I could try and get a place in Paia?"

"No, *lani,* your place is right here in my arms.

Epilogue

"I look bloated." I can't help but frown upon inspecting the profile of my torso in the full-length mirror.

Adele waves a dismissive hand in the air. "You look beautiful."

"You look knocked up," Kayla snorts.

Adele gives my bridesmaid—one of two—a disapproving look. "Not helpful, darling."

Kayla looks stunning, of course, in the knee-length blush-colored dress that she picked out herself. Jamie opted for a full-length gown in the same shade, presenting as a tiny, exotic goddess with peach-colored flowers in her hair.

"I'm not that pregnant, am I?" I do my best to smooth back the loose curls framing my face.

"You definitely don't look that pregnant," Jamie reassures me, but meanwhile Kayla has a huge grin spread across her face.

"Whatever you want to tell yourself," she says.

In truth, I'm only about four months pregnant and not showing much yet, but the bloating makes it clear that things are getting real. It turns out that mine and Kane's christening of the newly minted restaurant floor served up *more* than just orgasms. It wasn't what either of us expected, and I take responsibility for being forgetful with the pill, but after enduring multiple rounds of fertility treatments with Dale, an unplanned pregnancy didn't exactly seem in the cards. When I peed on the stick, I nearly lost my mind with worry, fearing his reaction. What if he thought that I intended to replace Kaiden? Nothing and no one could replace his son, nor the memories Kane carries of him. I knew that, and it wasn't easy for Kane to learn that I was *hapai*.

It took him a while to come to terms with the news, which felt at odds with my joy. It's so strange to feel guilty and elated at the same time, but that's the space I lived in for a while. Eventually he came around, and I know deep down that he's excited. The hardest part has been managing his anxiety. He hovers around me like a helicopter-parent, monitoring my every move. Right from the start, he hasn't wanted me running around, driving the car, or even putting away groceries in the kitchen.

While I understand the source of his fear, it hasn't been easy. One moment, Kane is blissfully building a crib for our new arrival, and the next he's tearful in my arms, wondering why he deserves this second chance. I love Kane though. His journey is my journey and we'll find a way through it together. Last week, I signed the divorce papers and haven't heard a word from Dale since. However, I did hear from Terry, my old assistant, that Dale is now dating Maggie, my former spin partner from accounting. I'm happy for him; I really am. Everyone deserves to find their one true love.

I sigh and twirl around once in my floor-length lavender gown. It's not exactly traditional, with low-cut sides and a deep-set V-neck, but we didn't exactly go about things traditionally either. The gown has a beautiful wrap around the front and elegant slip along the side, and the style is a thousand times more *me* than that poufy princess number I wore with Dale. Most importantly, it's loose enough that my little bump isn't too distracting.

Adele places the *Haku Lei*—a beautiful crown of orchids—atop my head, and I notice her eyes watering as she steps back. "Thank you, Adele," I say, touching the crown gently. "And thank you for agreeing to walk me down the aisle."

When Adele heard that my parents weren't coming for the wedding, she was the first person to offer her services. My parents were about as supportive as I'd anticipated, given that I'm 2500 miles away and marrying some man they've never met. Still, they sent along their well wishes with a nice card and a personal check for $500.

Adele takes my cold hands in her warm, well-weathered ones, giving me a good squeeze. "I wouldn't have it any other way. You're as much my daughter as if I'd given birth to you myself."

"Not a visual I need right now," Kayla says, but her voice betrays her with trembling.

"Enough sniveling, girls. We have a wedding to get to."

I find myself in a daze on the ride to Baldwin Beach, staring out the windows as Jamie and Kayla bicker non-stop. I think I've probably created a monster by introducing the two of them, but I can't help but smile at how similar they are. The sun is setting when I step barefoot from the car. It's a short walk to the stretch of beach where my friends and loved ones are seated on the sand. A line of torches lights a path towards the clear blue water, and I catch a glimpse of Kane at the end of the aisle, head down with his strong hands clasped together. He's wearing a short-sleeve white button-down shirt, which shows off his beautiful olive skin.

Pancho smiles when he sees me, beginning to strum his ukulele, an instrument that I didn't even know he played. He starts to sing Bob Marley's "High Tide, Low Tide" and his low, soulful voice sends chills up my spine. Just then, Kayla steps ahead of me and starts down the path, followed immediately by Jamie.

"Are you ready, darling?" Adele asks, and I give her a little nod.

"Absolutely." I stare at the cloudless sky, where a gorgeous orange-pink sunset fades to dusk. I look back down to see Lance smiling at me beside Kane. Much to my surprise, Lance was a licensed Minister all this time—not one of those internet ministers but an actual student of theology.

My heartbeat picks up as I get closer. Kane's eyes flash and lock with mine, drinking me in from head to toe. We don't break eye contact as I walk down the aisle, and the look on his face wipes away my nerves. With my last few steps, it actually feels like I'm floating. As soon as Adele releases my arm, Kane pulls me against his chest and kisses me passionately, earning him a laugh from the small crowd.

"I think that part comes after," Lance says, clearly amused.

"Before, during, after…" Kane trails off. "Just try and stop me, Lance." As always, time seems to stop when I'm near Kane, the world blurring around me like a dream. "Lani, you know I'm not great with words, but words aren't enough to explain what you mean to me anyways. You saved my life, and I'm going to spend the rest of that life cherishing yours. You are so beautiful, inside and out, and yet somehow you're mine. I love you."

I don't try to wipe away the tears staining my cheeks, instead struggling for words. "I was empty and you made me whole, Kane Keo. You helped me find my passion and supported me in doing what I love. You love without expectation. You are so selfless and so kind. You let me be me, even when it's hard for you. You make me feel safe, beautiful, valued, and heard. I don't know how I lived my life without you."

Lance pronounces us man and wife, and Kane lifts me into his arms and kisses me. At the same time, the sun dips below the horizon, the sky flashing an intense emerald green. Our friends get to their feet and cheer, before swarming us with breath-stealing hugs. After he's had enough attention, Kane scoops me into his arms and carries me to his Jeep. He sets me down on the passenger seat and buckles me in with great care, trying not to wrinkle my dress.

"Mrs. Keo." He speaks in that gravelly voice that I've come to love so much. "Mmm…I like the sound of that. I might want to hear you screaming that later tonight."

"Make me then," I tease, and his eyes darken a shade.

"Oh, I plan to."

Kane parks in front of Salty's. When he leads me into the backyard, my jaw hits the floor. The space is transformed by tropical flowers, palm fronds, flickering candles in mason jars, and twinkling white lights draped over every surface.

"It's beautiful," I whisper.

"It's what you deserve. I'd do anything for you." Kane lifts my hand to kiss my knuckles.

I wander towards the white linen tables, each displaying a veritable smorgasbord of food. I offered to cook everything myself, but Kane wouldn't have it and Adele insisted on catering. I drew the line at my wedding cake, which was important to me, and I'm filled with happiness at Kayla's display of my macadamia-crusted coconut cupcakes on a hand painted surfboard. Once the last of our friends have arrived, Adele asks everyone to take their seats.

Kane leads me onto the makeshift dance floor in the center of the dining area. Elvis Presley's "Hawaiian Wedding Song" plays in the background; Kane shakes his head at the musical choice, but he's smiling. It was my pick, but as he moves effortlessly across the wood planks with me in his arms, I know it's a tune we'll never forget. The feeling is one that I'll never forget either, and my eyes brim with tears as I gaze at the bright starry sky.

"Why are you crying, Lani?"

My eyes find his as salt droplets drip down my nose. "Because I'm too happy."

"*Too* happy?" He laughs, but I can see the understanding in his eyes.

"I feel like my chest is about to burst open."

His eyes dip into the low neck of my dress, and he traces the hemline with his thumb. "Now we can't have that, can we? I love this chest."

I try to swat his arm away, but he laughs even harder and tugs me close. "I never thought I'd find happiness again. I never thought I'd deserve it."

"You deserve everything, Kane Keo, and I want to give it to you."

"You already have," he whispers, his lips grazing the shell of my ear. "More than you'll ever know. I'll never be the person I was before meeting you, even if I'm always a bit broken. Losing a child, I guess you never come back from that, but you've shown me how to find joy again. You've shown me that despite everything, it's possible to take risks—and to love, even if I'm not good at it."

"You're good at it, Kane."

"I'm trying."

"Besides, there's no right way. It's whatever you feel in your heart."

"*You* are in my heart. Only you."

His answer brings tears to my eyes, but I swipe them away, like memories I don't need anymore. The song ends and Pancho switches to something more upbeat, hoping to get the guests on their feet. Kane and I sample the food, handing out cupcakes as we visit each table. The evening is casual but intimate, and far more than I could've asked for on my wedding night. The night wears on and Adele heads home for her beauty sleep. A few others, including Pancho and his family, say their goodbyes as well. Eventually, it's just Kayla, Taylor, Lance, Kane, and myself left inside.

Kane pours everyone—including himself—a small glass of champagne. We toast to good food, good friends, and Paia, which Taylor follows up with "And to us!" He's about to throw back his drink, when his eyes lock with something behind my head. I glance over my shoulder to see what's so interesting, and I can't help but smirk at Kayla's surf calendar tacked to the wall, open to none other than Miss July.

"What the hell is that?" He snaps, getting to his feet.

"What?" Kane's eyes flit around the room.

Taylor gets off his stool and stalks behind the bar, ripping the calendar from the wall. "This!" He waves the glossy paper in Kane's face.

"A calendar?" Kane answers, giving him a funny look. "Ashley put it up."

"Why did you put it on the wall?" He shouts, turning his wrath on me.

"Because Kayla is beautiful and the calendar is awesome," I say with a shrug.

"It's not appropriate."

"She's fully clothed."

"You mean barely clothed?"

"Something about my ass must really offend you." Kayla says.

The two of them lock eyes in one hell of a stare down. I let myself fade into the background, not wanting any part of this moment.

"So, you like having your ass on display for everyone to see?" Taylor asks.

"It's just a surf calendar, man," Lance starts, though he wisely shuts up upon seeing the look on Taylor's face.

Taylor speaks through clenched teeth. "It's not going up on that wall again."

"Shove off, Akana! It's not your decision to make. It's not your bar!" Kayla shouts.

"I'm Kane's best friend and occasional business partner, so it damn well is my decision. Kane?" He snaps, turning his attention to my husband.

Kane raises his hands in surrender. "I'm staying out of this one."

"Yeah? What if it was a calendar of Ashley?"

"On second thought, burn the goddamn calendar if you want. It's not going up again."

"Real helpful, Kane," Kayla snorts, turning to me instead. "Men think that they have domain over everything."

Aloha in Love   241

"Not everything," Taylor begins, his eyes lingering a little too long on her face.

"Ugh!" Kayla throws up her hands. "Keep the fucking calendar, for all I care! I'm going home. Sorry guys, congratulations to you both." She kisses my cheek and nods to Kane.

"Don't be sorry," I say, softly. "Get home safely."

"I'll take you," Taylor offers.

"Uh, hell no?" She shakes her head like he's crazy. "Lance is giving me a ride."

"I said I'll take you!" I watch Taylor's hands curl into fists, scrunching the calendar into a ball.

"And I said that I have a ride."

As entertaining as I find their banter, I'm relieved when Kayla and Lance finally make their exit. Jamie comes to say goodbye and surprises me with a hug for Kane. She's been cautious with him, giving him a hard time at every opportunity, but she has a newfound respect for Kane that warms my heart.

"Take care of my best friend," she says.

"She's my best friend, too—and I will, always."

"I know you will…or else." She grins and punches him in the arm. Jamie barely comes up to his chest, but he mock-flinches anyways and rubs his wound.

Taylor lets Jamie know that he's leaving, having agreed to take her home. He bids us a distracted goodbye and stalks out of Salty's with a confused looking Jamie in tow.

"What the hell was that about?" Kane asks, sliding his arms around me from behind and resting one hand on my swollen belly.

"You know exactly what that was about."

"Believe me, I don't."

"Me Tarzan, you Jane." I do an impression, and he spins me around.

"Taylor? And Kayla? No."

"Remember how you acted after my date with Lance?"

"My sweet, sexy wife," he murmurs, pulling me closer. "If you want that guy to continue breathing this beautiful Hawaiian air, you will never mention that date again."

I roll my eyes. "You're calling him *that guy*? Lance was *your* friend first, remember?"

"Some friend," he responds, but I can tell he's joking—sort of.

I shake my head. "What's with island men and marking their territory?"

"He knew better. From the moment you set foot in Salty's, you were mine and I was yours, even though it took us some time to realize it."

"Well, I'm glad it took another man to help you come to your senses," I tease.

He takes my cheeks in his hands. "You know it wasn't like that. From the second you opened that luscious mouth of yours, only to demand the biggest margarita that I could make, I ached to be near you. Keeping my distance was almost physically painful."

"So glad that I could put you out of your misery," I laugh, not realizing my words.

Kane's eyes soften. "I'm getting there, day-by-day, thanks to you, and now this little gift." He drops his hand to caress my belly once more. "*Aloha au iā 'oe*. I love you, Ashley Keo, more than any language can adequately describe."

He kisses me with soft warm lips, and we stay like that for awhile, wrapped up in each others' arms under a brilliant blanket of stars.

Acknowledgements

Thank you to my husband, Thor, and to my two little men, James and Andrew, for giving me the space to write when I needed it, for helping me select titles and fonts and storylines, and for always being your sharp, curious, and inquisitive selves.

To the island of Maui: unmatched in your beauty, you are truly one of my favorite places in the world. There aren't enough words, in any language, to convey the magic you hold. And to our own Hawaii of the North, Savary Island, for being a constant source of inspiration. I written more on your shores in the last six years than I think I have in a lifetime.

A big, heartfelt thank you to Megan Watt and The Self Publishing Agency for your guidance: to Sarah with her launch expertise, and to Kelsey Straight for her amazing, unmatched, incredible, ninja-like editing skills.

To my friends and family - my cheer squad - who support and encourage me every day and continue to share my writing with others.

And to my mom, the woman who gave me a way with words. I am forever grateful, aspiring always to create narratives as beautiful as yours.

For more titles and information visit www.jenniferwattsauthor.com on Facebook and Instagram @jenniferwattsauthor.

Made in the USA
San Bernardino, CA
19 May 2019